Praise for

"In *Rubies from Burma* we meet Mae Lee Willis, a child in the rural South of the 1940s, and watch her grow up in the shadow of her beautiful older sister, Ava. Ava marries handsome Duke, but the war intervenes, and he goes off to fight in Burma. Duke returns emotionally damaged, and when their marriage begins a downward spiral, it's up to Mae Lee to help mend the broken family in this engrossing family saga."

Anne Webster, Author of *A History of Nursing*

"Anne Lovett's unique story is a masterpiece of lush writing, telling of a young girl's growing-up years at a time in history when innocence was not so rare. Scenes of life on a Georgia farm of the 1940s and '50s will stay in your mind and heart as you come to understand Mae Lee and her family."

Judith Keim, author of *The Beach House Hotel* series and other books

"As a fellow member of a writing group, I listened with interest to the development of *Rubies in Burma*: to the range of imagination behind it and the scary pivots of its plot and the lovely turning of tones in movement and relationship. I am glad to discover that it is now being published. Cheers to Anne Lovett!"

Barbara Knott, award-winning author of two chapbooks of poetry and host of online literary/art journal *The Grapevine Art & Soul Salon*

"*Rubies from Burma* tells the WWII coming of age story of Mae Lee Willis, in the hateful shadow of her beautiful older sister, Ava. Much of the novel focuses on Mae Lee's gawky stage, her voice, and the South Georgia setting reminiscent of Carson McCullers's *A Member of the Wedding*. As she matures the voice changes subtly to match events. The talent shown in Anne Lovett's debut novel makes her an author to watch. I can't wait to read her next story."

Louise Richardson, writer and past president of
Sisters in Crime, Georgia Chapter

"Anne Lovett makes an impressive debut with an appealingly spunky young heroine. Mae Lee has the odds stacked against her in rural Georgia. But she creates her own opportunities for love and growth in order to discover that true love is as rare and precious as rubies."

Sarah Parsonson, PhD, former Dean, Atlanta Art Institute

RUBIES *from* BURMA

a novel

anne lovett

WORDS OF PASSION • ATLANTA

Published by Words of Passion, Atlanta, GA 30097.

Editorial: Nanette Littlestone
Interior Design: Peter Hildebrandt

ISBN: 978-0-9960709-6-6

Library of Congress Control Number: 2016919448

Acknowledgments

My heartfelt thanks to those who have journeyed with me on this adventure. My first readers, including Anna Montford Shepard, Annette and Peter Mayfield, Judy Keim, Betty Hamrick, Mary Louise Crosby, and the Midtown Writers' Group: Linda Clopton, Anne Webster, Diane Thomas, Bill Osher, David Darracott, Fred Willard, Gene Wright, and Jim Taylor. Thanks to later members for their support and encouragement: Barbara Knott, Joshilyn Jackson, Atticus Connell, Jim Harmon, Sandi Curry, Jill Patrick, Eric Allstrom, Matt Johnson, Steve Archer, and Brent Taylor.

Thanks also to Terry Kay for sage advice, to Rosemary Daniell for her careful manuscript comments, and to my Zona Rosa friends for their support. Thanks to Kent Nelson and Ann Kempner Fisher for their teaching. Thanks to Chris Tilghman who saw this tale in its first incarnation as a short story and saw its potential. And of course, thanks to the judges of the Pacific Northwest Writers' Association contest, whose comments gave me the encouragement I needed.

Sisters in Crime provided support and education, and my friends from Georgia Romance Writers, especially Haywood Smith, have been so helpful and inspiring.

And of course, thanks to my great editor, Nanette Littlestone, for her expertise, to Peter Hildebrandt for layout, to Clarissa Yao for the fabulous cover. Thanks to Jerry Richardson for his great photography and Louise Richardson for friendship and willingness to help.

Thanks to my late parents, and my brothers, who were and are always at my back. And of course, to my husband, to my children, and to their father, who believed. Hugs and kisses.

For all who fought, and for those who loved them

Chapter One

1944

I am looking through a lace curtain at a dead man's feet. I am ten years old, the mist is rising on a fall morning in 1944 in Sawyer, Georgia, and I am standing on a front porch painted gray with white trim.

The smell of wood smoke and wet leaves and wild olive clings to the mist; a dog barks in the distance, the phone inside is ringing and ringing. I know the person on the other end of the line is Ava. Ava is nineteen and too beautiful for words, as I am not.

A car pulls up behind me and stops. My father gets out.

Before my father takes me away, I see a rosary inside, on the floor. It's the silver rosary of red beads and crystal I will be given later—much later—to keep.

It was Hardy Pritchard's feet I was looking at, and he had the bad luck to be beautiful too. A lawyer should never be beautiful. Clients cannot trust him, though they want very much to, so he did not have enough of them. Even though he was thirty-five and married, he did odd jobs for his daddy such as collect rents, which is why he was standing in the July heat on our porch one Saturday morning three years earlier.

July 1941

Momma was inside lying on the bed with a cold cloth across her face. I could hear the radio crackling with Glenn Miller music and Hardy Pritchard was saying to me, Where's your daddy? and when I told him he was out he said that I ought to get Momma up to pay the rent, the rent was late, and why was it late.

And I was looking at how beautiful Hardy Pritchard was. Even a little girl can appreciate things like that, even if she doesn't know quite why. He had blond hair streaked by the sun, and blue eyes that were deep and sleepy and a shirt that was full of muscles and blond hairs on his tanned arms. He smelled like tobacco and sweat and Old Spice and had a straw fedora pushed back on his head.

But he wasn't looking at me. He was looking in the window at the far end of the porch, the window of the bedroom Ava and I shared in our house next to the railroad tracks. She had been standing before the mirror in her white cotton underpants and a bra which was stitched like a bulls-eye, fixing her hair because she had a date. I saw the blinds come down with a whap and then Ava appeared at the door in a pink housecoat.

The July flies filled the air with the racketing and the mimosa tree was wafting sweet smells from its powderpuffs and Ava and Hardy Pritchard looked at each other like they had never laid eyes on one another before which was ridiculous. She turned a little pink and his eyes got a little bigger.

Mr. Pritchard, she said.

Ava Willis, he said, my how you've grown. His eyes were on the front of the pink housecoat which stood out like a billowing sail.

If you can't be more original than that, get off my porch, she said.

Is that any way to talk to the rent man? he said.

How would you like me to talk? she said.

Well, now. Honey talk.

Sorry, that's not my beeswax.

He grinned, slow and snaky. What I would really like, he said, is a glass of tea.

She looked at him then with her head tilted like she was measuring things up. Come on in, she said. Her voice was making honey now, rich and thick.

I stayed out sitting on the porch in the swing, and before I knew it here came another car stirring up the dust on the road and it stopped and a man got out and walked up. This man wore a uniform, and he was not beautiful but tall and rugged and strong-looking, with dark hair cut short and caterpillar eyebrows and gray eyes cool like a well.

You must be Mae Lee, he said. I'm Dulany Radford.

Loo-tenant Duke Radford? I asked, because that was how they had been talking about him.

He nodded and my heart started beating fast because he told me to tell Ava he was here and I thought about Ava and Hardy Pritchard drinking tea in the kitchen. I ran inside and when I got there they were standing up with glasses in their hands, still looking at one another, and Ava turned to me and looked at me like I was a roach that showed up out of the woodwork.

Your date is here, I said.

Duke Radford, she said to Hardy Pritchard in that careless way she had, and shrugged.

You is in high cotton, said Hardy Pritchard in a voice like a colored person.

Higher than yours? She raised one eyebrow and had a tiny little smile.

Ain't no man got higher cotton than mine, he said.

I have to go, she said. I have to dress.

How about the rent?

Come back later, she said, when Chap's home.

I'd like to come when he's not home, he said. Why do you call him Chap anyhow? Is he your stepdaddy? But she was already heading down the hall and pretended like she didn't hear him. I guess he thought little girls like me were deaf, dumb, and blind.

Hardy Pritchard was right behind me as I marched to the door. I said over my shoulder, Chap is our real daddy. I opened the door wide. He saw Loo-tenant Duke Radford and said, Hey Duke, you ain't goin' to war.

The hell you say. How about you, pretty boy?

Hardy Pritchard's fists clenched up. I'm a married man.

You could have fooled me.

I don't have to take this, Radford. He balled up his fist.

Right here in front of this sweet chile?

I'll fix your clock later, he said. You and me got a date with destiny. He clattered down the front steps and out to his car. It roared away, spinning dust.

Arrogant bastard, said Duke. Sorry, honey, you weren't supposed to hear.

My daddy Chap says stuff like that, I said.

In front of you? He frowned.

I like to listen in where nobody can see me.

A fly on the wall, he said.

I see you are having such a good conversation with my sister, but ain't we going to the movies? Ava clip-clopped into the living room, wearing a slinky blouse with big sleeves and a yellow skirt and open-toed shoes with the high heels.

Don't say ain't, I said.

Miss Priss. You are such a pill.

I love you too.

Good-bye, Mae Lee, said Duke, and they walked out on the porch, down the steps, down the walkway to the street and he opened the car door for her, a Buick convertible, and then drove off. Clouding up that dust again.

I went back to see Momma and she was just stirring from her nap. Sweat was on her forehead and there was a fan turning back and forth, blowing the dotted-swiss curtains.

Ava get off? she said, her hand to her forehead.

I scuffled my toe on the rag rug. Yes, ma'am.

Come on, we need to get started on that corn.

Elmo Conable had brought us some Country Gentleman that morning when he came to pick up Chap and it was still in the paper sack in the kitchen. I followed Momma into the kitchen, almost tripping on the cracks in the blue linoleum floor and sat down at the table. She piled the corn in front of me and told me to put the shucks in the sack.

She spotted the two glasses by the sink. You are supposed to use the jelly glasses, Mae Lee.

It wasn't me, I said. Ava gave some tea to Hardy Pritchard who was coming for the rent.

Momma bit her lip. Hardy Pritchard was in here with Ava?

He said he was coming back later, I told her, but I didn't tell her the part about he wanted to come while Chap wasn't home.

I finished my pile of corn and Momma put it on to boil. She had already cooked the butterbeans with a ham hock and they smelled real good. She had sliced ham and fresh tomatoes from the garden. She told me I could go outside to play till Chap got home.

I went outside where Chap had built us a barbecue pit. It had an iron cover and that's where I made my mud pies. I stirred up some dirt and mixed it with water out of the faucet, using Momma's watering can. Then I added some chinaberries for flavor and patted the pies out on the hot iron sheet. I thought about God patting dust into clay and clay into people. Does he care when they dry and crack, and blow away, or get drowned by the rain?

I had just made the last pie when Elmo Conable's pickup truck came rumbling in our driveway and stopped behind Chap's car, which was in front of the garage. The garage had double doors and was locked with a padlock hanging from a chain. That was where Chap kept his project.

Chap got out and grinned at me, and I knew he and Elmo had had a good day. His clothes were dirty and his black hair curled down over his shiny forehead. He held out his arms and I ran into them.

Hardy Pritchard came by, I said.

He held me out by the shoulders and frowned. Did he, now.

He said he'd come back later, I said.

Elmo got out of his side and came around, said, Hi, there, little lady. He was a giant of a man with hair bleached white from the sun. They walked toward the house. Son of a bitch, Chap said to Elmo. I told him I'd have it Monday.

I hosed the mud off my hands and feet and dried them with some of the old towels Momma kept on the back porch, then slipped through the kitchen door and went back to my room to change. When I got back to the kitchen Chap was scrubbing his hands at the sink with Lifebuoy.

Elmo was sitting at the table and Momma put a plate of ham in front of him. Mabel not cooking tonight? she said.

She went to see her cousin, Elmo said. Them girls could talk from here to Sunday without stopping for breath. I wish they was quiet like you, Gwen.

Oh, how you do go on, Elmo, said Momma but I could see she was pleased. She opened the icebox and got out two bottles of beer and set them on the table. Chap popped the tops with a church key and took a long swallow of his before he sat.

Where's Ava? he said.

Got a date, Momma said into the pot she was dishing butterbeans out of.

Oh? One of them Braxtons?

Dulany Radford, she said, and set the butterbeans and corn in front of the men. I put out the potato salad and the slab of butter and a stack of light bread and a jar of green tomato pickles and the glasses of tea.

Y'all go ahead, she said. Return thanks, Chap.

Ain't you eatin', honey?

I want to show Mae Lee the moon coming up, she said.

Chap said thank you to the Lord for the food, but nothing at all about Duke Radford which was more scary than if he had. Elmo kept shaking pepper over his food till it looked plumb dirty. Momma fixed our plates and we went out to the back porch and sat in the rockers there and the moon came up just like she said above the garage, even though it was still daylight.

O inconstant moon, she said.

What does that mean? I asked.

It's just a line from a play, she said. Romeo and Juliet.

What's it about?

She was quiet for a minute. About a boy and girl who loved each other a whole lot.

And they got married?

They died.

Why?

A misunderstanding.

I don't like that story, I said. I like happy endings.

Sometimes happy endings don't teach you what you need to know, she said.

I had a feeling she wasn't telling me everything. We took our plates back to the kitchen. Chap and Elmo had already cleared the table and had the radio on and the cards out and a bottle of whiskey.

They drank out of jelly glasses and Momma and Chap and Elmo played there under the low-hanging light, a circle of them in the warm dark night, and Momma was more happy and laughing than I had seen her in a long time.

They sent me off to bed but I lay there in the dark hall and listened to them talking about Church Hill and Rosavelt and my eyes got heavy. Somebody picked me up and carried me to bed.

Hardy Pritchard, I heard somebody say. He could ruin that girl.

I didn't understand what they meant. I didn't think Ava would let anybody do anything to her she didn't want.

Chapter Two

That night I snuggled down into the warm sheets smelling of sun and grass. Boards creaked, a faucet squealed, the radio sang faint and tinny, and I could hear an old hooty owl. I woke to voices outside and stripes of moonlight on my quilt. Somewhere down the street where the colored people lived a guitar picked out sad and bluesy notes.

I pulled myself up over to the open window, and out by the car Ava and Duke Radford were kissing. The smell of the honeysuckle drifted in, and the racketing of the katydids and the July flies was loud, loud, loud. The moon lit up the sky above the chinaberry trees.

Ava smiled at him, then turned and hurried into the house.

I heard Momma scrape a chair in the living room, then her voice and Ava's hushed and excited.

Did you like kissing him? I asked Ava when she came in and started peeling off her clothes in the moonlit dark.

You're supposed to be asleep, she said.

I would like kissing him, I said, better than stupid Hardy Pritchard.

I never kissed Hardy Pritchard, she said. It was dark but I could feel sharp eyes on me.

But you wanted to.

You don't know anything, you little fool.

I want to marry him when I grow up, I said all of a sudden.

But you think he's stupid, Ava said, pulling the brush through her hair.

I didn't mean Hardy Pritchard, I said.

You can't marry Duke Radford, she said, because I'm going to. She kept brushing, flipping, her hair falling like curling silk.

You are not.

Just watch me, she said, with another stroke of the brush. I will have him.

You can't have them all, I said.

You want to bet? She just laughed.

I won't let you.

You silly kid. Go to sleep.

The next morning Ava told me she didn't have any clean church clothes so she would stay home and have Sunday dinner ready for us when we got home. Of course Momma had already cooked it the day before except for the corn sticks, and Ava knew how to fix those.

So what's Chap gonna say about church? I said.

He can't make me, she said. I'm sixteen. I'm not his property.

So are you Duke Radford's property?

I am my own property, she said.

Chap was sitting at the breakfast table in his suit and tie reading the Macon Telegraph as he did every Sunday that ever came around. I slid into my place. The birds outside on the wire were jumpy, flying up and settling back down. I split two crispy biscuits and roped cane syrup over them and helped myself to bacon and some peaches.

Ava wandered in her pink housecoat that billowed like a sail and kissed Chap on the cheek and sat down and got some biscuits.

How was your date last night? he said.

Duke is a fine gentleman, she said. And kind and considerate.

An officer and a gentleman, Chap said. You couldn't do better than that.

Momma didn't say anything but I could see her eyes were sparkling. I hear he's a wonderful young man, she said.

Kinda old, for you, though, said Chap.

Twenty-two, said Ava. Graduated from Georgia Tech in Industrial Management.

I won't have him takin' advantage, Chap said. A girl in your position has to be careful.

What position is that? said Ava, tossing her curls.

You know what I mean. I'm a mechanic for his daddy at the plant. He is not our kind of people, Chap said.

I stopped eating syrup and biscuits then. Money was talked about a lot in our house, mostly that there was never enough of it. Chap used to have a repair shop but lost it when somebody sued him and he had to take the job at Radford Industries. Momma had gone back to teaching second grade and we moved to this rented house. I didn't remember our last house but they talked about it a lot. It had a picket fence and roses and was closer to town and Momma grieved over losing it.

Ava told of her plan to stay home and Chap sat up very straight. You will not stay in this house alone. You will not miss church. His look was so dark she stuck out her lip but I guess she thought better about smarting off.

I'm gonna stay home, he says, and see who comes by.

I sat in the John Wesley Methodist Church chewing on my nails the whole time Pastor Ben Higgins was preaching on THE GATES OF HELL, according to the board outside. It was hot and the windows were cracked open at the bottom from the stained glass leaning in, except we didn't have but two stained glass windows and the rest green milky glass. People were fanning with fans with Jesus on them holding a lamb in his arms.

Nobody knows what hell looks like, said Pastor Ben Higgins, but I think it is a dark place. We know it is a place where glowing, red coals of fire are heaped on the head of hapless sinners. Get right with the LORD! Remember Jesus loves you! He will gather you to his bosom!

Ava looked bored and pouted, like she couldn't wait to get home, but she knew all the boys were looking at her the way they never would look at me, slinky and shifty and hardly daring to breathe. Ava showed she knew she was being looked at in the way she sat, in the way she lifted her hair in back. She wasn't listening to talk about sin.

When we got home Chap was out in the garage working on his favorite project, and he came out and wiped his oily hands on a rag and said, Guess who showed up to collect the rent? Hah!

Well, said Ava, shrugging, I told him to come back when you were here.

That man must have radar in his head, said Chap, to know I was here when all of Christendom is supposed to be at church.

So you paid him the rent, what about it?

Get out of here, missy smart mouth, before you get switched.

You would not dare lay a hand on me.

He thought about it. No, he said, but ask me for a few bucks and see what happens. She gave him a black look and flounced away. Chap wiped his forehead. That child will be the death of me, he said.

No, Chap, no, I said. It scared me when he said things like that.

It's just an expression, he said.

The whole week they just tiptoed around each other and no gentlemen at all came to call. I wondered what Chap had said to Hardy Pritchard.

Saturday Chap and Elmo went out again; this time they were out looking for parts for Chap's project. Almost every Saturday they were either doing some repair jobs on the side, or working on Chap's project in a barn out at Elmo's farm or in the garage.

They were building an airplane. Chap had learned how to fly in the big War and had had a dream to build his own plane ever since.

I was crunching the sugary top on cinnamon toast and Momma was telling me my grandmother Mimi was coming to see us when Ava walked in dressed in her flouncy yellow skirt and her yellow shoes with the fat heels and her white blouse with the poofy sleeves.

Where do you think you're going? Momma said with a spatula in her hand.

I just want coffee. I'm going to town to look for a job.

A job.

Yes, ma'am. Chap said he won't give me any money.

What kind of a job?

Woolworth's maybe.

Chap will have a fit, Momma said.

I don't see why.

Why don't you do what he tells you?

I do, most of the time, but Momma, if I'm going out with Duke Radford I need some better clothes.

Momma thought for a minute and put the spatula down. Better clothes, she said.

Ava pouted. What if he wants to take me home to meet his family? How can I go in some old homemade outfit?

The serpent's tooth, said Momma under her breath. You thankless child.

Oh, you sew good, Momma, but we have to buy cheap material, 59 cents a yard.

I do my best. Maybe you ought not to get ideas above you.

You don't really mean that, Momma. Don't you want to see me in a big fine house with a Cadillac car and a maid and a cook and a—

I need to go lie down, said Momma. Take Mae Lee with you to town.

Mae Lee? She'll just be in the way.

I looked at her then. I made a motion, two fingers up together like somebody smoking a cigarette and grinned. Ava's face looked black as thunder because she knew I had been snooping and found her cigarettes under her bras. I am bad to snoop, everybody tells me, but I just want to know things and nobody will tell me because I'm a kid.

She just nodded and grabbed my arm and we went out the door. Almost as soon as we were out of sight of the house she lit one up. Holy Jesus, Mae Lee, she said.

Momma ought to wash your mouth out with soap, I said.

Shut up, she said.

The yellow skirt flared around her knees as she clicked along the sidewalk. I pattered after her, short legs flying to keep up with her clicking shoes. Houses gave way to stores and then sidewalks filled with people, jostling fronts and rears, blue bags and red baskets and calico bundles, dark people and light people smelling ripe from the sun. Then I lost her.

I stood terrified in the swirling crowd.

I felt a hot moist breath on the back of my neck. I wheeled around and I was looking at a big gray nose attached to a mule tied to a parking meter and behind the mule there was a wagon.

The mule drew back his teeth like he was going to bite and I jumped back.

Hee, hee, somebody said.

Willie Pennyman was slapping his knee. Scairt of ol' mule, he said.

Shut up, Willie, I said, fanning myself to cool down. See if we buy any more barbecued chickens from your daddy.

I ain't worried, he said. Your daddy do love them chickens.

Go on, Willie, I said.

We see you tonight, he said. We have them chickens ready for your delectation.

I elbowed through the crowd and found myself standing in front of what looked like a tunnel. People were hunched over on stools and the red tips of cigarettes glowed, smoke drifting out. Maybe it was Hell.

A sign at the entrance read LUNCH 5 cents.

A hand gripped my shoulder and I screamed. Then I saw the red nails. Where have you been?

Where have you been? I could tell she was plenty mad. Let's go, she said.

Ava. I think that is Hell.

She threw back her head and laughed. It's a beer joint, you ninny.

She didn't let go of my elbow till we got to Woolworths. It felt funny to be creaking across the oiled wooden floors, the store smelling of popcorn and candy and perfume, rows of bins down the aisles crammed with sparkly treasures. Ava handed me a nickel. Go shopping, she said, while I go see the manager.

The candy counter at the front of the store was my first stop. My mouth watered over chocolate creams, licorice whips, red and white peppermints, gumdrops, jelly beans, caramels. I bought four cents worth of jellybeans because you got a lot of them, and one chocolate cream.

You could see people passing through the plate glass window and I stood there eating my chocolate cream and who did I see but Hardy Pritchard. He was walking along with a lady who looked very refined, as Momma would say, in the way she dressed and carried herself. I decided it might be a fine thing to be refined and I wondered how you got that way.

I peeked out the door and saw them go into the bank on the corner.

Just about then Ava came up behind me. What are you doing, twerp?

Oh, just checking the weather, I said.

I can tell you. Hot today, hot tomorrow. No rain in sight, no job in sight. He said he didn't need anybody right now.

So we can go home?

Maybe the dress shop needs somebody, she said.

So we went down the sidewalk and stared in Rosenberg's window at a red dress with polka dots and red shoes to match. Just my style, Ava said. We went in and talked to a lady with black and gray hair and a rose colored dress with lace around the collar and she said, my dear, I got so much family to employ. Let me take your name just in case.

Back on the sidewalk heat was really rising and my hands were sticky from the chocolate and jelly beans.

How about the bank, I said, the devil in my soul. Maybe you could be a bank teller.

She just glared at me. You have to be good at math, she said. Let's try The Paris Emporium. She set off so fast she didn't see the Help Wanted sign in the window of the drugstore we were passing. I grabbed her hand. Look, look, I said.

Ick, she said, pulling her hand away. Mae Lee, you're sticky. You're hopeless. And I don't want to work in a drugstore.

You know, I really should have kept my stupid mouth shut.

Chapter Three

S he couldn't go to the Paris Emporium with sticky hands.
Inside the drugstore a high ceiling fan cooled the medicine-smelling air. A smell of bacon and coffee floated over from the lunch counter, where three men ate hunched on stools. Ava went to the thin redhead with frizzy hair behind the counter and asked her for a wet napkin.

You want to order something, Ava? She handed it over.

Thanks, Vernile, but not right now. She wiped her hand and then mine. She nodded her head toward the window. Just out of curiosity, what about that job?

It's behind the counter here. Jimmy up and joined the Navy. Go on back and see Doc Weir. A new customer sat down and said, Hey, Vernile, how about a Coke?

I got to go, she said.

Ava shrugged and I followed her past shelves full of witch hazel and iodine and mercurochrome, peroxide and bandages, soap and toothpaste and cologne, shaving cream and shaving brushes. Doc Weir stood behind a counter in back and when he saw Ava coming his way he accidentally hit the scale in front of him and set it swinging.

She told him her name and explained that she was inquiring about the job.

The bristly moustache twitched. But do you have any experience? he said.

This stopped her short. I cook a lot at home, she said. I know how to make grilled cheese and club sandwiches.

I opened my mouth in surprise and was going to say, No you do not, but she gave me such a look.

Hum, he said.

I'm a fast learner, she said before he could say anything else. What's the pay?

You're Chap Willis's girl. Ain't you in school?

Not for another month, she said, and I could come in after class.

Let me see your hands, he said, and she held them out and he nodded. You ain't engaged?

No, sir, she said.

You have a beau, he said.

You might say that, she said, and I was not sure if it was the right or wrong thing to say.

I don't like my girls to flirt with the customers.

No, sir.

He cocked his head to the side and I swear he was looking at her bosoms. That remains to be seen, Mis' Ava. You come in tomorrow and we'll see about a uniform.

You haven't yet told me what the pay is.

Thirty cents an hour to start. More if I see you work hard.

She appeared to be thinking it over. Yes, sir, she finally said. I'll be here.

We went up to the counter and Ava ordered us Cokes. We were sitting on the stool drinking them when guess who should come in the door but stupid Hardy Pritchard. He slid onto the stool next to Ava and grinned like the snake he was.

Whatcha doin', Mis' Ava.

Oh, that smile and dimple. I just got a job, thank you very much.

Gimme a cherry dope, Vernile, he said.

Vernile gave him the fish eye. I didn't know you liked cherry dopes.

I like anything sweet, he said. Like Ava here.

The door opened with a jingle and in came the lady I had seen him talking to. Oh, there you are Hardy, she said. I wondered where you got off to.

I got tired of waiting for you, he said, looking up at the list of ice cream flavors in black letters stuck in a white board.

The lady carried a white patent leather pocketbook in her hand. She had been to the beauty parlor, I could tell, because her light brown hair was all in perfect waves against her head and she had that perfumy smell about her. She wore a neat linen dress and looked delicate, like a field flower. Oh, Hardy, she said. I'd like some ice cream, but there's nowhere to sit.

He slid down. Take my seat, hon, he said, but he didn't look happy.

We're just leaving, Ava said, tossing that mane of hair. She paid Vernile and I slurped the last of my Coke and slid the glass on the counter and we jingled out through the door.

Who was that lady? I asked on the way home.

She hooted and giggled. That was Mis' Celia Pritchard, she said, and she was once a debutante in Savannah, and they say she is holier than the Pope.

His sister you mean?

His wife, she said.

Who is the Pope?

God, Mae Lee don't you know anything?

I won't if nobody answers my questions. Why did you take that job? I asked. I thought you didn't want to work in the drugstore.

She shrugged. I changed my mind. I thought it might be fun.

A horn beeped behind us and it was Dotty, Ava's friend from school. She gave us a ride home in her Chevy and all Ava could talk about was the drugstore and the folks she was going to see when she worked there.

I resolved to find out about this Pope business but I didn't get a chance because by the time we got home Mimi was there.

When I ran into the kitchen Mimi and Momma stopped talking and had that look on their faces like they had been saying something we weren't supposed to hear. Mimi sat at the kitchen table, her big carpetbag beside her, smoking a cigarette in a holder, and Momma was at the counter slicing tomatoes. My sweet Mae Lee, said Mimi, and I made a face. She smooched me on the cheek and I wanted to rub off the red but didn't know if I'd hurt her feelings so I let it stay. I've been telling your momma she needs to go to the doctor.

They could talk through me all day. I said, Mimi, what did you bring us? Pickles, said Mimi, green tomato pickles. There were three jars on the table. She twisted one open with a pop and the pungent smell tickled my nose. Now we can have them for lunch, she said. Your momma says she didn't have the energy for pickles this year.

Momma didn't say anything but started slapping mayonnaise on light bread.

If it's the money, Walter will help you out, Mimi said.

It's not the money, Momma said.

Walter had a good crop, she said. Bought me a Cadillac. Used, but still.

Ava came in just then. She had changed to a pair of shorts and a blouse. She kissed Mimi and got lipstick on her cheek too. Cadillac? she said. She went over to the back door, hands on her hips, and looked out at the car. One day I'm gonna have one of those. A new one.

You thinking of marrying a Vanderbilt, honey?

She turned around and smiled. Better than that, she said.

Mimi stubbed her cigarette out in the ashtray and looked at Ava and nodded. I think you will, she said.

If she doesn't mess it up, Momma said.

He's crazy about me, Ava said.

So who is this fella with all the dough?

Ever hear of Radford Industries?

Oh, yeah, they make work pants and all that.

Well, his daddy owns it and he's gonna run it someday, Ava said.

Sounds all right, said Mimi. A very eligible bachelor.

He's in the army right now, she said. You can meet him tonight.

He's the most wonderful man I ever saw, I said.

Well, listen at her, said Mimi. You'd think she's sweet on him herself.

She is, Ava said. Lot of good it will do her.

Momma set ham sandwiches on the table oozing with Miracle Whip and juicy tomatoes. Now Ava, be sweet, she said.

I got a job, said Ava, and Momma and Mimi both looked at her at the same time.

Momma set her lips in a thin line. You're going to be the one to tell your daddy.

Sure, said Ava, and reached for a sandwich.

Wait till we say grace, scolded Momma.

By suppertime Momma was lying down again and Mimi was in the kitchen heating up butterbeans, an apron tied around her waist.

Chap pushed open the door and grinned at Mimi with just his teeth, no eyes crinkling up. How you doing, Irene? He walked over to the icebox and found a cold beer and crunched it open with the church key.

Tolerable, she said.

How's Walter? Chap said, taking a long sip of beer. Surprised he let you come.

Gwendolyn's my only child, Mimi said. I come to see about her.

I can't do nothin' with her. Can't help nobody don't want help.

You ought to take her to the doctor and make them tell you what's wrong. That's what I did with Walter. I shake my stick at them.

Chap looked at his beer. That don't work here, Irene.

Mimi looked like she was going to hit Chap with her stick but Ava came in just then. She said real quick in one breath, Chap I got to tell you something I got a job I'm going to be working at Doc Weir's drugstore.

Say what?

She's gonna be working at the drugstore, said Mimi. That's a mighty enterprising young lady.

Goldang, said Chap. Did I say you could get a job?

You said you weren't giving me any more money.

I ought to take a plum switch to you.

She crossed her arms and looked down at him, like she couldn't believe he had said that. That was uncalled for, Chap, said Mimi.

Who asked you to butt in? This is between me and Ava.

I'm the child's grandmother. You going to need me if something happens to Gwen.

Nothin's going to happen to Gwen.

They were fixing to get into it again, so I said, Ava wants to buy a nice dress for when she has a date with Duke Radford. He's coming tonight, right?

Chap was hunched over the beer and now he raised his head. Every mornin' I stand out in front of the shop and watch that goddam D.B. Radford ride to his office in that goddam big Lincoln. I work on that car and keep it like a goddam sewin' machine. We started out in nineteen-eighteen, both went to Souther Field to learn to fly. They said I was too hotheaded for combat. Spent the war workin' as a mechanic, flew a few ground missions. He gets to be a flyin' ace, but who kept him in the air? I come back with my hearin' shot and he comes back with the glory.

He took a long swig of beer and wiped his mouth. Hell, I hope she does marry his son. Go to the drugstore, lassie. You have the blessin' of your pa. He made a cross in the air.

I wish you wouldn't swear Chap, said Mimi. Or be sacrilegious.

Who, me? Chap said.

Well, I better get ready, Ava said, looking confused about whether she had won or not.

Momma came in then and said she was feeling a little better. Lord. I just live to see that child in a white gown. She will be the most beautiful bride this town has ever seen.

Don't get the cart ahead of the horse, Mimi warned.

There's gonna be a war, Chap said. We'll see what kind of stuff this boy is made of.

Chap was waiting out on one of the old metal porch chairs when Duke pulled up in front of our house. He walked up on the porch and Chap said, You like my daughter so much, looks like you could sit down and talk to me.

Momma and Mimi were in the living room, hovering around, murmuring that Chap was gonna scare him away.

Duke smiled. Sure. But we're due at a party.

I won't keep you now. You willin' to fight?

That's my intention.

Ava came out dressed in the yellow skirt again. She walked down and slid her arm through Duke's and smiled up at him. See you later, Daddy.

Got something for you, punkin, Duke said to me. He winked at me and I wanted to run to him and throw my arms around him but Ava would pinch me for sure. He handed me a rolled-up handkerchief. Don't unroll it till I'm gone.

They walked down the walkway and to the car. He opened the door for her and she got in and settled back into the seat. When the roar from the motor had died out I unrolled the handkerchief.

What's that? said Chap. What did he give you? Let me see.

I laid it in Chap's outstretched hand. He smiled. That damn boy is gonna be a paratrooper.

He threw the handkerchief into the air and it was rigged up, string tied to the four corners tied to a bolt, and it floated down, swinging this way and that.

I played with it until it got dark, and I slept with it under my pillow.

Ava didn't have everything.

Chapter Four

February 1942

A bright cold sun came up on Valentine's Day of 1942, sparking through the bare limbs of the pecan trees, turning the frost on the scraggy front porch bushes to wisps of fog. The leaves on the ground crackled underfoot, and the air was so still you could hear a piano playing early morning blues from a block away.

I took my new binoculars out to the porch and pointed them at the sky looking for enemy planes. Chap had told me how to spot them by their shapes, but all I saw this day were clouds and crows, pecan hulls like black tulips and wrinkled chinaberries.

Whut you got there? I heard Willie Pennyman say. I hadn't seen Willie since he was in town laughing at me for being scared of that mule.

I lowered the binoculars. He wouldn't laugh at these. Hey, Willie, I said. I walked over and showed him. Look what I got for Christmas, I said.

Yeah, he said, I didn't have so good a Christmas.

Santy Claus not come?

He shook his head. He come, all right. But my brother Cyrus, his ship got sunk by the Japs.

It was like the time I fell off the jungle gym, all the breath knocked out of me. The war had gotten close to home. I sure am sorry, Willie, I said. Is he—

His dark face looked up at the sky. He ain't dead. He in the Naval hospital. Missing a arm. How he gone work now? My momma is still wailin'.

Maybe he can help with the chickens.

Uh-huh. I guess he could slop on the sauce. That ain't no proper work.

There seemed nothing else to say and Willie scuffed his toes in the leaves. See you, Willie, I said.

He moved on along, his hands in his pockets, jingling some change. I guess he was headed to the store for his momma. Just as I turned to go back in the house I saw stupid Hardy Pritchard's car coming down the street. I found Momma laying the table for supper.

She grabbed my hand. Freezing cold, Mae Lee, you'll catch your death. Don't go back outside.

Willie Pennyman just told me his brother lost his arm at Pearl Harbor, I said, and started to tell her that Hardy Pritchard was coming. But she looked so tired and I didn't want to worry her. I shut my mouth.

Wash your hands, she said.

I heard about Cyrus Pennyman, Chap said, coming into the kitchen. He's lucky to be alive. Was a steward.

Lucky, said Momma. Was it his right arm or his left?

Willie didn't say.

Momma dished up soup and cornbread, and Chap put his paper aside, and Momma told me to go get Ava who was in her room dressing for a Valentine's dance. Then somebody knocked at the front door.

Before I could say anything Ava popped out of her room in a flowered housecoat and went to the door. Chap's here, I heard her say.

Hardy Pritchard in a big leather coat followed Ava into the kitchen, grinning and scratching the back of his head, saying I sure hate to disturb you folks but I was just in the neighborhood and thought I would stop by, see if the rent is ready. I looked at the calendar. He was a day early.

Hell, I got it, said Chap, and he reached in his pocket and pulled out some cash. Momma passed it to Hardy Pritchard while Chap went back to his soup and cornbread.

Won't you have a bit of supper, Mr. Pritchard? Momma asked, in a polite voice but not a specially encouraging one.

Hardy Pritchard chose to listen to the words. I think I will have a cup of that coffee, he said. It's mighty cold out there. You folks go ahead with your supper.

Momma turned her back and poured him a cup and handed it over. Here you are, have a seat. He pulled up a chair while Ava hung over by the door, saying she had a date.

How's it goin'? said Chap.

Hardy Pritchard blew on the coffee. Had a bit of a problem with the draft board, but it's all straightened out now. Course I'd go, but you know how it is, when you got responsibilities.

Yeah, said Chap. I think we all got to think about our responsibilities. How's Mis' Celia?

Well, you know, said Hardy Pritchard. She's got them nerves.

She don't seem nervous to me, said Momma, when I go to the library.

The library's good for her, Hardy Pritchard said. She likes doin' volunteer work. It was clear he didn't like the way the conversation was going but now he had his coffee and couldn't leave without being rude. Ava looked at the floor like she wanted to be anywhere but here.

Would you like some cornbread, Mr. Pritchard? Momma said.

Ava's head came up when somebody else knocked at the door. Oh Lord, he's early, she said, and I'm not dressed.

I guess I'd better be going, you folks got comp'ny. Hardy Pritchard got up from the table, his coffee only half drunk.

I'll see you to the door, said Ava.

Hardy Pritchard smirked but I got up and ran to the door first and flung it open. Duke Radford stood there holding a corsage box.

Ava looked from one to the other and Hardy Pritchard grunted something and slapped his hat on his head and stormed out the door.

If looks could kill you'd be dead, Radford, said Chap, grinning. Your daddy is on the draft board, I know that.

What are you talking about? Ava said, opening the box. The corsage was red roses, and she buried her nose in them. I love red, she said.

Nothing but the best for you, sweetheart, Duke said.

I heard Momma in the kitchen rattling dishes and in a minute she came out wiping her hands on her apron. How do you do, Dulany? We've just finished, but there's still some soup if—

I'm early, ma'am, and I apologize.

Of course, said Momma. What beautiful flowers.

I'm going to put my dress on now, Ava said, would you hold these?

There's apple pie, Momma said, taking the flowers. Dulany?

We'll get something to eat, Ava said. She whirled out of the room.

You should be about finished with your trainin', said Chap. Where they sendin' you? Washington?

Not much call for paratroopers in Washington.

Just thought with your old man—

I'm going to the Pacific, said Duke.

Thought that was navy territory.

Special assignment, said Duke. My brother-in-law.

Yeah, I know the colonel.

Ava came in wearing the red polka-dotted dress she had bought with the drugstore money and Momma pinned on the flowers and she borrowed Momma's wool coat, the black one with the big buttons she had bought before Chap lost his business.

You'll be the prettiest girl at the club, he said.

She really did look like a movie star with that red red lipstick matching the dress and the roses. Edging out the door, I followed them out on the porch. Ava was saying, Duke, can't that colonel get you assigned somewhere close to home?

I want to be out there, said Duke.

I don't understand it, said Ava.

He kissed her on the nose. You're young.

She stuck her lip out. Not too young to know I love you, Duke.

Oh mush, I said. Ick.

She turned and saw me then. Where did you come from, brat? She reached out to yank my hair but I dodged. Go back inside, she said. And it was cold out there and she had on Momma's coat and I didn't, but I stayed put.

Duke looked down and winked at me. You look after Ava while I'm gone, punkin. Promise.

Cross my heart and hope to die. I left them then and went back inside where Momma was cleaning up the kitchen.

Momma, I think Duke Radford should marry me instead of Ava.

She almost dropped the pan in the sink. And what made you think of such a thing, may I ask?

I don't make goo goo eyes at Hardy Pritchard.

Ava doesn't either, Momma said.

Yes, she does. I saw them.

She smiled then, like she thought I was being funny. Well, he's easy on the eyes, that one, too much for his own good.

Beauty is as beauty does, I said. That's what you always say.

I do, she said.

Ava doesn't listen, I said.

You two, Momma said. Don't be jealous.

I'm going to grow up one day, I said. Then Ava better look out.

Can't you do something with her hair, Gwen? Chap frowned at my stringy dishwater locks.

Take me to the beauty parlor like Mis' Celia, I said.

Hush your mouth, girl, Momma said. Mind your own business.

I wanted to say, Why should I? But I couldn't say that.

Chapter Five

After Duke left for training, somebody began to call Ava on the phone, somebody she talked to in that slow, honey-purple voice, the voice she used when Momma and Chap weren't home. She didn't mind me, because she thought I was too dumb to figure anything out. I wasn't too dumb to figure this mystery caller was stupid Hardy Pritchard.

She thought I was such a little bit of nothing she didn't bother to hide a letter from Duke. I found it lying right between her bed and mine, partly covered by the rumpled bedclothes.

When I picked up the blue paper, I smoothed out the crackles and looked at the words. Even though they were written in cursive I could read most of them.

I love you honey and I miss you and think about you every night when my head hits the pillow. Now you are mine forever and don't you forget it. Maybe it was wrong.

I didn't hear her come in.

She shrieked and snatched it out of my hand. How dare you.

It was on the floor, I said.

Momma made a bad mistake teaching you to read, she said. She looked around for the envelope. She jerked the bedcovers off, and the envelope tumbled out. One day, Mae Lee, you're going to get in bad trouble being so nosy, she said, stuffing the letter back in.

I'm just interested in the world around me, I said, which is what I heard Momma tell Mabel Conable about me one day.

I can interest you in this, Ava said, and curled her fist around a hank of my hair, which was thin and silky like Momma's and not thick curly dark like Ava's and Chap's. She yanked, hard.

Ow, no fair, I said, and ran to the door. Then, still mad, I turned back and shouted at her, What did you and Duke do wrong?

What the hell are you talking about?

Duke said, *maybe it was wrong*, neener neener.

She lunged for me but I was out the door and running for Momma.

I didn't tattle, but I slept on the sofa in the living room for a week after that. I was afraid she was going to smother me with a pillow while I was sleeping.

Then I got sick. They told me it was glandular fever and I missed weeks of school. Momma taught me at home, and there we were, two sick folks together. I had to take spoonfuls of nasty-tasting tonic and baby aspirin, and I felt too bad to snoop or listen to what Ava was saying on the phone. Hardy Pritchard never came around anymore, because Chap started going by his father's office to pay the rent.

Momma remarked one day that she had seen Mis' Celia Pritchard at the library, and she really did feel sorry for her. She thought she was lonely. What she needed was a baby, she said.

I don't think so, Ava said.

But why not? asked Momma.

People say she's too nervous to be a good mother, Ava said.

Momma just looked at Ava. Well, I think she's lonely.

Ava just got up and went to paint her nails.

Ava graduated from high school and went to work at the drugstore full-time. There were hardly any soda jerks left in the whole county; they had all enlisted or been drafted and like Chap said, Radford Industries was taking up any slack in the job market. They had switched production from work pants to army uniforms.

That summer it seemed there was a wedding every weekend. I went to three at John Wesley Methodist Church, wearing my black patent shoes and pink organdy dress and stuffing myself at the reception with ginger ale punch and chicken salad sandwiches and green and pink and white mints. After the Conables' oldest boy, Elmo Junior, tied the knot right before he shipped out, Ava started talking about the wedding she was going to have when the war was over.

She would have a white dress of lace and satin, with a long train, and orange blossoms for her hair ordered special from Florida, and for her troo-so silk nightgowns and slinky slippers, and folks would give her gold-rimmed plates and crystal glasses, real silver for the table, and closets full of smooth white bedsheets with scalloped edges, towels in all colors, and damask tablecloths. She would have a hope chest made of cedar to put everything in.

Hmph, said Momma. You need pots and pans and a sewing machine and a housecoat you can cook in. And some cheap dishes from Woolworths because they get broken. Especially with kids.

Ava just kept reading her magazines, cutting out pictures of things she wanted and pasting them in a scrapbook.

I'm going to live a different kind of life, she said. Rich people don't have to be afraid of breaking something, because they can afford to buy another one. I'll have dinner parties like they do in the movies, she said. Maybe even a butler. I'll have a maid to iron my clothes. And I will wait to have children.

So what does Duke say about that? Momma said.

He wants me to be happy, she said.

And what makes him happy? Momma said.

Ava slapped her scrapbook shut. He'll be happy if I'm happy, she said.

You know the fairy tale about counting the chickens before they're hatched? Did he ask you yet? I held my breath. Maybe he hadn't.

That's my secret, she said, and I knew she was saying that just to be mean.

I wanted to know if he was really planning to marry her. The very next day after she left for work, I looked for another letter. I searched the dresser under the underwear, the bedside table drawer among the gum wrappers and pencil stubs, on the high shelf of the closet, under the mattress, even behind her old Nancy Drews in our little bookcase. I dared not go snooping in Momma and Chap's room, and she wouldn't have put them there anyhow.

Later on that afternoon, Momma was in the kitchen ironing clothes and listening to *Stella Dallas*. In my room I turned the pages of a Nancy Drew, puzzling out the words I didn't know. Nancy usually found what she was looking for, and this time she had found something in an old clock.

Too bad we didn't have an old clock. All we had on the wall was a picture of Jesus, all smiling and holding out his hands to the little children. It was pasted on a sort of tin plate that covered up a pipe in the wall.

Well, Brother Ben Higgins always said that Jesus was the answer.

I put down my book and scrambled up on the dresser. I tugged at the pie plate little by little, and then all of a sudden it came out of the wall with a *sproing*, and some papers flew out. I almost fell off the dresser but caught myself just in time and held on breathing hard. There were letters on the dresser and on the floor around me. I hurried down and gathered them up, hoping Momma hadn't heard. If I got caught my goose would be cooked.

I held my breath and listened to the radio voices. *Darling, I didn't really mean it. (sob sob)*

I opened a letter and unfolded it. No secrets—the camp, the chow, the buddies, how he missed her. The next one was just about some of his old friends, did she have news. And the next was all about stuff to eat. But the next one read like this, all the way at the bottom: *Doll, we'll have a bang-up wedding when I get back. It would only upset my folks to know we jumped the gun. After they get to know you as well as I do they will love you just as much.*

Mae Lee! Momma called me to come help put away the clothes. My feet felt like somebody had cemented them to the floor and my throat felt like I had swallowed a bucket of sand. I finally croaked I was coming, just a minute.

I climbed back up and stuffed the letters back in the pipe and was really, really careful not to get any handprints on the wall. When I got to the kitchen, Momma said, what's the matter, you're all out of breath. Have you been up to something?

I'm afraid I just stood there with my mouth open and Momma said have you been jumping on the bed again?

Well, um, I said and looked down at my feet.

You are too big for that. It will collapse and one day it might break and I'll let you off this time but next time you'll get a switching.

All right, Momma, I said, and took the basket of clothes and went and put the socks and undershirts and slips and step-ins away in everybody's room. There were no more cigarettes in Ava's underwear drawer. I came back to the kitchen.

Can I have a drink of water?

Use the jelly glass, she said.

I poured some cold water from the icebox and drank about half of it down. Then I took the glass to the table. Do you think Ava and Duke got married? I said.

She turned around so fast and had such a look on her face. What makes you say that?

I was just wondering, I said. So many weddings this summer.

They most certainly did not, she said, and don't say anything like that in front of your daddy. And do not mention it again.

My face was burning but I turned to the butterbeans.

She had taught me well. I knew how to slide my finger down and slip the casing off, and it was fun to pop the cool beans off the sweet-smelling pods. For a while anyway. I soon got bored listening to the soap opera but perked up when a dashing pilot came into the story. When is Chap going to be finished with that plane? I asked. I sometimes went into the garage and watched him work on the engine, when he'd let me.

I hope he doesn't get in trouble, she said.

Why?

It's the law, she said. All airplanes now belong to the war effort.

But it's still in pieces, I said. Part here and part out at the farm.

I don't know if that makes a difference, she said. It's a good thing he got most of the parts already, or he'd never find them. He got the flying bug back in the first war, and he'd be out there now if it wasn't for his hearing. She sighed. Now hush and let me listen to my story. Get him to tell you all about it.

I was quiet while the dashing pilot flew across the country to save a dying boy with the serum with ice forming on the wings. The engine sputtered and coughed and the pilot said, Oh, no, I'm losing altitude! There was this keen whining sound and the announcer said in this low disturbing voice, *tune in tomorrow.*

Ava came roaring in the door, and when she got to the kitchen she looked like she was fit to bust. I got something to tell you that you ain't going to believe, she said.

Don't say ain't, said Momma, frowning. She switched off the radio.

I quit, Ava said.

You what?

She giggled like she was my age. Momma—Hardy Pritchard offered me a job!

Momma's face was calm but her pale blue eyes looked like ice on the wings of a plane. You are not going to take it, she said.

I am, Ava said.

But Ava, I said, and gave her a look. What about—

What about what, twerp? The way she looked at me, I was glad she didn't have an iron poker in her hand. She might look soft, all curves and curls, but inside she was full of nails and bricks.

The back door opened.

Everything got quiet all of a sudden.

Chap closed the door. What the hell is goin' on? Why are you all sittin' around like somebody died?

She says she's going to work for Hardy Pritchard, Momma said.

Ava put her chin up. He'll be paying me enough to move out of here. I'll move out if you stand in my way.

I'll kill the bastard first, said Chap. I seen the way he looks at you and now he's tryin' to break up my family.

Ava spoke very calmly. He needs a secretary. His old one got on the bus and rode clear across the country to be with her husband at the Navy base in California.

But you aren't a secretary, Momma said.

You're a soda jerk, I said.

Shut up, Ava said to me, and then to Momma and Chap, I studied shorthand and typing in school. They were my best subjects.

It ain't right, Chap said.

I can't go back to the drugstore, she said. The Doc blessed me out.

What the hell did you do?

Well, she said, you know there are regulars who come in every day and have their coffee and breakfast before they go to their offices.

Yes, I know, Momma said.

Sometimes Hardy Pritchard sits with them and sometimes he doesn't.

He should be having breakfast at his house, Momma said.

I think she sleeps late, Ava said. You know she has nerves.

What does that mean, nerves, I said, since it was the second time I had heard it.

Never you mind, Mae Lee, said Momma. Go on, Ava.

Well, I was refilling their coffee and one of them said, So what's really going on with the Jews over there?

Nothing, it's just propaganda to get the Jews to finance the war.

Wait a minute, Hardy Pritchard said. I expect there's a lot we don't know.

I poured coffee into their cups, Ava said. I think you are right, Hardy Pritchard, I said. You guys are sitting in the drugstore drinking coffee and eating doughnuts and some of us have loved ones out there fighting.

Who asked you, girlie? one of the men said.

Yeah, women should be seen and not heard.

Hey, lay off her, said Hardy Pritchard. They all turned to look at him but he didn't back down. She is entitled to her opinion even if it ain't the same as some of ours.

You are right, I am, Ava said, and I think—

Ava, come here for a minute, called Doc Weir from the back of the store, and she asked the men to excuse her and she went back there to the scales.

I did not hire you to air your opinions, he said.

Ava told us that she started to open her mouth and thought of her job, because what she was earning was helping us out a lot since it didn't look like Momma would be well enough to teach next year. So she shut up and said yes, sir and when she went back to the counter all the men had left. She smashed two eggs by accident when she was putting supplies away.

The next day who should come in for lunch but Hardy Pritchard. She didn't see him at first because he was early and she was making a new pot of coffee, dumping the old grounds and cleaning the basket and putting in fresh coffee, then she scraped the breakfast bacon grease off the grill, getting it ready for grilled cheese and hamburgers. When she turned around there he was sitting at the counter and had not said a thing, just sitting there watching her work and it made her sore.

What do you think you're doing sneaking up like that?

I didn't sneak; I'm sitting here big as day.

Well, what can I do for you? She took her pad out of her pocket.

You're a good worker, he said. It's what I can do for you.

I don't know what you're talking about.

Can you type?

I can, she said. Second best in my class. Why?

I'll have some iced tea and a club sandwich, he said, looking at the person who had hunkered down on the stool beside him. How you, Jimbo? he said. She took the other order because she could do two orders at once and fixed him his club sandwich and his tea and then those red stools started filling up with people and the fans were turning overhead and I could just see it there, cooler inside the store while outside it was hot beating down and everybody drinking their milkshakes and eating their hamburgers and club sandwiches and tuna fish and grilled cheeses while she brushed off the sweat from her forehead.

Hardy Pritchard ate the club sandwich and went back to talk to Doc Weir and got a prescription filled and then he came back and ordered an ice cream sundae and after he had finished that he ordered a cup of coffee and Ava thought he was never going to leave but finally the people had left and took a glance back at Doc and when he saw Doc was busy, he leaned over and said, come to work for me.

She looked at him like he was kidding but he looked serious. I don't know if I want to, she said, but then he told her how much she was going to make, and she thought about how tired her feet were and how she came home every night with her hair smelling of grease and medicine and Doc Weir's grumpiness.

Hardy Pritchard is not so bad Chap, she said, and we really could use the money, and this is my big chance to be a secretary instead of a—she looked at me—*a soda jerk*.

Chap just looked at her, his hands turning his beer bottle around and around. He lays one hand on you and I'll blow his head off.

Thank you Chap, she said, and smiled. Momma did not protest. Maybe because she suspected I knew something because of my question. If Ava was really married to Duke Radford, then it might be okay.

I wish I had said something. But they never listened anyhow.

Chapter Six

I t was the second week in September, and there hadn't been any letters from Duke in a long, long time. And Ava didn't care.

She never looked in the mailbox, never asked if anything had come for her. She went out with Dotty and Barbara to dances on the weekend, and as the weeks dragged on by it seemed my sister wasn't ever at home.

Momma and Chap sat at the kitchen table with beers and talked in low voices about her. Better for her to enjoy herself, they said, than sit home and mope. What if he never comes back?

I popped out from behind the living room sofa. He's got to come back, I shouted at them. He's just *got* to!

Little pitchers have big ears, they said. Why do you care so much?

I had no answer that they would like.

On the fourteenth of November, I pulled a letter out of the mailbox, a letter all crumpled and stained, a letter from *him*.

I ran in the house with the letter, to the kitchen, where Momma was standing at the stove where a pot was coming to boil. A letter, I said, and she turned and saw from my face who it was from.

Ava needs to see it first thing, she said. Put it on the hall table on top of the rest of the mail, she said. Is there anything for me?

I don't know, I said, scuffing my toes on the floor. I left it in the box.

Momma had infinite patience with me. Go get it, she said, then come in here and grate this cheese. I looked at the cheese, bright orange, a good kind of smelly, resting on a cracked plate.

But Momma—

Just go.

I ran to get the mail, legs pumping across the cold yard, then put it on the hall table all out of breath, Duke's letter on top. I settled at the yellow Formica table with the cheese, running it across the grater and watching the little curls drop onto the plate. The pot on the burner hissed and sizzled as she dropped macaroni into it.

Chap's car rumbled up in the back and then he came in the door, grinning at me, and I shoved the plate of cheese aside and leaped up to get a hug and then I got him a beer and opened it. He shrugged off his leather jacket and hung it on the back of the chair. He settled down with the beer and took a long guzzle.

Then he ran his hand through his dark curls. Go play in your room a few minutes, Mae Lee, he said.

But the cheese.

Dinner can wait. Your momma and I have to talk.

I washed my hands and went to my room, then I slipped back out and tiptoed into their room, into their clothes closet, behind Momma's Sunday dresses. I pressed my ear to the wall.

You heard what that Glenda Shale has been sayin' around town, Chap said.

I heard, Momma said, but I don't believe it.

Talk is she's jealous. She and Pritchard, huh.

I thought she went to San Diego with her husband.

He went without her.

Momma was quiet for a minute. That girl was always lazy, she said.

I am tellin' you, Gwen, our Ava is gonna lose her reputation and there goes Mr. Dulany Radford and anybody else worthwhile.

Poor Celia. Hardy Pritchard is some cross to bear.

Poor Celia! Is that all you can say! I'm gonna shoot the sumbitch.

Hush, Chap. It's just loose talk. We have got to hold our heads up like we heard nothing at all. If she quits now it'll just prove what they say. And she can't go back to the drugstore. What'll she do? Work at the plant?

Shit, said Chap. Over my dead body.

Hush, said Momma.

Then I heard the chair scrape back and steps were coming my way. I had nowhere to go so I scooted back to the far corner and held my breath. Chap took off his work boots and stuck them in the closet and got out his old slippers. I sucked breath, afraid he'd hear my heart slamming in my chest. As soon as he shuffled out, I shoved the coat aside and jumped out into sweet air smelling of Momma's powder. I ducked back into my room and opened a book, and then I heard, all at once, Momma calling me and the front door bumping closed. Ava was home.

Going back to the kitchen, I saw her looking through the mail on the table. When I got there, Momma had finished the macaroni and cheese and Chap was drinking another beer. I took the plates and laid them on the table. Ava walked in. It seemed like God had stopped the world from spinning.

What's going on? She looked from one to the other.

You've got a letter, I said, and the world wobbled a little and began to turn again.

This? She reached in a pocket and pulled it out.

Read it, read it.

She pocketed it again, her eyes narrow. All in my own time. It's *my* letter.

We waited for her to say something else.

She shrugged. Can we have supper? I'm hungry.

Chap turned on the radio so we could hear the news while we ate, which filled up that empty space Ava was making. The announcer was saying the Americans had landed on some islands and were advancing against the Japs and it made me think of

Willie and his brother. The British, he was saying, are advancing in the BCI theater planning to take back Burma.

Ava looked up then, got up from the table, and hurried back to her room fast as she could without running. No fair, I called, because that would mean doing the dishes by myself.

Leave her be, said Momma. Let her read her letter in peace.

Why oh why was she so soft on Ava? My hands deep in soap bubbles, I knew I was going to find that letter.

When I got home from school the next day, all ready to look behind the Jesus plate for the letter, Momma had milk and molasses cookies waiting for me in the kitchen, a treat because of the sugar and butter rationing.

They're not too bad, she said. I used that oleo. We're raking leaves and gathering nuts this afternoon.

She needed the pecans for Christmas. I ate my milk and cookies, all the while thinking of the letter, and she tied on a headscarf and bundled up in her old coat and her gloves and we went out and raked and picked up nuts, plunking them into a tin bucket. Her face was shiny and rosy from the sun and the cool air, but she soon got tired and left me to finish up. I sure wished the doctors could fix whatever it was that was making her so weak.

I was hurrying, trying to finish, so I could search for the letter before Ava got home. And here came Willie Pennyman walking down the road, whistling one of those gospel tunes that sounded happy and sad at the same time.

Hey, Willie, I said. How's your brother?

He gon' be home for Christmas, Willie said. Your momma pay you for raking?

No money. Just milk and cookies, I said.

I rakes for money, he said. Mis' Celia Pritchard, she pay good, and Mis' Lila Potter too.

I leaned down and picked up a handful of nuts. Want some?

Don't mind if I do.

I walked over to the fence and handed them over. Where does Mis' Celia live, Willie?

Over to Oakdale Street, he said, cracking two nuts together in one hand. It ain't far.

I know, I said. I cut through that street sometimes on the way home from school.

Not me, Willie said. I go the long way round so I don't have to pass that haint house right down from her. He ate the nuts.

But that's fun, I said.

You ever go up on that veranda?

No, I said, but I had heard the boards squeak when I looked through those dusty windows at long cobwebs. I didn't want to hear what Willie would say about that.

You be careful now, Willie said, cracking two more nuts. Don't let them haints get you. He walked off, and I had a feeling he was on the way to the store for his momma, because I got sent to that same little store on the corner where Mrs. Moses kept penny candy, Dr. Pepper, and a big wheel of cheese.

When I finally finished picking, I put the nut basket on the back porch and piled the leaves in a big metal trash can for Chap to burn. Then I hurried into the house, stripped off my sweater, washed my hands, and climbed up onto the dresser to the Jesus pie plate. But the letters were gone.

I searched the room like a doodlebug digging a hole: the underwear drawer, the shoeboxes under the mattress, all everywhere. I gave up when I heard the front door shut and Ava's heels on the floor. Momma was sleeping, and no supper had been started, and now Chap was coming in the back door.

Ava sized the situation up. I'll make grilled cheese, she said. There's some soup in the pantry. It was tomato soup, my favorite.

The next day it drizzled, and rained for almost a week. The tags in the cotton fields sagged, and the whole town looked like it was bathed in pink light with gray, empty pecan branches against the sky. Puddles glistened in the streets, the buildings reflected in wavy patterns, and the horses in the field across the way moved through the mist munching damp brown grass.

I searched behind some loose bricks, the way Nancy Drew would, and checked to see if we had any loose floorboards, but they were all nailed down tight. The letters were not between the mattresses on any of the beds.

At the end of the rainy week Momma was feeling better, and she got up and fixed meatloaf and mashed potatoes and English peas and apple pie. That night Chap came home with the flat face he used when he and Elmo Conable played cards, and I had a feeling something was up. He waited until we were all seated around the table to tell us.

The Radford boy, he said, is in Burma.

How do you know? Ava's voice was a little cry.

It was goin' around the shop today. His daddy got word somehow.

I knew he was somewhere awful, Ava said.

What's he doing there? Momma said.

It might be better not to ask, Chap said. Stilwell said he'd be back. He shook his head. Jungle fightin'. It was bad in the trenches, but this has gotta be worse.

Please don't talk about it, said Ava.

Whatever you say, princess, Chap said, and he cut his eyes at Momma and I knew they would talk about it later.

He'll come back, said Momma.

Maybe he won't, said Ava.

Yes, he will! He's got to! I started waving my arms around. Oh, Jesus help!

If he didn't, there would be nobody to ruffle my hair and make me parachutes and call me punkin. Momma was always tired and Chap was always busy. And Duke had told me to look after Ava. I couldn't do that the rest of my life.

You little fool, Ava said, getting up. I can't stand it. I'm going out tonight.

Behave yourself, said Momma, looking at me.

Where you off to? said Chap.

To the office. Hardy is preparing a case.

That sumbitch doing some actual work?

Chap, please, said Momma.

He's coming by for me, she said.

Maybe I'll have a word with him, Chap said. He scooted back his chair and folded his arms.

Chap, it's important, Ava said. Her voice was sharp as a knife.

Nobody said anything for a long minute.

Can I have your pie? I said.

She got home about ten-thirty, and Chap was looking out the window when they got home. She jumped out of the car and ran to the house and by that time I was sobbing about a tooth that had started paining me right after I ate that second piece of pie.

Our dentist had joined the navy. Momma didn't know who else to call so late and there we were in the kitchen, me with cloves in my mouth and Momma crushing up an aspirin tablet and mixing it with orange juice.

Ava wanted to know what was going on and when she found out she said there was a dentist down the hall from Hardy Pritchard's office who was a buddy of his, and he would work us in, she was sure.

Dr. Carruthers was on the third floor of a five-story building, white and shining like a steeple in the sun. The elevator inside was creaky and scary, a cage, and I was afraid it would get stuck and we would be stuck there between floors forever.

Our shoes clacked on the marble floors as we walked down the long hall to the dentist's office. Above us, cobwebs hung from the high ceilings, and we passed doors with frosted snowflake glass panes, names painted on them in black letters. The hall felt cold, with a sharp smell of rubbing alcohol and cloves.

We passed a door marked *Horace C. Pritchard, Attorney at Law.*

Can't we stop and say hi? I asked. And see what the office looks like?

No, we'll be late. Momma hurried me on to the office of *Z. C. Carruthers, DDS.* Almost as soon as I got settled on the green plastic sofa, the little window at the front snapped open. The lady said the doctor will see the little girl now, and I went in and he seated me in a chair and made me breathe some air through a mask and the last thing I remember was the dentist bending over me with white hair combed up on both sides so that his head looked like a giant tooth.

I was never one to mind Momma too well. While she was making arrangements to pay the bill I slipped out and tiptoed down the long, echoing hall.

The metal knob was cold on my palm. I turned it ever so slowly and pushed the door open inch by inch, peeking through the gap. Ava sat at a desk typing, Hardy Pritchard standing behind her looking at the paper. Then he touched the back of her neck and rubbed it the way Momma did Chap sometimes when he got in from work. Ava stretched like a cat, and then he leaned down, and my nose tickled, and I sneezed, spluttering into my hands.

Is someone there? called Ava.

I pushed the door all the way open but Hardy Pritchard was gone and the door behind her was closed. Well, twerp. You saw Dr. Carruthers? Where's Momma? she said.

Paying the dentist bill, I said, but before I could say anything more I felt Momma's warm body behind me, a firm hand gripping my shoulder.

Do not run off like that, I told you, she said. Sorry, she said to Ava. She turned to me sternly. You must not keep Ava from her work, Mae Lee.

But—

Not another word, she said. And we left.

As we drove home, I gazed out the window at all the leafless trees and the gray sidewalks lined with cotton lint. When I turned back I saw that Momma was gripping the steering wheel like it was going to fly away from her.

I saw something, Momma, I said.

I wonder if I should take you back to school, she said.

No, I said. I saw something. In there.

Maybe I won't take you back to school, she said. You can help me get the last of the leaves. Maybe it'll be dry enough for Chap to burn them tomorrow.

I gave up then. Okay, I said.

And it turned out that Momma was too tired and I finished the leaves all by myself. That turned out to be lucky.

Chapter Seven

After I got the leaves all done I took them over to the big trash can and started to stuff them in, but I was careless and knocked the can over. And it rolled around on the ground before I could stop it and leaves came out. Nothing to do but pick it up and start again but when I bent down to pick it up I saw some newspaper in there. Now Chap hated for anything to be in there but leaves so I pulled at the paper and it came out and a lot of other stuff came with it. The letters. She had meant for them to be burned with the leaves.

Feeling strange, I took them behind the garage so nobody could see me from the kitchen window and I hunkered down on the cold ground, my back to the wall, and I read those letters, every last one of them. The one that had arrived the night I was grating cheese said

June 15

My Ava,

I can't say much about what I'm doing or where I am, or the censor will have this so full of holes it will look like one of my target practice cans. When you write me, make it on one side of the paper in case they cut anything out. It's going to be a damned hard mission, harder than any of us thought. But just thinking of you over there waiting for me keeps me going. It's hot here, muddy, bugs the size of bats, poisonous snakes, leeches, parasites, man-eating tigers. We keep busy.

I hope your job at the drugstore is going well. Dad says things are rolling at the plant. I can't wait to get back to you and the folks and the job, in that order.

God, how I want to see your sweet face. I wish I was holding you now and loving you. One day we'll have everything you want, sugar, a good life with our own house and kids. Keep smiling for me.

All my love,

Dulany

That last one put an ache in my heart. I was so sorry for him that she was not thinking of him at all but stupid Hardy Pritchard and what was going to happen there with him, married to Mis' Celia? Grown people were so confusing. I couldn't ask my friends at school, not Faye or Carol Jean or Lourdes Sanchez who had come here from Cuba, and I sure couldn't ask Starrett Conable.

Maybe Momma and Chap were right. Maybe Ava would ruin her reputation and there would go Dulany Radford, and was she married or not?

I'd write to him myself, I would. I was writing pretty well, Momma helped me. But it would make Ava so mad. And I might be nosey, but I wouldn't be a tattletale.

I didn't want to put the letters back in the leaves to get burned up. I wrapped them in some of Momma's sewing scraps and stuck them in the bottom of my school bag.

I worried and worried about Duke over there fighting that war and dreaming of Ava and her about to burn up all his letters. But there was Mis' Celia Pritchard to think about. I wondered if she was jealous of Ava. I would just walk by her house and I would go up and ring the bell and when she answered I would tell her to watch out.

I came that way after school the next day. All the houses on that street were nice trim houses, not too big and not too small with azaleas and other bushes out front and mowed lawns of fat-bladed grass that Momma called St. Augustine, and one even had a goldfish pond with fish in it, which I thought was very fine. I wanted to have fish one day. But I didn't know which one was the right house, and Willie wasn't there to tell me.

I was about to lose my nerve when I saw her. She was sitting in a rocker on the front porch like she was waiting for somebody. Me? I looked at her, and she looked at me, and she got up from her rocker and came over to the edge of the porch and put her hand on the rail.

Yoo-hoo, little girl, she called, and I stopped cold.

Yes, ma'am?

Aren't you Ava Willis's little sister, Mae Lee? I thought I saw you in the library with your mother.

My knees turned to jelly. Yes, ma'am, I said.

She smiled. Well, Mae Lee, would you like to come in and have some cookies? I'm expecting Father Shepherd for tea and I would love it if you could join us.

My heart pounded like a galloping mule. I better be getting home, my momma might worry.

Oh, she won't mind. They're lovely cookies and some little cakes and some tiny sandwiches.

What's a father shepherd? I asked. The only shepherd I knew was on the wall of my Sunday school room, and that shepherd was just a boy.

Father Shepherd is my pastor, she said.

Like Brother Ben Higgins? I asked.

You might say that, she said. Oh, do come.

I took a deep breath and thought about Duke and the letters. Okay, I said, maybe for a little bit. She smiled from ear to ear, making her earbobs dangle. She led me up the steps and into her entrance hall where there was a telephone stand and then into the living room.

Oh, my. A maroon velvet chair begged to be petted like a kitten and I longed to sit on the shiny satin sofa of maroon and gold with fringes on the bottom. We stepped on a smooth carpet that smooshed underfoot, and the sun was slanting in through the windows sprinkling the air with fairy dust.

On the side table were figurines of ladies with fans wearing robes, and she told me they were Japanese, and I said Japs? all surprised, and she looked at me with a mournful face and said, please do not say that, they have a beautiful culture and this war breaks my heart.

I'm sorry, I said, though I did not know what culture was.

Please, have a seat, she said, and she went to the kitchen and I sat down on the satin sofa and stroked it. On the other side table I saw a picture of her in her wedding gown with lace all around her head looking down at a bouquet of lilies. She was very beautiful then, and I don't know what happened to make her so thin and worried-looking as she was now, like somebody could break her in two. And standing behind her was stupid Hardy Pritchard looking beautiful too, like a man in *Life* magazine, looking out of the picture like he wanted to kiss the camera.

She came back in with a tray of tea and cakes and little tiny sandwiches, and some thin cookies, butter wafers she said, and poured me a cup of tea and fixed it with sugar and lemon, and poured herself a cup. The cups had violets on them. She passed me the plate and it was full of violets, too. I took a cookie and then a sandwich and she let me eat a few, just smiling, before she said a word.

How does Ava like her job? she said.

I took a swallow and it was hot going down, but I didn't choke.

Hardy says she's very efficient, said Mis' Celia.

Yes ma'am, I said, she took typing and shorthand in school.

Does she work much in the evening? Mis' Celia asked sweetly.

I shrugged. Sometimes. I started to feel I was sliding into a big black hole of trouble and I backed up. Not very much, really, I said.

She has a boyfriend? Mis' Celia asked.

He's in the army, I said. A long way away. Duke Radford, I said, just to say his name.

Oh dear, she said. I know the family. She must really miss him.

Yes ma'am. He writes her lots of letters. I thought of the letters down in my book bag and I could bring them out and show her. But then she would know I had stolen them. Mis' Celia, I said, I—

A car door slammed outside.

Oh, she said with a smile, that must be Father Shepherd, but before she could get up the door opened and Hardy Pritchard came in big as you please, looking me up and down. What's going on?

Oh, Hardy, it's Ava's little sister. I invited her in for tea.

No kidding, he said. Well, little girl, he said. You do get around. You better be careful.

Why Hardy, whatever do you mean?

Nothing he said. Kids ought to be careful of strangers, that's all. He curled his lip.

Poof. I'm hardly a stranger. What are you doing home?

I've got to go out of town, he said. A funeral.

Who died?

Nobody you know, he said. I'm going to pack.

I need to get home, I said. Momma will be looking for me. The phone in the hall rang and he answered it, and Mis' Celia walked me to the door.

Thank you for the tea and sandwiches, I said.

Do come again, she said. It's so nice to have a child around.

When she opened the door, there was a man there, all ready to ring the bell, a man dressed in black with a little round white collar. He had wavy gray hair and little round glasses and rosy cheeks like Santa Claus.

Father Leo! she exclaimed.

Cecilia! He leaned over and kissed her cheek. And who might this charmin' young lady be?

I'm Mae Lee Willis, I said.

Ava's sister, Mis' Celia said, and they looked at each other with some kind of wordless understanding.

He leaned down to shake my hand. And a lovely child you are. Shall I see you at church?

Oh, no, I said, I go to the John Wesley Methodist Church. But the way he talked made me want to giggle, and later on Mis' Celia would explain that he had come from Ireland. I liked his smile. Maybe I can ask Momma to bring me to your church, I said.

It's called St. Lawrence's, Father Leo said.

Okay, I said, and started down the steps.

Wait, Mis' Celia said, getting all excited. Why don't I take you to church? I sometimes go to early Mass but I would wait until later for you. More like you're used to at the Methodist church.

Now Cecilia, Father Leo said. Have a caution.

I'll have to ask Momma, I said.

Well, do let me know, she said. We have a new child there about your age, Lourdes Sanchez, who has moved here from Cuba. Her father is a doctor and her mother's a nurse.

She's in my class, I said. I like her. She tells me Spanish words.

Well, then.

I've really got to go. Goodbye, Father Leo, goodbye, ma'am and thank you for the cookies. When I finally got to the corner and turned out of sight, I ran all the way home. Could I really go to church with Mis' Celia?

When I got home, Momma was peeling potatoes in the kitchen and looking sleepy, like she'd just woken up from a nap.

I made some fresh oatmeal cookies, she said. Did you get kept after school?

Not this time, I said, and bit my lip. Lourdes Sanchez and I were playing on the playground after school. She told me about her church. It's called St. Lawrence's.

It's a Catholic church, she said. It's very different from ours.

Yes, I said. Lourdes is allowed to wear earrings. Her mother pierced her ears when she was just a baby.

Well, said Momma. I don't know what that has to do with church.

What if I wanted to go? I said.

Why would you want to do that?

Just to see what it was like, I said.

You have your own church, said Momma.

Christmas came at last, and Mimi and Mr. Linley came over for dinner. She had married him after my grandpa died and always called him Mr. Linley so the rest of us did too. We swapped presents and had a good time, all except for Ava, who looked like she wished she was somewhere else, lonesome as a hound baying at the moon, and Mimi asked her if she was missing her army boyfriend. She said yes, it was hard to think of him all alone over there with the tigers and the snakes, and Chap laughed and said he wasn't exactly alone, and Momma huffed and said, Chap how could you, and he said, I just meant the boy had good buddies.

We had all packed a box to send to him full of books and insect repellent and Baby Ruth bars and Camel cigarettes and coffee. I had written him a Christmas card all by myself and signed it lots of love forever, your friend, Mae Lee Willis, and hoped he would get the message. Ava held up her wrist and showed us a beautiful gold bracelet and said it had come from him. I asked how he had bought it out there in the jungle but she said they have ways.

I thought about that bracelet a lot and decided to ask Momma to take me to the library to get some books. And sure enough, back in the picture book section, putting books back on the shelves was Mis' Celia. My heart dropped to about my feet when she said, Hello, Gwen, hello, Mae Lee, and then leaned over and whispered when are you coming to church with me?

Momma stared at me as hard as if I had come out of the house buck naked. Oh, Mis' Celia, I said. I don't know. I want some horse books. I really love horses.

Over there, she said to me, winking. Second shelf. I walked over to the right bookshelf but not before I heard her say, Oh Gwen, do let her come. I promise I won't try to convert her.

Momma waited until we got home with my stack of horse books as well as a book on Maisie Flynn, Reporter, which Momma said was too advanced for me. I wanted it because Maisie was nosy and asked questions. Then she said, what was that all about with Mis' Celia? Going to church?

I got all red and said, well that day I was late from school, I told you a story. The real thing was, I stopped and had some tea and cookies with her and I met Father Leo.

Start at the beginning, Momma said. Why were you over there?

Willie Pennyman said there was a haunted house. I wanted to see it.

I told her most of the story but left out the real reason I went.

Well, your father would be against going to her church.

And I thought that was that. But then Mabel Conable came over.

Chapter Eight

M omma was out in the backyard with a basket full of wet clothes when Mabel Conable rode up in the truck and parked in the driveway. Momma finished pegging up a blue work shirt of Chap's and I handed her another clothespin and we watched Mabel walk over, the clothes flapping in the breeze. Mabel gave me the eye.

Gwen, I got something to tell you, she said.

Mae Lee, go on in the house and get Mabel and me some iced tea, Momma said.

I watched them out of the open kitchen window while I took out the ice trays and pulled the handle and banged them on the edge of the sink to make the ice come out. I filled the glasses and poured the tea.

I started to carry out the tea and got as far as the screen door when I saw Mabel lean over and fish some boxer shorts out of the basket and hand them to Momma to hang. Gwen, she said, you are my dear friend so I am going to tell you what people been saying. She couldn't see me behind the screen and didn't lower her voice.

And what is that, Mabel? Momma pegged the shorts and took an undershirt.

Mabel got kind of red and said, it's about Ava and Hardy Pritchard.

You do know she works for him. Momma took two clothespins out of her pocket and snapped the undershirt on the line.

Mabel picked up another damp shirt and turned it in her hands. Well they were at the drive-in barbecue down by the river last night, three people saw them.

Momma passed her some clothespins. Here, you can hang that as good as me. She bent for a towel. Ava sometimes works late, and there's no place else open. Mabel, maybe they were hungry after all that work.

It's dark under them trees, Mabel said, moving down the line to find room for the shirt.

What are you trying to say, Mabel? said Momma.

There's the bracelet. Mabel could be stubborn.

Dulany Radford gave her that bracelet, said Momma.

Jane Peabody was in Webb's jewelry buying a silver cup for her grandbaby and she saw Hardy Pritchard buying a gold bracelet.

So you are going to ask Celia Pritchard if she got a gold bracelet from her husband, Mabel? I am sick of all this gossip. You will be surprised to know that Celia Pritchard is a friend of this family and has asked Mae Lee to go to church with her.

What? said Mabel and her mouth hung open.

I figured this was my cue to go out the door with the tea glasses so that was what I did. Momma looked relieved to see me. Aren't you planning to go to church with Celia Pritchard, Mae Lee?

She was looking at me with a bedsheet in her hand like she knew I had been listening. Yes, ma'am, I said.

She's going this very Sunday, Momma said. Come here and help me with this bedsheet, Mae Lee.

Mabel took the tea glasses and I helped Momma with the bedsheet. Mabel drank her tea like she had been out in the burning desert with all the camels. Well, I can see you're busy, she said, wiping her mouth with the back of her hand.

Mae Lee, you forgot to bring the napkins, Momma scolded.

I ran into the house to get them, but when I got back, Mabel was gone.

Are you sure about this, Gwen? Chap said at the breakfast table Sunday morning with the house smelling of bacon and pancakes.

It'll do her good, Chap, to see how other people worship. She had braided my hair into two fat pigtails and buckled my feet into my black patent Mary Janes and I was wearing my best dress. I stirred the food on my plate. I was too nervous to be hungry.

What is Ava going to say? Chap chuckled. Maybe you should have told her. Maybe you shouldn't have let her spend the night out.

Momma shrugged. She'll have to like it, she said, and there was flint and steel in her voice.

Don't let the Pope tell you what to do, Chap said to me, and winked.

Who is the Pope? I said.

Father Leo's boss, Chap said.

I thought that was God, I said.

That's just the point, Chap said.

Don't confuse the child, Momma said. One day it will become clear to you, she said to me. Now go outside and wait on the porch for Mis' Celia.

I waited on the porch swing, pumping back and forth, and the Cadillac stopped in front of our house a few minutes later. This time it was for me.

Where's your sister this morning? Mis' Celia wanted to know, even before I got the door shut good.

She spent the night over at Barbara's, I said.

Would that be Barbara McIntosh?

Yes, I said. They're best friends.

How fascinating, said Mis' Celia, but I didn't see anything fascinating about it. What were they going to do? Mis' Celia asked.

I shrugged. They like to go to movies. And dances.

Does she dance with lots of boys?

They both do, I said.

Thank the Lord it wasn't far to her church. It wasn't much different from the outside from the Methodist or the Baptist churches. Like them, it was made of red brick with a white steeple, but it was smaller and set on a little grassy hill and we walked up about ninety steps to get there.

Once inside, I decided they had John Wesley beat six ways to Sunday. The inside was painted a soft cream color and the carpet was red, and the stained glass windows were red and blue and green and purple and gold, and the figures in the glass wore crowns and sad eyes and held onto their robes to keep them from dragging the ground, and there were statues in niches on the walls, and the smell was rich and perfumy.

John Wesley with its brown wood and white plaster and milky windows and smell of musty hymn books seemed awfully dull, and while we had a plain cross, St. Lawrence's had a golden cross with Jesus hanging from it that I couldn't quit looking at.

I heard a familiar giggle and turned to the left. Across the aisle sat Lourdes Sanchez and she grinned at me and I grinned back and then the organ started and Mis' Celia patted my hand and I had to be quiet.

Father Leo gave a sermon about Love beareth all things and believeth all things and endureth all things, which I liked, and Mis' Celia wiped at her eyes with a handkerchief and then they took the Lord's Supper but I did not and I later found out it was not saltines and grape juice.

After the service, Father Leo smiled his Santa-cheeked smile and told me to come again. Cecilia needs a child in her life, he said.

On the way home Mis' Celia chattered on about the service, explaining it all, and I was only half listening because I wondered why she and Hardy Pritchard did not have any children. I was going to ask but I heard the voice of Momma in my head telling me not to be so nosy all the time even though Maisie Flynn, Girl Reporter, would get no stories if she was not nosy, and Nancy Drew would solve no mysteries. Well, yes, they got in trouble in the books, so I guess trouble did go with being nosy. When Mis' Celia pulled up in front of our house, lo and behold there was Barbara McIntosh's father's car and Ava was getting out of it with her pillowcase gripped in one hand. She turned around and saw us. She opened her mouth halfway as if she had seen a giant boulder coming at her from out of the sky. Then she closed her mouth and hurried into the house.

Mis' Celia just sat there a minute looking thoughtful. She could have come over and spoken to me, she said. You would think she would. After all, my husband pays her salary.

Maybe she had to go to the bathroom, I said.

No, dear, she said, and patted my hand. It's all right. She was just afraid, that's all. Now she sounded tired and weary as though she had gone on a long journey instead of church.

Mis' Celia, you're not scary. I don't see why she should be scared of you.

She started to say something but stopped. Then she gave a short little laugh. Thank you, dear. I must pray, she said, and right away took a set of beads out of her pocket and half closed her eyes and started saying something so fast and breathlessly I couldn't understand. I did not didn't know what she was doing and her fingers were moving on the beads. They were pretty beads, red ones and clear ones and there was one of those Jesuses on the end.

When she had finished she opened her eyes and she was smiling.

What's that? I said.

It's a rosary. Next time I'll show you how to use it to pray, but I think you'd better go in now.

Yes, ma'am, I said. Thank you for taking me to church, Mis' Celia.

Will you come again sometime?

I stopped. If they let me, I said, and then I leaped out and walked to the house. I didn't look back as she drove off.

Unfortunately, Momma and Chap were not back from church yet. They were probably still out front in the sunshine talking with the preacher or Mabel or Lord knows who all and it was just me and Ava in the house.

She had a terrible look on her face, the only way in the world she could ever look ugly, and she was ugly now, and she said, What in hell were you doing with Celia Pritchard?

Going to church, I said. To make me good. Not like some people.

She reached to yank my hair but I stepped back and stood my ground. Momma asked her if I could go, I said.

Ava stood there, her hand out in midair, nails ready. What? Doesn't she know that woman is crazy?

She is no more crazy than you are, Ava Willis.

She has bad nerves.

She has beads, I said, and she prays with them. She is going to pray for you.

Ava turned pale then and turned around and went to our room and locked the door.

No fair, I said, I want to change out of my Sunday dress.

I could hear her crying into her pillow. When Chap's car came rumbling in the driveway she unlocked the door and came out.

It's all yours, she said, but the tears were gone and there was a hard look in her eyes.

Chapter Nine

Ava got more and more distant from all of us and went around with this faraway look. She still put money in the family pot, and if anybody tried to ask what was on her mind, she just said, I help to pay the bills around here, leave me alone, which was rude but nobody could do anything with her. We needed money to help pay the doctor bills because the doctors finally decided what Momma had was something called lupus and kept trying different medicines. Nothing seemed to work.

When the doorbell rang one day in October, Ava was still at work and Momma was in the kitchen slicing carrots and potatoes for soup, a hambone simmering in the pot, and that pot would get all our leftover vegetables for the week. I went to the door, and there was a soldier standing there.

He was tan and sun-blond, eyes as blue as a butterfly wing, grinning like a fool. There was a redheaded girl waiting for him in a green convertible at the curb. Hello, cutie, is this where Ava Willis lives? he said.

Yes, but she's at work.

Got a letter from her sweetie. Carried it a long way.

I held out my hand. I'm her sister. I'll give it to her.

He frowned and said, I was supposed to put it into her hands and give her a kiss from old Duke. Can I kiss you?

My cheeks burned then because he was really cute and I figured he was teasing me. I'll get Momma, I said.

He laughed and handed it over and bowed. With my very best wishes, princess. Tell her Jack Austin was here.

I hugged the letter to my chest with both hands and remembered my manners. Would you like to come in? I asked.

He glanced back to the girl in the car. My ride's waiting, he said, otherwise I would love to. Then he leaned over and kissed me on the cheek and ran out to the car and leaped in and they sped away. I rubbed my cheek, feeling like I wanted to cry and laugh at the same time.

I ran into the kitchen where Momma was bent over the cutting board chopping celery for the soup. Who was at the door, Mae Lee?

A man from the army.

Ohmygod, she said, and she grabbed the letter I was holding out. It's from Duke, she said, looking at it, and slumped back down. Don't scare me like that.

I wasn't trying to, I said.

I'm glad he wrote. I hope it's not too late, she said, scooping up the celery and dumping it in a bowl. She reached for a peeled carrot.

What do you mean?

She just shook her head and sliced the carrot into strips. She's tired of waiting, Momma said. She can't see beyond tomorrow. She thinks he won't come back. I just hope she doesn't write him a Dear John letter.

What's that? I watched her work crosswise on the carrot strips, making them into tiny blocks.

She dumped the carrot blocks into the bowl. It's when you write somebody and say you met somebody else. It's especially bad for soldiers because it makes them give up. They quit fighting. They quit wanting to live. If Chap didn't love me like he does—

Hush, Momma, I begged. I knew she was talking about her sickness. You have to keep fighting.

She lifted the lid off the stock pot already smelling like tomatoes and sweet ham and poured in the vegetables, along with bowls of peas and beans and corn. I will, she said. I've got the three of you to live for. Now go get me the cornmeal from the pantry.

I don't know when Ava read her letter that night because she didn't say anything to any of us. She knew we were all waiting around for her to tell us, but nobody wanted to ask for fear of getting their head bitten off.

I only found the letter because she tried to flush it down the commode and it didn't go down. Some came floating back up, four soggy pieces where she had torn it. I fished them out with a stick and spread them out on the top of the space heater after Ava went out.

I was glad he had written in pencil.

What happened to the tender loving girl I left behind? Your letters are so vague lately. We are having a god-awful time of it here. The tigers and snakes are bad enough without the bones and rotting corpses. The Japs are never far away. We never seem to get enough to eat except when we encounter a friendly village. Then they give us a big feed of curry.

The work is interesting and dangerous, but don't worry about old Duke. He is a tough character, at least that's what my buddies tell me after I've cleaned them out at poker. We pay the natives with dope, and they work like hell for us. I got banged up a little, but I'm here at the base hospital recovering. They were going to send me home but I asked to stay. Out here it's patch up and keep fighting.

I keep going by the thought of defeating the Japs and bringing this war to an end so I can get back home to you. It's a great feeling knowing you're waiting for me. I kiss your picture every night. It's torn and ragged from traveling.

What was the matter with her, anyhow? How could she like that stupid Hardy Pritchard?

I watched her every day but far as I could see, she didn't write back.

Finally on Friday I asked her, Have you written Duke?

She folded her arms. Is that any of your business?

I shrugged. Momma said that if they get a Dear John letter they will quit fighting and give up and get themselves killed.

What makes you think I'm going to write any such thing?

So what are you going to write then?

Look, she said, if you care so much, why don't you write to him?

I will, I said. He's coming back, you know. He needs to know somebody loves him. He needs to know you love him.

I'll write in my own good time.

So can I write him?

Suit yourself. She walked out of the room like she just didn't care, and I knew then she wasn't going to write.

I wasn't going to let him give up and die. I wanted him to come back and be in our family, to be my big brother if I couldn't marry him. A brother who thought I was special.

Momma gave me some thin blue stationery. But I couldn't find Ava's purple ink.

My dearest Duke, Mae Lee is writing this for me bcause I broke my rist. I love you and I cant wait for you to come home. Mae Lee loves you too very much. Momma and Chap love you. Get well soon. All my love, Ava and Mae Lee XXXXOOOO

I wanted it to be longer but I didn't know that many words. I got Momma to help me address it and mail it. I just had to get him home, and after that I would worry about what to do next.

Time went by the way it does when you're waiting for something, molasses or boiling pots or Christmas all the same. Ava clicked into the house on her high fat heels and she clicked out again like a sailing ship, proud and haughty, and we did not speak of Duke.

Chap listened to Walter Winchell on the radio every night and told us what was happening. We listened all through the news which was getting better except for the kamikaze attacks, and Chap said They are not tellin' you how many have been killed. They will never tell you the truth about that.

One day the phone rang and Mabel was crying and she told Momma that a telegram had been delivered to the Conable's farm that said Starrett Conable's brother Elmo Junior was missing in action in Europe, and we had a very bad day. I hoped Duke would write back, and I hoped Ava would not write him unless she could tell him she loved him.

Sometimes one thin thread of hope is all you have to tie you to the rest of life.

Mis' Celia called from time to time and Momma let me go to church with her, and I asked her to tell me more about the rosary. She gave me one, of really pretty milky white beads and taught me to say the Hail Mary and the Our Father, but before she could teach me any more prayers, Momma found out, and said she was trying to prosartize, and I was to give it back. I was going to be a Methodist if Momma had anything to say about it. Ava sneered. I told you about Celia, she said. Crazy lady.

And then Mis' Celia stopped calling me.

Momma swore she didn't tell her not to call me. After two weeks of no calls I missed her. I picked up the phone and told the operator her number, I could do that as well as Momma. Stupid Hardy Pritchard answered and said she couldn't come to the phone and I better quit calling.

What has happened to her? I asked Momma.

I don't know, honey. Maybe she went down to Savannah to see her people.

Looks like she would have told me, I said. She likes to talk about Savannah. Maybe he's keeping her locked up, I said.

Momma and Chap just looked at each other. Locked up? Momma said. Why would you think of something like that?

Because he's mean, I said. And because Ava keeps saying she is crazy and ought to be locked up. Dr. Manifold locked Tess up on *The Shadow* last week.

They looked at each other again.

That night it was hard to sleep. Momma had told me to just forget about Mis' Celia, but I felt sorry for her. And if Ava ran off with Hardy Pritchard I might never see Duke again in my whole life. I didn't know I'd fallen asleep until a car door slammed outside and jolted me awake. I listened for Ava's heels on the front walk but only heard the faint whistle of a far-off train and the bumping notes of jive down the street.

I rolled over and scooted across the covers on my belly to see out the window. The full moon hung high above the chinaberry tree, and there they were, Ava and Hardy Pritchard wrapped around each other in the soft yellow light, kissing and kissing like *they* were never going to see each other again and his hand was feeling of her rear end.

When Ava finally broke away and came up the walk, I scrambled back under the covers and pretended to sleep while she undressed and climbed in bed and gave a long happy sigh.

I woke again when the sun was just peeping through misty pink. Light was coming from down the hall, and the smell of coffee drifted in. I slipped out of bed and padded to the kitchen in my socks and pajamas.

The clock read seven-thirty. The light was on in the garage, and I knew Chap was out there working on his plane.

I knew Mis' Celia usually went to early Mass. A Catholic, she said, never misses Mass. Surely Hardy Pritchard wouldn't keep her from going to Mass. I could meet her outside and see if everybody was telling me the truth. I could take her back the rosary she had given me.

I dressed in my dungarees and Keds and red hooded sweater, scrubbed my face and combed my hair. There was no time to eat, but I drank some of the coffee with lots of milk and sugar in it. I took the rosary and said my prayers.

I headed for the front door, but then the toilet flushed and Ava came out of the bathroom.

Where do you think you're going? she said.

I bolted for the door but she must have seen the rosary sticking out of my pocket.

You better not go over there, I heard, just as the door was closing behind me.

I ran and I ran, down the dirt of Pickens Street, hit the pavement at Seneca Avenue, got on the sidewalks, footsteps pounding, pounding, echoing in the still morning. Fog swirled around me. Maybe Ava was throwing on clothes to chase after me, but I was way ahead. I turned the corner onto Oakdale, not slowing.

The house at 127 looked dark, only one light behind the lily-frosted front door window. The Cadillac sat in the garage. I ran around back, climbed on the back porch, and peered in the kitchen door at the dim kitchen, where wilted flowers stood on a wooden table.

I listened for sounds from inside, but all I heard were children's voices next door, a passing car, dogs barking in the distance, and the flap-flap of one of the high school football players who ran up and down the street every day.

Then the phone started ringing.

Thumps came from upstairs—footsteps—then I heard Hardy Pritchard's voice, shouting *goddam*, then a thumpy-thumpy-thump, and a kind of smack, and then everything was quiet. I went around the house and rattled the back door, but it was locked. I ran around to the front door again and peered in the glass. I saw two legs lying on the floor at the foot of the stairs. Two feet were poking out of pajama bottoms, one bare, one with a slipper on it. Beside one foot was Mis' Celia's rosary.

I couldn't see the rest of him, but it had to be Hardy Pritchard. What was he doing on the floor? And what had he done with Mis' Celia?

A car screeched to a stop in the street, and Chap called my name.

I ran down the steps crying hard, choking, and fell into his arms.

I don't know if the phone ever stopped ringing.

Chapter Ten

The town talked about it for weeks, how Hardy Pritchard had fallen down those stairs and broken his neck.

Chap said it was a good thing Mis' Celia wasn't home to see it, but Momma said it wouldn't have happened if she'd been there, if Hardy Pritchard had not taken her to that sanitarium and had her committed. There was talk as to whether his shoe had come off and tripped him up. People also asked whether God put that rosary on the stairs or Mis' Celia left it there on purpose. I knew she would never have gone off without it.

Momma and Chap and I went to the funeral, but Ava wouldn't go. She cried and walked around like a zombie for weeks, getting thinner. I didn't tell anybody about the packed suitcase I'd found in Ava's room when we got back that day. I unpacked it and put all her clothes away and she didn't fuss at me or pull my hair or call me names.

Doc Weir called and asked her if she'd like to come back to work at the drugstore, but she just said, *hell no*, and Momma and

Chap stared at each other like they were doing as they had been more and more these days.

Mis' Celia checked herself out of the sanitarium. Since Hardy Pritchard was dead and there was nobody to pay the bill, the doctors found she was all right and less nervous than she used to be. In fact she was downright calm and what Momma called serene. When she decided to move back to Savannah, I went over to her house and helped her pack her things, the picture and books and little Japanese ladies with fans. A For Sale sign went up in the front yard.

She gained a little weight and roses bloomed in her cheeks. She still prayed on her same rosary, and one day, when she asked me over for a last cup of tea, she got all thoughtful and told me he wrenched it out of her hand and threw it behind when he grabbed her to take her to the car. I guess he didn't care where it landed.

The day the moving van left, I went over to wave good-bye.

Chap got angry at Ava for the first time in her charmed life. Look here, he said, you keep carryin' on like that and people will think the talk was true. You get your caboose up and out of this house and help to put some greens and cornbread on the table.

I can't, I can't, she said. I have burnt my bridges. I'm going to kill myself.

I wonder what would have happened if a certain letter hadn't arrived in time. I took it up to her. It's from Duke, I said, wagging it back and forth. You want it, or can I have it?

She stared at me, eyes wide, face white as cotton in the field. Give it here, she said, snatching it out of my hand like the Ava of old.

After she read it, she buried her face in her hands and the letter came floating to the ground. I picked it up and started to read it and she didn't even yell at me, she was weeping so.

> *My Ava,*
>
> *Give Mae Lee a big kiss for writing that letter for you. Hope your wrist is well now. Glad you got the letter I sent by my buddy Austin who was an airman we rescued from the jungle. He was flying the Hump when his plane was shot down. He got to go home, lucky dog. I don't know how much more of this I can take. I sure want to get out of this ole army and come home to you. I know it's hard on you, waiting for me, but I've always had faith that you would be there.*
>
> *Our boys are winning. I'm mostly recovered from my little dust-up, just a little gimpy. They're not sending me on missions, but I'm useful at HQ.*
>
> *Be a good girl and sit down and write me a lot of "sweet nothings" that I can dream about during some of these boring hours when I'm not on duty.*
>
> *All my love,*
>
> *Dulany*

So he would come back to Ava, but he might find out the truth about Hardy Pritchard. Would people stay quiet, or would they talk without Mis' Celia to protect?

Chapter Eleven

Duke was coming home.

It was March 17, 1945, and Ava had gotten a telegram from San Diego three days ago *and* a phone call this morning.

I sat out on the steps in the sun with my new green cardigan pulled around me, shivering with excitement. The wind ruffled my hair, and the sun sparked through the pale green leaves in the pecan trees.

Daffodils nodded and bobbed everywhere—in our yard and across the street, where they bloomed in clumps in front of the fence. The old horse frisked like a colt in the field.

I saw that Buick convertible way at the end of the street and ran back into the house. He's coming, I hollered, and I got up and jumped up and down and twirled around. He's coming!

Ava threw down her *Life* magazine and smoothed her silky red blouse, twisting around to look at her rear end in the mirror. Her dark hair was as shiny as the mink coat in the *Life* magazine.

She stepped out on the porch just as the Buick rolled to a stop in front of our house, lips apart, holding her two hands together.

Duke opened the car door, squinting at the sun. A long metal cane appeared first and then he heaved himself out of the car, leaning on it. He straightened and Ava gave a little cry and she ran to him, and he folded her in.

Ava touched the cane. Oh, Duke.

It's nothing, honey. I'm all right. It'll just take time.

Duke was drinking her in like she might disappear in a poof of smoke. They couldn't quit touching each other—a hand here, a hand there, a brush of lint off his coat. With his free hand he stroked her face and then he kissed her.

I was hanging back a few feet from them, the bratty kid sister Ava didn't want around, wanting him to see me, and then Duke held out an arm. Come here, Mae Lee. It's time for my hug.

I let him squeeze my small body against his big one and then I looked up at him to see if he was the same Duke who had left, and from the look in his eyes I got the strange feeling that he wasn't, that he had lost something out there in Burma.

But then he looked into Ava's eyes. I have something for you, he said, right before the screen door banged behind us.

Chap stood on the front porch, pipe between his teeth. He and Duke sized each other up. Chap walked down the steps past the rusty metal chair and across the swept-dirt yard and the pointy bricks and the daffodils toward the shiny Buick.

He shook Duke's hand. I held my breath. The wind stirred the daffodils, and then they both smiled. Chap said Momma was waiting inside with dinner. Duke squeezed Ava's hand and whispered, After dinner.

Momma had made fried chicken, mashed potatoes, peas with pepper and butter, slaw and pickles, and fresh biscuits. Duke grinned and said, The best part of getting back is all this good chow.

Are you sure, said Ava, and nudged him, and everybody laughed. She was back to her old self.

I knew it had to come sometime, but it came sooner than I thought. It came during the second helping of mashed potatoes.

Duke set the empty bowl down on his end of the table and said, Talley told me a funny story. I did not dare look at Ava. Duke said, Talley told me you had been working for Hardy Pritchard and now he's dead. How come you never told me that in any of your letters?

Chap sat on the edge of his chair like there was a coiled up spring inside of him. Momma sort of smiled and passed the peas. Ava's fork clattered on the floor and I dived down to retrieve it but she waved it away. She propped her elbows on the table and laced her fingers together. I know you didn't like him, she said with a little smile. I didn't want to worry you. He was paying me good money and we needed it.

Well, I guess it doesn't matter now. Duke rubbed his chin. Remember what he said to me that day we had a run-in? Got a date with destiny, you and me, he said. Well. What happened to him exactly? Nobody said anything and then he turned to Chap. Didn't you find him, Mr. Willis?

Chap was inspecting a chicken bone to see if there was any more meat on it. Chap was no good whatsoever at lying.

Chap and me found him, I said. He slipped and fell on Mis' Celia's rosary.

You don't know that for a fact, said Ava.

Mis' Celia thinks it's so, I said.

I could just see Ava was itching to say she was crazy but she just swallowed and said, Well, let her think what she likes.

How did you two happen to find him? Duke said.

I was going to church with Mis' Celia, I said.

It's a long story darlin', Ava said sweetly, laying a hand on his arm. Let me tell you all about it later. Momma let's have our pie now.

Yes, Momma said brightly, lemon meringue.

After all the pie and coffee were finished Duke said he wanted to take Ava for a drive in the country.

He has something for her, I piped up.

Shut up, you, Ava said.

Thanks, kiddo, Duke said and winked at me.

Enjoy yourselves, Chap said. I think he was glad to get them out of the house.

They stayed out late. I was in bed still awake when Ava came back. She was laying her coat on her own bed when I popped from under the covers.

Well, Mae Lee, she said. I hoped you'd be asleep.

Come on. What happened?

She pulled off her clothes, stretching like a cat: sweater, skirt, socks, loafers, underwear, and on went the gown under her pillow. Then she sat on the bed, opened her pocketbook, and took out a packet of paper tied with twine.

Here, she said. Feast your eyes, twerp.

I took it and that knot was hard to untie but I did it.

And oh, wow. On the grayish paper lay a pair of ruby earrings which were like two big drops of blood dangling from a diamond. I touched one and it felt warm, a heart beating.

Okay, give back, she said and took the paper away and refolded it and tied the twine back with a double knot. I'll have to get my ears pierced, she said.

Momma will have a fit, I said. The only girl I knew with pierced ears was Lourdes Sanchez.

Too bad. I'm not going to lose these, Ava said.

Please, can I see them again? They made me feel all funny, like all the mystery of things I didn't know was hiding in their red fire.

One day I would know how much they had cost.

Go to sleep, kiddo. Ava pulled the covers over her, closed her eyes, sighed, and sank right into the bed and that was all I heard from her that night.

It was a long time before I slept. Ava had the earrings to tell the world that Duke loved her, and she didn't deserve them. I wished he had brought me something. But the look in his eyes when he saw me would have to be enough for now.

One day when I got home from school I found Momma hunched over some sewing at the kitchen table, white material in her lap and jars of little pearls and shiny things beside her and a big bolt of lace. The pouches under her eyes looked bigger.

Duke brought back a silk parachute, she said.

So Ava finally thought Momma's sewing was good enough to make her wedding dress. Momma, I thought you were supposed to rest, I said.

I'm going crazy sitting at home, she said. This makes me feel useful. She paused. But this is my swan song. So Mae Lee, don't you ever get married.

Momma, you're teasing.

She nodded. Yes she said, but let me tell you something, honey. It starts out all satin and lace and pearls, flowers and candlelight and a big tall cake like young girls dream of. Nobody wants to tell you about the time when the dress is laid away and the flowers dry up and the cake becomes crumbs that the ants carry away. And then you have this. She touched her old slipper toe to the bare spot on the floor where a linoleum patch had gone missing.

Momma was scaring me talking like this. Duke's rich, Momma, I said, in case she had forgotten.

Rich or poor, if it gets too hard, a woman can be tempted by anybody who shows up with a branch of sweet shrub in his hand, sweet shrub bless me, not much to look at but heaven in its heart.

Momma, you're talking crazy.

I suppose I am, she said. Ava will have pretty things. Like those rubies.

Oh Momma, they are so beautiful.

She nodded. I should be happier about this wedding. I liked Dulany before he went away, even if your daddy minded that he was the boss's son. He used to be a sweet young man. But now he's harder. Disconnected from things. Sometimes he goes into his own thoughts, and it's like he's not even here.

That was it, the part he left behind. I didn't say so to Momma. She was worried enough.

Dulany Bennington Radford and Ava Dell Willis were married in the First Baptist Church on the sixteenth of June, the day after the war ended in Burma, and so many people came that chairs had to be brought for the aisles and the vestibule.

Ava's parachute gown outdid any creation from Paris, everybody said, and they said that Momma had outdone herself. Everybody cried, including me.

Mabel Conable and the ladies from the John Wesley Methodist Church helped Momma put on a reception in the church hall. They made green and white mints that melted in your mouth and chicken salad sandwiches and creamed chipped beef in patty shells and a three-decker wedding cake with wedding bells on top and beautiful pink punch with a floating ice ring made of ginger ale and strawberries.

Mrs. Norma Radford, Duke's mother, donated bouquets of pink roses from her garden, and it was as fine a reception as that old church had ever seen.

Duke and Ava left for their honeymoon on St. Simon's Island.

Shortly after that I started to save up my nickels and dimes to be able to buy some ear studs. I made friends with Lourdes Sanchez. And when I had saved enough, I convinced Mrs. Sanchez that my momma had said it was okay to let her pierce my ears. Momma was really mad, so to make her happy I promised I would go to church with her every Sunday, and when I came to the *age of discernment* I was received into the John Wesley Methodist Church.

PART II

Chapter Twelve

1945

It was right after they dropped the atomic bomb on Hiroshima that Chap and Elmo finished the plane, the beginning of the end of the war, the beginning of the end of my childhood.

Chap asked me to help him one Saturday afternoon out in the garage, handing him bolts and screws. The place smelled like dust and oil and airplane dope, and the door was thrown wide open, now that he didn't have to keep his hobby a secret. All sweaty and arms black with grease, he tightened the last bolt on the engine, put down his wrench, and asked me to run get us some tea before we cleaned up.

I hurried to the kitchen and came back with two fruit jars full, sweet and strong. We stood drinking it, feeling the cold wash through our insides. Chap wiped his mouth with the back of his arm. We'll be taking her out to the airfield soon, he said. There's an abandoned hangar we can have, and we'll put her all together, put the wings on and give her one last coat of dope. Then she'll be ready for a spin.

With me? I was all excited now. I couldn't wait to fly.

Why sure, you're my boy, you know.

That old thing he used to say, that old thing I used to like. Couldn't he see I was growing up? I was still flat-chested, but you could tell something was beginning to happen, and I longed for a bra to at least cover me when I wore a T-shirt. Chap, I said, I'm a girl. I want some girl stuff like Ava has. Dresses and jewelry.

Chap laughed. But you hate dresses. Look at you.

Okay, so I was wearing dungarees and a T-shirt, but still. I couldn't tell him about wanting a bra. Maybe I need some earrings, I said.

Earrings, hmmm, he said. He sat on a wooden box and motioned for me to sit too. I perched on an old kitchen chair one nail away from collapsing. Outside, the katydids skirled in the trees. He took a long drink of tea and rattled the ice. Ever hear of Amelia Earhart?

Sure.

She was a flier, he said. And she wore dresses—well, some of the time. I don't know about earrings. I just don't want you to give up bein' you, honey, to copy Ava.

Yes, sir.

I can give you flyin' lessons now and earrings when you're older. How's that?

How much older?

As long as it takes for your momma to get used to your ears having holes, he said, and that was that.

Then Japan surrendered, and the war was over. We had a celebration at our house. We bought barbecued chickens from Willie Pennyman's father and the Conables brought cake and Duke and Ava brought champagne, and it looked so fresh and bubbly I begged for some and she poured me a glass without a word.

Starrett Conable laughed at the face I made. Well, she won't ever be a drunk, Chap said.

Ava's rubies glittered and they both drank a little too much and got tipsy. Starrett whispered to me, the big hero's fixing to fall off his cane.

Shut up, Starrett, I said under my breath. He was a year older than me and thought he was so smart.

Let's go out to see the engine, Starrett said. We all trooped out to the garage, and we stood there under the bare electric light admiring it. Does it run, he asked.

It will, I said. It's going to carry me up one day when I fly the plane.

But you're a girl.

Chap's going to give me lessons.

He says.

Bet you ten million dollars, I said.

Something real, he said. If I win I get to kiss you.

And if I win I get to slap you, I said.

I was looking forward to smacking him.

One morning in September I was sitting on the back porch with Momma shelling butterbeans. It was a cool day, the first real blast of wind from the north, a wind to push summer all the way back to Florida. By this time Duke was out of the army and had gone back to work for his father at the plant and they were tooling up to make work pants again. The whole town thought of him as a hero. Like father, like son.

I was dropping the littlest butterbeans into a special bowl. I liked their earthy smell—it made me shiver and I didn't know why. Momma was faster than me, though her fingers often got swollen and she found it hard to do that kind of work.

We heard a car door slam out front and then Ava came tripping along around the house in her high heels, all dolled up in a new skirt and polka dotted blouse with puffy sleeves.

Momma's eyes lit up and mine narrowed. Hi, honey, she said.

Hello, Momma. Ava planted a kiss on her cheek.

There's coffee in the kitchen. I'm about ready for a cup, Momma said. She pushed herself out of the chair, panting and straining. Here, let me help, I said, and Ava and I exchanged the kind of glance sisters give each other when there's something wrong with their mother.

I'm all right, Momma said crossly, and limped into the kitchen. My knee is gimpy, that's all.

We poured our coffee, mine with half milk, and sat down at the kitchen table just as cozy as you please. So what brings you here? Momma said.

Does it have to be something? Ava said.

You have that look, Momma said.

Ava set her coffee cup down and her bird-wing brows came together. Duke found us a place, she said.

Well, what's wrong with that? I thought you hated living with the Radfords.

I like their house. I wanted one of my own.

Well, then.

Duke wants us to live in a bungalow. On his grandfather's farm.

Grandfather Dulany?

Yes, ma'am.

Sweetbay Plantation? Ava, that's wonderful.

No, it isn't! It's where the maid used to live!

I'm sure he'll fix it up for you.

But I want to live in town. I was expecting something swell.

Ava, he has to work his way up at the plant. I'm sure he wants to save money for a better place later.

I want it now. She gave the pout I knew so well.

I stared into my coffee cup and wondered if Ava had learned anything at all.

And Duke is going to teach me to ride, she said. She might have been saying he was going to teach her to eat worms.

I jumped up. Oh, Ava, you're the luckiest girl in the world! What I wouldn't give to have a horse!

She examined her nails. It will be very hard on my manicure, farm life.

At the mention of nails, Momma went out to the back porch to get the butterbeans. She hated to sit and talk when she could be accomplishing something useful. She pushed a handful at each of us and started shelling. Beans we plunked into the bowl and hulls into a paper sack. I reached for a pod.

Ava, she said, this is a battle you cannot win.

I'll die, she said. There's manure out there.

You won't have to shovel it, Momma said, smiling.

I'll have to smell it. Fresh country air, huh.

Momma didn't even glance at me when she said, Do you love him, Ava?

What does that have to do with it?

Momma ran her finger expertly down a pod, splitting it. Did I leave Chap when he lost his business? When we had to sell our house and move here? It hasn't always been easy. I've been tempted by—well, never you mind. But now we prop each other up, and I swear to God I don't know what I'd do without him. He is my strength and I am his.

Momma's eyes looked older than they should have, and I thought of what she'd said about the soft dirt and the sweet shrubs and I wondered if anybody had loved her besides Chap. But even if they had, I knew she would not have gone with them.

Ava picked up another bean and tore at it, trying not to use her fingernails. I came here hoping you'd be on my side, Momma.

I am on your side. I want you to be happy.

What do you mean?

You can win a battle, Ava, and lose a war, if you know what I mean.

Ava picked up another bean. She was getting good at not using her fingernails.

In a war you have tactics, she said thoughtfully.

One warmish Thursday evening toward the end of September, Mabel Conable stopped by the house, pulling the pickup around to the back. It was nearly seven o'clock, and the light was fading to gold around the vines on the back fence while I was unclipping clothes from the line, surrounded by air so full of the smell of ripe muscadines it could make you drunk. When she got out of the truck, I tossed a shirt into the basket and called hello. She looked as though somebody had taken a giant bottle of Clorox and dipped her in it. All the color was gone from her face, her hair was white-gray, and she was wearing a housedress as washed-out as a dishrag. I noticed the grim look on her face and my heart sank. It couldn't be Elmo Junior because we'd heard he got out of a prison camp.

I told her Momma was inside scraping some late corn off the cob to put in the freezer locker. Mabel went on in.

When I finished taking down the clothes, I carried them inside and found Mabel helping Momma scrape corn, scoring the kernels down with a sharp knife and then scraping down with the flat of a table knife to get all the good out. They both had glasses of tea by their elbows.

While I put away the clothes, I could hear them talking. Mabel was just like a radio announcer. It seemed that she was looking for Elmo and couldn't find him anywhere and felt he was off someplace with Chap. He could be with some woman, she said. They both could.

I think she's silver with blue and white stripes, Momma said. Her name is Matilda.

What the hell? Mabel said. Matilda?

You been out to the airport looking for them? It's the plane, Momma said.

She wouldn't go first try, Momma said. Elmo tell you that? They need to work on the engine.

He's close-mouthed, Elmo, said Mabel.

There was a silence as the women scraped and scraped.

I heard something, Mabel said. Duke Radford spends a lot of time down at the Bisons Club bar.

Oh well, said Momma. There are some vets there.

Aren't you concerned?

It's Ava's business, said Momma, and she has not seen fit to come to me.

I think she goes too, Mabel said, and there was a darkness in her voice.

You had better go to the airfield, said Momma, while it's still light, and her voice was even and calm.

Mabel got up then. Yes, she said, I had better go there.

I came into the kitchen just as the screen door banged closed behind her. Help me with the corn, honey, said Momma. It's almost done. She scored and I scraped. When we finished, she gave me a sack of boiled peanuts for a reward. I was sitting on the back steps eating them when Chap came home with Elmo.

The screen door banged and I heard the crunch of beer cans being opened. I waited for Momma to ask where they had been, but she never did.

There was a frost between Mabel and Momma, and the Conables did not come over the next Friday night. That was okay with me, because then there would be no Starrett to bug me and tell me I was his favorite dish. I had not forgotten our bet. Kiss or slap, and I was going to win. Then Chap said they had fixed the engine and maybe next Saturday we would all go out to the airfield.

I was so excited.

On Monday I got sent home from school for being sick. It came on me all at once, dizziness and fever, and the doctor said it was flu, there was something going around. I felt so bad I thought I would die and never see the plane take off, and I wondered if this was how Momma felt every day.

On Tuesday, Momma fixed me aspirin and a glass of orangeade about lunchtime and went out, closing the door softly behind her, telling me to sleep again. I drank all of the orangeade and set the glass on the bedside table, snuggling under the pile of covers she had mounded to try to ease my chills. Through my sick-fuzzy mind I heard a tapping at the front door, so faint I could hardly be sure there was anybody on the porch at all.

I heard a voice, a rumble, asking, How's the girl?

Doing all right, Momma said.

Despite the chills, I crawled out from under the covers and slid over far enough so that I could see out the window, and it was Elmo, and that was strange because he usually came to the back. Momma had her arms folded and they lowered their voices so I couldn't make out what they were saying. He put a hand to her cheek. Gwen, he said, and then she stepped back as if his hand had been red-hot.

I have to go now, she said, Mae Lee's calling. She turned and hurried in the house. I had not called her. Elmo walked away with his hands in his pockets.

Maybe I had the answer to my question, and I wished I didn't.

I tried very hard to get well by Saturday. I begged Chap to put it off, and he said if the weather was perfect, he had to go then. Momma explained that he didn't have many free Saturdays, and I did, so that I could go another time if I missed this one.

But I want to see it fly first, I said, thinking of the bet with Starrett. I just knew he would make it a point to be there. Maybe he would get Chap to give him a lesson.

We'll see, said Momma. Duke and Ava want to come.

I looked up at Jesus on the wall, and then I got the rosary out of my top drawer where it hid behind the socks, and prayed harder than I ever had in my whole life.

Chapter Thirteen

I hunkered in the corner of the back seat on the way out to Sweetbay, hoping no one would notice how pale I looked, trying to tell myself I felt fine. I'd pretended to have an appetite earlier and got down my eggs and grits, but my stomach rebelled at the greasy bacon, and I stashed that behind the stove. If Momma ever found it, she might think she'd dropped it by accident, because she wasn't so steady these days.

The drive to Sweetbay was even prettier than I imagined it, down a long dirt road bordered with huge oak trees draped with long swags of Spanish moss, then past neat fields, then rows of pines leading to the house itself. We parked in the circular dirt driveway under a huge, mossy live oak. There were a couple of trucks parked there too, the moss touching their roofs.

The house itself was one story, with a porch that wrapped all the way around held up by square white columns. Ava and Duke walked out and came down to greet us.

Granddad sends his apologies, Duke said. He's got a sick cow.

He never lets up, does he? Chap said.

All he's ever done was work, said Duke. Worked even harder after Grandmama died, like she was up there watching him.

More to drive away the loneliness, Momma said to me under her breath.

I blinked when I really looked at Ava. She wore a pair of jeans and a calico blouse, and a scarf was tied around her head, the two ends sticking up like rabbit ears. She saw me looking and twirled around. How do you like the latest farm fashions?

Oh, Ava, Momma said.

I've spent the morning stripping turnips, she said, wiggling her fingers and making a face.

Good, Momma said. I noticed that Ava's nails were not polished.

Come see my bungalow, Ava said.

Chap wanted to talk to old Mr. Dulany, so he went with Duke to hunt down his granddaddy in the barn while Ava took Momma and me to show us the bungalow. We walked around back of the big house and I saw the barn and some outbuildings, and heard people talking and chickens gabbling and horses snorting and smelled gasoline and manure. And here was a little white-painted bungalow with green shutters. A chimney stood at one end, and some new bushes had been planted under the two front windows. Ava jerked open the screen door. Welcome to my world.

We walked into a tiny front entrance with a little kitchen on the left, a breakfast bar separating it from the living room. It reminded me of a doll's house, with white ruffled curtains at the windows and a brown-and-pink slipcovered sofa. And there were Ava's movie magazines, of course, arranged on the coffee table, which stood on a rag rug.

Why, Ava, Momma said. This is charming.

I nearly died when I first saw it, she said. Dark and musty and dusty, no one had been living in it for years. It didn't even have electricity! Thank God I have a phone. I'd die without it.

You're on a party line, said Momma.

You have to be careful, she said. No telling who's listening in. Who am I going to talk to out here? Duke's always working, and the old man's always working. There's only Elzuma, and I don't think she likes me. Duke told me she used to tell fortunes, and I asked her to tell mine, but she said she didn't do that anymore.

Who's Elzuma? I said.

You don't need a fortune, Momma said. What you need is a baby.

I'm not ready for one, Momma. Maybe when we move back to town.

You think he's going to do that?

He'll get his fill of farm life.

Who's Elzuma? I said.

They weren't listening to me. An argument had started and I wandered outside. I walked by a gas pump and inspected an open shed that sheltered a tractor, a wheelbarrow, a pile of timbers, three old signs, and some rusty tools.

I headed toward the sound of chickens and came on a chicken-wire pen, and behind the wire stood a short, squat colored lady with a bandanna tied around her head. I knew she had to be Elzuma. She was wringing the neck of a chicken.

Rooted to the spot, I watched the scrawny claws kicking, the strong brown hand tighten. There was a powerful odor of chicken mess, and my stomach heaved right then and there.

Hey, chile, she called but I was running fast as my legs would carry me back to Ava's bungalow. I almost made it.

The sound of sickness brought Momma and Ava out, and Momma sent Ava to get a cold cloth. They cleaned me up, walked me back inside, and made me drink flat Coke which was disgusting.

Right in the middle of all the commotion Chap and Duke came to the door. Hey, girls, time to go, they said.

Mae Lee can't go, Momma said. She's messed up her shirt and she's sick. You all go on and I'll stay here with her. No need, said Duke, Elzuma can look after her. At that my stomach heaved again and I bent over.

All over my rug, said Ava.

I'll get Elzuma, Duke said, but while he was gone Momma cleaned up the mess and Ava found me a T-shirt of Duke's to wear. She sure wasn't going to let me wear anything of hers. Little did she know that T-shirt made me stupidly happy.

Duke stuck his head back in the door. She's coming, he said, soon as she finishes with the chicken.

Don't say that, I begged.

I guess we can go, Ava said. Momma put me in their double bed with the chenille bedspread and turned on the radio to some music. You rest here, she said. Do not get up. I would stay with you but Chap really wants me there.

I lay back, dizzy again, and listened to the mutter of the car until it died away. Out in the fields I heard the swishing of the wind in the broomsedge and hoped the day would be too windy to fly, and they would have to put it off till I could come. I turned over, squealing the saggy springs.

Still Elzuma did not come. The radio played "Oh! What it Seemed to Be," which sounded sappy, and "Shoo Fly Pie and Apple Pan Dowdy," which sounded silly, and then they played one I liked, "Laura," singing about the face in the misty light.

Bored, I slid out of bed and looked at the books in the bookcase. I picked out *The Foxes of Harrow* and was disappointed it wasn't about animals. Then I saw a small, slim book kind of wedged in, and I pulled it out. I opened it; it was a kind of diary. When I saw Duke's writing, I sucked in my breath and read:

We are quartered in a tea plantation in the hills of Assam. Officers in the main house and enlisted men in a converted tea shed. Tea bushes cover the hillsides. We are not far from Naga territory where headhunters still roam the hills. Met the first batch of Kachin recruits I'm supposed to train. We pay them in opium.

Just then I heard the screen door squeal open. I shut the book, slid it back on the shelf, and hopped back into bed just as Elzuma appeared in the door. She grinned at me. You mean to tell me killing a chicken makes you sick? How else you gone eat,

girl? You think them chickens grows on trees? You can't make
no omlet lessn you break eggs.

I was already sick, I said in a small voice. And I don't want any
eggs or any chicken ever again.

Don't you worry none, honey, she said. She smiled like she
was full of sunshine and peaches instead of chicken blood. You
change your mind soon's you get hungry.

I was half scared of her, but since Duke said she would look
after me, I trusted him. I hitched myself up in bed. Do you really
tell fortunes?

She frowned. Who say that?

I just heard it, I said.

I use to, she said. Don't do it no more.

How'd you do it?

Diff'rent ways, she said. Some work better'n others. Tea
leaves, chicken feathers. Onct my old auntie down on the island
show me how to do the cards, but that just a parlor trick.

Will you show me about the cards?

She frowned then. Better not.

But if it's just a trick, why not?

She sighed, a long windy sigh with Africa in it. I guess it
can't do no harm. She went in the other room and came back
with a pack of cards, just ordinary cards like Momma and Chap
used for playing gin rummy. She shuffled them, talking all the
while, like wanting to fill up the house with talk, while the radio
played.

Elzuma told me about when she used to live in the bungalow
when Mis' Catherine, Duke's mother, was a young lady, and then

marrying Link Handy and having babies of her own, and moving out when it got too small for all of them to another house on the farm, and walking down the lane to work from there, and coming back here to look after old Mr. Robert, and living in the big house now in easy shoutin' distance.

She sat on the end of the bed and laid out cards on the cover like she was going to start a game of solitaire. Queen of clubs, queen of diamonds. Two queens, two ladies in your life, she said.

Six of spades, trouble and strife.

I held my breath.

Two of diamonds, love to spare. King of clubs, friend always there. She smiled at me. Jack of diamonds, won't be true. Four of clubs, he'll make you blue. I giggled. I didn't even have a boyfriend, if you didn't count Starrett Conable. He was more like a pebble in your shoe you couldn't shake out. I wondered if he was at the airfield.

Then she started to lay down a card, glimpsed at it, and it slid out of her hand. Done dropped one, she said, and scooped it up. I better start over.

She gathered up the cards, but not before I saw the one on the bottom. The ace of spades.

Something was howling, faint, in the distance, like a train whistle, like a ghost wolf. What's that? I said, my heart beating fast. I felt dizzy.

That sick wagon, she said. She prodded me with her gentle, chicken-strangling fingers. You lay back down. It ain't nothing.

She took the cards away and came back with some cool lemonade for me and held the glass while I sipped it. I finally lay back and closed my eyes.

I don't know how long I lay there until I heard the car in the driveway and the voices. The door opening and closing and Ava's hysterics. More voices in the other room and then Duke appeared at my bed. He took me in his arms then, and I had one moment of happiness with my head on his chest before he told me.

Chapter Fourteen

Where are they, the shadow-people? They hover between life and death, between absolutely alive and absolutely dead, and I have noticed some people are like that all their lives. Chap was never a shadow-person. He was in the sunshine all his life, except for those two days he lingered in the hospital. And if I had known that Duke was coming to tell me Chap was heading toward the shadows, I would have run. I would have run to the far reaches of the world, to the Pacific, where the news sometimes gets lost, and news unfound, news delayed, news unheard, is not ever true.

He had landed the plane perfectly. It was the stress, they told us. An occult heart condition, they called it, which sounded peculiar, and made me think of the ace of spades. Lion-hearted as he was, nobody suspected his heart might be weak.

They tried to break it to me gently. Chap's in the hospital, they said. He's going to be all right. But children look at actions more than they listen to words, and all the red eyes and hollow faces, what they weren't saying, made me scared and shaky.

They wouldn't let me go to the hospital, and I had to imagine his arms around me, telling me he'd be home soon, and then he'd teach me how to fly.

I didn't get the story of what happened until Starrett Conable told me one afternoon when he came over with a pan of chicken and dumplings from his mama and we sat out back on the steps. He told me because I asked him.

Chap and Elmo had each had a turn taking the plane up, then Chap took Mama for a ride and Elmo took Starrett because Mabel wouldn't go. Mama had loved the ride, he said, and her eyes were all sparkly when she got out of that plane.

They were about to call it a day when Ava decided she just had to try it and posed for a picture by the plane—Chap with his old style leather flying helmet and Ava with her hair all windblown. Chap took off, telling her he'd give her a thrill.

The climbed higher and higher, circled, and dived. Ava must have liked it, even if she did scream, because Chap climbed to dive again. On the next dive, though, the propeller stopped, the plane bucked, and then it stalled.

Chap managed to glide it in perfectly, but then he slumped over. Ava had hysterics and Momma fainted. Elmo pulled him out of the plane. Starrett ran to the hut on the field and called for an ambulance.

Starrett shook his head. My poor dad, he said. He ain't never going to get over it if your dad don't make it.

Chap fought long and hard. We thought he was too tough to die. The second day after the heart attack he cussed out all the doctors, but the third day he passed away along toward evening. He told Momma he loved her. She said she hadn't heard it in years.

I know better now, but I always looked at that moment as the time when everything began to fall apart.

Maybe if Chap hadn't died things would have turned out differently.

His funeral was one big blur of faces and flowers, a scent of lilies and roses, folks hugging me and burly men calling me little lady. I could hardly see who they were, my eyes were so red and wet. And at the end they played Amazing Grace on the wheezy little organ and I broke down and Elmo Conable had to carry me to the car.

During the weeks afterward, poor Elmo wandered around like a lost soul. It didn't help that Elmo Junior was still over there somewhere. During that time we didn't see much of the Conables, though Momma went over from time to time with something she'd cooked. She fretted that we might have to move, but we could pay the rent because Chap had taken out some life insurance a long time ago, and she got a little bit from the Army.

I was missing Chap like crazy. Every once in a while I'd look out back at the garage and get a big lump in my throat, but I didn't let myself cry. As long as nobody played Amazing Grace, I could keep it in. I thought I had to be strong for Momma so she wouldn't worry about me. Maybe then she wouldn't grieve so hard.

She kept on going to church every Sunday and I went with her, though I didn't love the John Wesley Methodist Church and Brother Ben Higgins as much as she did. I was getting worried about her—I missed the old Momma I was used to. She was getting weaker and complained about the pain in her joints, saying it was rheumatism. Please, Momma, go to the doctor, I'd say. When Brother Higgins came by, I'd take him aside. Make her go to the doctor.

I'm working on it, he said.

But I thought she was just giving up.

And then it was fruit basket turnover time, time for Mr. Higgins to leave for another church, which I hated. Why did the bishop make them leave? The Reverend Mr. Hayworth, who replaced him, was blond, with a long solemn face, and looked about nineteen years old. Momma didn't like him. One Sunday, after we got back from church, she pulled the hatpin out of her navy straw hat, stabbed it back in the hat, and threw the hat down on the bed. She closed the door. I thought I could hear her weeping in there.

She stayed in her room all afternoon, and I bounced around the house feeling lonely. I liked to go into the old garage sometimes because I could make myself believe any minute Chap would come in and laugh and crack a joke. I walked out there then and saw the light streaming down through the boards onto the spot where he'd had kept the engine. Some oil still lay on the floor, oil from the engine, and I dipped my finger in it and looked at it for a long time before I wiped it off on my play clothes.

I supposed Elmo had the plane now. Momma said she didn't want to see it again or have anything to do with it.

I looked at that oil drying up and I knew he wasn't coming back.

And then I broke down and cried.

Chapter Fifteen

Deaths always happen in threes, they say. But it was more than a year after we lost Chap when Duke's grandfather died of a heart attack right after he got home from church on Easter Sunday. He left Sweetbay Plantation to Duke.

The very next week Momma was talking on the phone, a serious look on her face. She did what? I'll talk to her. She hung up the phone with a sigh just as Ava's Cadillac screeched to a stop in front of our house. I ran to the door and flung it open to see what was happening, and there she was struggling to lift a heavy green Samsonite suitcase out of the trunk. I ran down to help her. What's happened, Ava? What?

She let me heft the bag. She fingered a small train case she used for her cosmetics and jewelry. I'm leaving him, she said.

You're what? It was hard to breathe all of a sudden.

I'm not living on that farm, she said. No more. He went back on his promise. And—she looked up at the door, where Momma was standing with her arms folded.

Duke called here, she said. He said to just come on back and he'll pretend like it never happened.

I'm never going back. He's already quit his job at the plant and says he's going to farm that place. I did not sign on to be a farmer's wife. She looked at me like the Wicked Queen in Snow White. Mae Lee, you've got your roommate back.

I looked at Momma but I couldn't tell what she was thinking. Her face was blank as a poker chip. I followed Ava with the suitcase up the steps, in the house, down the hall, into my room.

Put it on the bed, she said, and flung open the closet door. Dammit, get your stuff out of my closet.

I folded my arms. Your closet is at Sweetbay, Ava. How was I to know you would want to come back? You have no right to just run off and leave him like that. Don't you love him?

It is not your business, she said, and started pulling my things off the hangers. I could have fought with her, but I just picked up my clothes and hung them in the other closet. Can I have him? I said. I would love to live on a farm. I could have a horse.

She whipped around and stared at me open-mouthed, and I hid my smile behind my hand. Very funny, Mae Lee, she said, turning to face me, smiling her crocodile smile. Why on earth would he want *you*?

I was too used to her jabs to be hurt. I looked down at my skinny self which was growing taller and filling out way too slowly. I knew I would never look like her and she knew I would never look like her. Still I hoped for a miracle. *Someday, Ava.*

Someday. Dog in the manger, was what I said. You don't want him but you don't want me to have him.

This conversation is too ridiculous to be believed, she said. I'm going back to get the silver and the rest of my clothes. He'll be out in his precious fields and can't stop me. Elzuma wouldn't dare.

Momma appeared in the doorway with her hands clasped. Ava, you shouldn't do that, she said.

Well, I'm going to do it anyway, she said. Are either of you going to help me?

No, we said in chorus, and she went out and drove away. Two hours later she came back loaded down with boxes which she stacked in the front room.

Duke called and she wouldn't talk to him. Momma talked to him and told me Duke said to just let Ava show her tail till it turned blue. He'd take care of the problem. I didn't see that he was doing anything, because she lay around the house for two weeks smoking and leaving butts in all the ashtrays and going to the movies and shopping and reading magazines. Pretty soon she spent up all her cash, and then, when she tried to charge things, found out he'd cut off all the charge accounts. She tried to write checks but found out the joint checking account was empty.

I have rights, she said to Momma later. How dare he humiliate me like this? Maybe I'll see a lawyer.

Lawyer? What lawyer? Some friend of Hardy Pritchard? You want his name coming up again? Momma shook a finger at her. You want to start the gossip while Duke does not know squat about any o' that? Honey, I know what you're doing, and it's not going to work. This Queen Bee mess could backfire you right into a divorce.

Duke sat tight out at Sweetbay and waited for her hissy fit to wear out. In the end she packed all her dirty clothes in a laundry bag for Elzuma to wash and went back to him, back to the farm, back to the big house that was now theirs, back to the fields and the crops and the cattle—and the horses. He invited Momma and me to come anytime.

Momma was not getting any better. But when she was having a good Saturday, she would take me to Sweetbay. I rode Ava's horse, and sometimes Duke would ride with me, and during those rides I felt like I was riding in a sunbeam. He never said much, just pointed out things to me, taught me how to hold the reins, told me about getting along with a horse.

Just once, I asked him about the war.

He got a faraway look in his eyes. Someday I'll tell you, he said. But not now. You're too young to understand.

No, I'm not, I said, but he gave his horse a little nudge and said, race you to the tree, and when we got there—he won, of course—he laughed and told me I had a good competitive spirit.

I lived for those moments.

Duke was a good steward, and the cotton and peanuts and cattle grew and made them some money. Ava calmed down and started fixing up the house. Elzuma moved out of the back room by the kitchen, out to the bungalow, and worked for them part-time. Life looked sweet for them.

I didn't know then that the sweet life could be like honey-suckle vine smothering a barbed-wire fence. I found out on the Fourth of July.

Ava and Duke invited the whole family out to the farm for an old-fashioned Fourth cookout—watermelons, boiled corn, barbecued ribs, potato salad, churned peach ice cream, Elzuma's pound cake, pitchers of iced tea and lemonade, and of course, beer and cocktails.

We gathered at a pavilion Duke had built not far from the barn on the edge of the small pond, cold from an artesian well. There was another pond the cows used for drinking and splashing in, but this one was for horses and fun.

Duke was happy to see his daddy and his momma, Mis' Norma, and especially his sister Talley. He didn't seem so happy to see her husband, Colonel Wilkes Davis, who was now at Fort Benning. I wasn't so happy to see the Davis boys, Harry and Chuck, four and seven, afraid I'd get stuck babysitting. Talley was unable to chase them, because she waddled about in a yellow maternity top and shorts, looking like a bathtub duck.

Momma wasn't happy to see the barrel of iced-down beer, the big shining bottle of gin, and the bowl of sliced limes and the tonic water.

What's wrong? I said.

Maybe nothing, she said. But she didn't lose the frown.

The party started with a lot of laughs. People told stories of old times, fourths of July in the past, election-year barbecues, politics. Duke and Mr. Radford and Colonel Davis drank beer.

Momma and I and Aunt Talley drank iced tea, and the kids had lemonade. Ava fixed herself gin-and-tonics.

After I'd polished off a good square of cake and a dish of ice cream, I got antsy, bored with the talk about Korea. I had a feeling I was about to get shanghaied into entertaining the kids. I spotted Duke over at the ice chest getting another beer, so I walked over and asked if I could go riding.

He slipped the can back into the ice. I'll saddle Dandy for you, he said.

I can do it, I said.

I want to get away for a minute, he said. Come on. He started walking and I followed. When we got out of earshot of the others he said, A little of that jabber goes a long way with me.

You didn't agree with what Colonel Davis said about Korea, did you?

He looked sideways at me. No need to antagonize my sister in her condition.

He glanced back at her, a half-smile on his face. He was fond of his sister and even those holy terror nephews. But now the smile faded and he stiffened ever so slightly. I followed his gaze, and saw Ava standing over by the Colonel, handing him a drink. Her other hand rested gently on the back of his neck. She gave it a teasing stroke. No one else there saw it, and I winced to see the shadow cross Duke's face.

I wanted to tell him that Ava didn't mean anything by it; it was just that she had to have any man this side of the grave under her spell. She suddenly glanced up at us, and her hand retreated from the Colonel's neck.

Where are you two headed? she called.

Mae Lee wants to ride, said Duke. I'm going to help her saddle Dandy.

Ava straightened and hurried over to us in that slinky way she had, bosoms swinging in her red halter top. She touched Duke's arm. Why does she always take my horse? she said. Maybe you ought to let her take Nimrod for a change.

Duke looked her steady in the eye. Nimrod's hard to hold, you know that. Dandy needs exercise. You should ride her every day.

Well, I always have so many chores, she said, pouting.

Not so many, Duke said. He picked up her hand which had red nails again. He kissed it.

Ava glanced back at Talley and the Colonel, who were looking at us as if they were waiting for the show to start. She leaned over and kissed him on the cheek. The boys want to shoot firecrackers now, she said. Roman candles when it gets a little dark.

I would rather they didn't, he said, and a little muscle began to twitch in his cheek.

Ava waved her hand. What's the Fourth without firecrackers? Their dad will take them out in a field. Can't you go inside if you don't like the noise?

Ava, I—never mind. A darker look passed over Duke's face and his jaw hardened. Go tell them they can do it. Out in the field. Go on, Ava. He walked away from her then, toward the barn. I hurried after him.

He told me to get Dandy while he got the tack. I led her out of the stall and bridled her, then held her head while he threw on the blanket and saddle, then tightened the girth. I laid my cheek against the mare's. This is heaven, I said. Ava is a fool.

Don't call your sister a fool, Mae Lee, Duke said, his voice stern. She may be restless now, but I think she'll come to love the place like I do. It gets in your blood.

Why?

Oh, I don't know. Maybe it's that peaceful way the trees sound when the wind is blowing through 'em, or the birds calling on a spring morning. Out on the fields you can smell the rain coming in the grass, see a calf stand up on new legs, and look out at land going on and on without a blessed soul to see you. It feels safe here.

She didn't understand why you quit at the plant, I said.

I tried to tell her, but she didn't want to listen, he said. It's hard to explain what I went through in the war. Some people, like my brother-in-law there, are born soldiers. Uncle Sam likes noise, and so do they. They've got the kinds of hearts that they can wall off from what they see. Some of us can't.

But you made it, I said. You came through.

Only because I disobeyed orders, he said. He jammed his hand in his pockets.

How?

I wrote about it. In a diary. We weren't supposed to. But when I was in the hospital, I would've gone nuts if I hadn't had some way to make sense of it all.

A memory tugged at me, a little leather-bound book I had looked at. Where is it, I said, the diary?

He shrugged. Put it away. One day I might look at it again. Come on, you'd better get going. He cupped his strong hands to give me a boost, and I stepped into them and swung my leg over the saddle. He handed the reins to me. Have a good ride, he said.

I headed out, watching him drag his bum leg back to the party. My heart ached for him. Oh Ava, Ava. Can't you be kind to him? She would never leave him, I knew, and would go right on being like she was and he would go right on putting up with it, hoping one day she'd be different.

I rode down to the Thompsons' farm, which had been sold after the old man died because neither of his kids wanted to take it over. My friend Lindy Yarbrough was living there now, and she didn't need much persuading to leave her own parents' barbecue and come out with me on her Tennessee walking horse.

That day, the July sun beating down on our heads, we idled in the sweetness of the ripening blackberries and plums, riding past farm after farm, cotton fields in bloom, corn tasseled out, cows taking the shade under huge oaks, colored folks barbecu-ing a pig in a pit.

We talked and rode, rode and talked, until the sun had sunk low in the sky, splashing silver-edged clouds with orange and pink. I realized dark would be falling soon, and I could hear fireworks in the distance already. Momma would be wanting to get home. We turned and headed back.

After I left Lindy at her gate and turned Dandy toward home, she broke into a gallop, eager for the barn and some hay. Loping over the rise to the pond, I saw Aunt Talley packing up the last of the picnic. Her hair was disheveled, she was damp with sweat, and her face was scrunched up like her head hurt. Harry and Chuck were sprawled on the grass, and the Colonel was busy folding up the chairs. I didn't see the older Radfords.

I slowed Dandy and trotted over. Where's everybody?

Talley turned a tired face to me and shrugged. You'd better put the horse up.

I put her curt answer down to her tiredness and rode on to the barn, hoping Duke would be there, but no one was around. I slid down from the saddle, took off Dandy's tack, pulled a rope halter over her head, and walked her. When she was cool and breathing easy, I let her have some water, and then led her into her stall. Nimrod wasn't in the barn. I looked out into the paddock, but he wasn't there either. I checked the tack room. Duke's saddle was gone.

I hurried up to the back yard of the big house and found Elzuma rocking on the back porch, a wad of snuff in her cheek.

Where's Momma?

She be to the house.

Where's Duke?

You ain't gone see Mr. Dulany tonight.

What do you mean?

At that minute my mother swung open the back door. Mae Lee, here you are. Let's go home.

But I was still looking at Elzuma. Tell me, Elzuma. Tell me what you mean.

She just shifted the wad of snuff in her cheek. Momma took my arm. We have to go. We'll talk about it later.

Please tell me, Momma. What is it?

The car, Mae Lee.

We got in the car and Momma cranked the old engine and there was a smell of oil. I watched the road speed by through the hole in the floorboard before it got too dark to see. It was black all around except for the stars twinkling above and the headlights picking out fenceposts. I was frightened of this Momma who sat still and thin-lipped, driving straight ahead. Momma, tell me, I pleaded.

I knew it, she muttered. I knew something wasn't right with him.

With Duke, you mean?

When they started with those firecrackers he got on that horse and took off like a banshee and nobody has seen him since. Ava is in her room crying.

I found out much later that Duke had spent the night with Nimrod down in the swamp. Down in the swamp he found shadows to shape the moonlight into visions. He found night sounds to drown out memories of the war.

He found peace.

Not long after my thirteenth birthday, a package came in the mail from Savannah. Mis' Celia had just found out about Chap from someone who came to visit, and now she sent her condolences along with her old red and crystal rosary. She hoped the gift would remind me of the happy times we had spent together, and I would find comfort in prayers. I made the mistake of mentioning it to Ava, which, of course, I should *not* have done. She turned as white as the cotton in the fields.

I put the rosary away and never looked at it again, not until the most horrible night of my life.

PART III

Chapter Sixteen

1950

The day they admitted Momma to the hospital, it was late August and rain had not fallen for weeks, and the heat drew every drop from the earth, browning the grass and turning ponds into puddles. Magnolia leaves curled under and clattered to the ground, while paint cracked on the ancient Victorian mansions of Grandview Avenue. At night people slept on porches hoping for a stray night breeze, and by noon their clothes clung to their damp and shining bodies. Even Ava's hair drooped in wilting tendrils of ebony.

I led her through drab hallways that smelled of flowers and floor wax and starch and the smell I knew too well, the smell of chlorine bleach on blood. The skirt of her white sleeveless dress, pouffed out by crinolines, swayed as she walked. Her waist was cinched by an elastic belt the same shade as the red gladiolas she carried.

For the first time in my life, I was looking down on Ava. Since last year, I'd grown a pair of long legs—coltish, Momma had told me. A doctor, balding and sandy-haired, came down the hall, stethoscope swinging. He gave us a polite nod, but he looked only at her. She was wearing the rubies from Burma, and I felt like an ostrich next to a bird of paradise.

Momma lay behind the second curtain in her double room, next to the window. When we pushed it aside, she smiled at Ava. I've been waiting for you, honey.

Ava set the vase of flowers on a side table and leaned to kiss her. How's the farm, how's Duke? Momma asked, and while she answered I turned away, my arms folded, looking out the window at the pecan trees in full leaf, their buds swelling green. It had taken Ava long enough to get here. I'd called her just after I called the ambulance, Momma insisting all the while there was nothing wrong with her. No, she'd just collapsed while she was trying to hang out the wash.

I heard my name and turned back to them.

You'll stay with Ava until I get out of here, Momma said.

I stared at them dumbfounded. Why? I'll be sixteen in a month.

You're too young to be staying in that house alone. You never can tell.

I won't be able to walk to school from Ava's, Momma. It's just a week till it starts. The day after Labor Day, you know.

I'll be out by then, Momma said.

How can I come to see you now? It wasn't fair.

I'll drive you, Ava said. I want to see Momma too. She drew out an emery board and rasped it across her nails.

Momma, please. Don't make me. She doesn't really want me.

Wash your mouth out with soap, Mae Lee, said Ava. Looks like you'd want to be out there with your precious horse that happens to be mine.

Girls, girls, Momma said. Don't make me worry about you.

I'm sorry, Momma, I said, my face reddening.

I'm sorry, Momma, said Ava. She leaned over and smoothed the wispy hair.

That's better, she said. I was afraid she would tell us to kiss and make up and was relieved when a knock sounded at the door. The old lady behind the next curtain said come in, and then we heard a deep voice. Gwen?

Momma's eyes widened and she put her hands to her cheeks. Oh Lord, a man, and I don't have on a speck of makeup. Go talk to him, Mae Lee. Get my lipstick and compact, Ava.

I walked to the door and met Elmo Conable, John Deere hat in one hand and a canning jar of zinnias in the other. Lines tracked deep on his rugged old face. How is she, girl?

Give her a minute, I said, and I walked out into the hall with him. How's Mabel?

Sorry she couldn't come. She's right poorly herself. He held up the bunch of neon-bright orange and pink zinnias. She wanted me to bring these, grew them herself. He cleared his throat. The boy says to tell you if there's anything he can do just call him.

I let that pass without comment. Starrett Conable, the pebble in my shoe.

Ava called for us to come in. Momma was sitting up in bed, nose powdered, lips slicked with red, hair combed, shoulders wrapped in the quilted blue bed jacket Ava had given her for her birthday. She looked pretty. I took the vase with Ava's glads and set it on the windowsill to make room for the zinnias.

When I turned back around Mr. Conable was looking at Momma in a way that would tear you up. I thought about the time I'd seen them through the window, and thought of him secretly loving her for years. I felt sorry for him. Now, at their ages, it didn't seem to matter. He was holding her small hand in his big one. When he saw me looking at them, he patted it and laid it gently down.

Ava looked from Momma to Elmo and said, We'll go and let you visit. I'll take Mae Lee to pack her things, and we'll be back tomorrow. Momma nodded, though Ava hadn't really been there very long.

Bless you, children, she said. We kissed her and then we left.

We said nothing until we got outside. Ava fumbled in her bag and pulled out a pack of Chesterfields. She whapped the pack till one popped out, then she put it between her lips and lit it with a small gold lighter. I swear to God I think old Elmo's got a thing for Momma.

Oh come on, Ava, I said. They're old. We were standing in front of the hospital and the sun was beating down on our heads, the sweet hay-smell of dry grass all around us. We walked around to the parking lot behind the building. I shrugged. You know he was Chap's best friend his whole life. I still missed Chap, and I got a lump in my throat thinking if he was here Momma might try harder to get well.

Ava trailed smoke, leading to her car parked under the pecan trees. Mabel's a piece of work. Imagine, Momma and Elmo.

Don't be disgusting, Ava, I said. They would never do anything. Not like some people I know.

Her eyes got hard. I don't know what you're talking about. She jerked the car door open. Get in.

We drove across the railroad tracks. Ava waited on the porch of our house while I packed a week's worth of clothes, including jeans for riding. I'd outgrown my boots, and thought saddle oxfords would be fine to ride in. I looked out the window at Ava pacing on the porch, remembering the first time Duke had driven up to our house in a cloud of dust. I reached into my jewelry box and drawer and slipped out the red and crystal rosary Celia Pritchard had sent me. I tucked it into my pocket. A few extra prayers wouldn't hurt.

At last we turned into the long dirt drive that led into Sweetbay, past fields where cows cropped grass and lazed in the sun. Ava had raced the whole way and she was still driving too fast, and the car bounced over the ruts. She pulled into the circular driveway in front of the house, skidding to a stop under a massive oak, its Spanish moss-beard trailing to the top of the car. The moss, the spreading live oaks, the square columns of the wraparound veranda—they meant Sweetbay, the house that had meant so much happiness to me, and so much pain.

I lugged my suitcase up the five wooden steps. Ava opened the door for me. Inside I got a shock.

The old chintz-covered settee and rockers and cane-bottomed chairs were gone from the living room, and in their place stood a new white sectional sofa, the latest style. It wrapped around on two sides, and in front of it Ava had placed a Danish modern coffee table holding some slick magazines and a vase of artificial flowers, just like something out of House & Garden.

Holy cow, I said.

How about them apples? Come on. She dragged me back to the bedroom. I blinked at the fancy bed and matching dressers and nightstands, finished in washed white.

French provincial, she said.

And a red carpet, I said. And a white satin bedspread. And one of those old-fashioned dolls with ruffled skirts on the bedspread. Ava, how can you stand those dolls with teeth? They give me the willies. Those staring eyes. Like a dead person.

She snorted. You're crazy, you know that?

Ugh, I said. I looked away, across the hall. Sunlight poured into a small, empty room, where paint cans stood on a dropcloth. The room had been painted sky blue with white trim, unfurnished except for a single white iron bedstead without a mattress.

This would be just right for a baby, I said, not understanding the clutch in my heart. Are you—

No, she said, giving me a look that meant I was not to pursue this line of conversation.

So where will I stay?

Back by the kitchen, in Elzuma's old room.

I picked up my suitcase and followed Ava down the hall. She waved her hand in the direction of the second spare room. This will be a guest room before long, she said. Old sheets covered the furniture and white plaster patches splotched the walls. Paint cans were stacked in the corner.

We passed Duke's paneled office and I peered in. Papers cluttered his old roll-top desk, and books crowded into a bookshelf on the far wall. Pictures covered the walls, and a leaping marlin hung above the books.

Ava, steps ahead of me, looked back. Duke won't let me touch it. It's such a rat's nest, I don't know how he stands it. Come on, quit lollygagging, Mae Lee.

I stumbled down the hall, remembering the house the way it was, sad for the memories that had been lost, but maybe Duke didn't care. I wouldn't have wanted our old house to change. I would've felt safe there with Momma's things all around me and the old garage behind me, where, if I closed my eyes, I could still believe that Chap was whistling away while he painted and patched on that plane, which, in my dream, would never take off.

We went through the kitchen and out to the room behind the laundry room. Ava pushed open the door. Dusty sunlight filtered through half-closed blinds, patterning bars on the chenille bedspread and faded patchwork quilt. So I was to sleep in this high old bed, its varnish black with age, and store my clothes in that tall chifforobe. The heat was stifling in the musty room, and I said so.

Ava walked over to a window and creaked it open, scattering dust. I'll get you a fan. Then she left me.

I lowered my suitcase to the floor and opened the doors of the chifforobe. The right half was for hanging clothes and the left side had drawers. It would be big enough for the few things I'd brought. I drew a finger through the dust and sighed.

Ava brought the fan and set it on the floor. I asked her for a dust rag, which she furnished with bad grace, and told me she'd see me in the kitchen to help with supper.

I dusted the chifforobe and stowed my clothes, and was just about to close the door when, on a whim, I opened the small drawers at the top. They'd never been emptied when Elzuma moved out. The one on the left held pencils, safety pins, receipts, scraps of cigarette tobacco, an empty snuffbox, and a tin aspirin box rattling with straight pins. The one on the right held nothing but a worn pack of cards with an oriental pattern on the back. I picked them up and riffled them. They might have been the same cards Elzuma had used that dreadful afternoon.

Two details came back to me in sharp focus: the look in Duke's eyes when he'd seen the pack of cards by the bed, and the way he'd held me, comforting me.

Ava hollered at me, interrupting my train of thought. I shut the cards in the chifforobe and walked into the kitchen. Ava had changed into jeans and was standing at the counter, sandwich fixings spread out in front of her. I asked her about Elzuma.

You know she's back in the bungalow, she said. She can't work like she used to, the arthritis has gotten her, but Duke lets her stay there, says it's the least he can do after all those years. One of her grandkids comes here to do cleaning once a week, but I do most of the cooking. Every once in a while Duke gets her to come up here and cook him some catfish or fried chicken. She pulled a face at me. Imagine me frying chicken.

I can't imagine, I said. I didn't remember her ever lifting a finger in the kitchen when she was home. She dug her knife into a bowl of pimento cheese and spread up a sandwich. Get a jar of soup down from the pantry, she ordered.

I found it and set it on the counter beside her. I'd like to go see Elzuma, I said.

The knife stopped in midair. Why?

Just want to ask her some questions.

About what?

Stuff. Old tales, you know. I set the table and poured the tea while Ava heated the soup. Take my advice and stay away from there, she said.

Why?

I never got an answer. The back door swung open with a squeal, and we both turned at once. Duke filled the door frame, giving me a big grin. Mae Lee, he said, holding his arms wide. Looking so pretty. Come here, honey. How's your momma?

I fell into his bear hug, comfort washing over me like a healing wave.

She had a small stroke, said Ava.

Duke released me, frowning. What do the doctors say?

It's the lupus complicating things.

She'll get better soon, I insisted. She just needs to rest. She won't quit. I told the story of how she insisted on hanging out the wash that day.

Duke went over to scrub his hands at the kitchen sink the way Chap used to when he got home from work. Ava handed him a dish towel. We hope and pray, she said. We sat down to our supper of soup and sandwiches, and Duke said a long grace.

He looked up. So is Mae Lee staying with us?

Maybe a week, said Ava.

Duke winked at me. Those horses have been mighty lonesome. I was beginning to think the girl had deserted us.

I've been real busy, I mumbled. Friends, you know? It had been a pretty good summer with the other kids, despite having to look after Momma. And I had a crush on a basketball player named Glenn Dorris, tall and dark-haired, who didn't know I was alive.

Uh-huh. Duke winked at Ava. Yep. Boys will do it every time.

I felt the red creeping up my neck. I'll ride every day, I said. I'll feed them too, if you want.

Good, said Duke, if Cyrus lets you. You remember Cyrus Pennyman, Willie's brother? He's my new hand.

I felt my eyes go wide. The one who—

Yep. And he can barbecue chickens just like his daddy.

How does he manage with just one arm?

Better than you think. Duke bit into his sandwich.

A little after seven o'clock, I finished with the supper dishes, hung my apron on a nail, and ran down to the pasture. The horses were standing by the fence waiting, along with a mule. In the glow of evening, the rich smell of horse manure mingled with the sweet scent of hay.

Dandy was glad to see me, her white-streaked muzzle sniffing for the apple I usually brought. Sorry, girl, I said. No apple today. I snapped a lead onto her halter and took her to her stall. I was going back for Duke's big gelding, Nimrod, when I saw a cocoa-skinned man, one sleeve of his work shirt pinned up, leading the mule my way.

Hey, missy, he said, and grinned.

Cyrus?

Yes'm.

I'm Mae Lee Willis. I used to know your brother Willie, I said, and reached up to stroke the mule's silky nose. What's his name?

We call him Francis, but he don't talk. Cyrus grinned like he'd made such a joke.

So what does he do?

He good for all sorts of jobs.

I'll get Nimrod, I volunteered.

No need, missy. They's used to me.

He was telling me he didn't want any help, and I knew Nimrod could be ornery. More power to him if he could handle him. Okay, I said. See you later.

See you, missy.

I turned back toward the house and met Duke coming across the yard, dragging that leg of his. I remembered the first time I'd seen him, how straight and tall he'd been, and it pained me for him. I met Cyrus, I said. And Francis.

Duke grinned and tossed aside the sprig of hay he'd been chewing on. Mules are good in places where a tractor can't go.

It's pretty swampy down at the creek, you know. I nodded, and, with a chill, thought of the night Duke had spent in the swamp on the Fourth of July.

Cyrus let me know he didn't need any help, I said.

He leaned against the rail fence and looked over at the barn. He's a fighter, determined not to have people look at him as a cripple. Elzuma told me about him. Said he'd been at Pearl and couldn't find a job with that arm. I decided to take him on, seeing as I have this bum leg. He's become a good buddy. You know, we were all there together in Burma—black, white, Gurkha, Kachin, Brit, Aussie. You forgot about colors after a while. And he's a damned wizard with mules.

That's a funny talent, I said.

Duke laughed. Yeah. You know, I never really appreci- ated mules until I was in Burma. They used them a lot because machines couldn't get through in the jungle. They used elephants too. It took machines and animals both to build that road over there. I'm glad that job wasn't mine. God, it was hard. Jungle's thick with weeds that slice a man's skin. Week's work could be washed away in a monsoon. His voice had taken on a faraway, almost wistful tone.

I dug my toe in the dirt. You sound like you miss the war.

His eyes met mine, those golden eyes. No, honey. I don't miss the fighting and the killing. The part I miss is feeling that what I did made a difference. What difference would it make if I worked at the plant or not? To make a better pair of pants?

What was your job? I asked. In the war, I mean?

He looked at me for a long time as if deciding whether he could trust me with the answer. Spying, he said. Sabotage. We parachuted behind the enemy lines. It's the kind of work that takes your beliefs and turns them inside out. He paused for a few moments, then wiped his hand across his face. Somebody had to do it. It was us or them. That's what war is. He dusted his hands as if he could dust the war off them. Let's go see Cyrus. I'll tell him you're good with horses.

I followed him over to the barn and found the animals snug in their stalls.

Guess he's gone home, said Duke. You can get better acquainted tomorrow.

Where does he live?

I leased him one of the old tenant houses. He's fixed it up and is talking about buying it from me, along with a few acres. I've got a mind to sell him some. Then he scooped a handful of corn out of a croker sack and gave it to me.

Go on, make friends with Francis.

I held the corn flat on my palm and let the mule take it, his rubbery lips tickling, and then I stroked the soft nose and the long black ears. I didn't mind Cyrus, if he didn't mind me. We could share the horses for the short time I'd be here.

That night I stared in the mirror of the chifforobe as I peeled the sweaty shirt and jeans off my body, thinking of how beautiful Ava had looked today at the hospital. I felt more gawky than ever. My reflection swam in the cracked and spotted old glass. Looking so pretty. Just one of those things Duke would say to be polite, never mind how lank my hair hung, or how skinny I remained—my bosoms had just started to fill out—or the freckles that pestered me every summer.

The house was quiet as I brushed my teeth in a bathroom with a sloping floor, its boards creaking. Then I mounted the steps to the high bed. I felt lost there, and the door to the chifforobe kept flapping open. I finally stuck a piece of gum on it to keep it shut, knowing that Ava would give me hell if she found it. The summer night sounds—the cicadas and the bobwhites—filled the darkness, and I could hear an owl's haunty call far away in the woods. The smell of late honeysuckle drifted in through the window. The old room seemed to be full of the spirits Elzuma had once talked about.

The fan whirred and turned for a time, and just as I was getting sleepy it stopped. I tugged the old frayed cord out of the socket and got back into bed. Muggy air settled around me. I pushed the white chenille spread down to the foot of the bed and lay on top of the sheets, then I peeled off the top of my pajamas. I lay back in the dappled moonlight, watching the shifting shadows of the trees on the wall. The chifforobe seemed to loom and grow.

The dry dusty way Momma had smelled bothered me, and a feeling of dread kept hanging over me. I didn't want to be here. But Momma would get better. She had to get better, and I would go home. I clung to that thought until I fell asleep.

In the middle of the night I woke up with a start, shaking, out of a dream that someone was screaming. Shivering, I clutched for the covers and found they'd slipped to the floor. I wriggled into my pajama top and leaned down to retrieve the faded chenille spread.

From the hall, the ancient boards squeaked. I lay still, telling myself it was the settling of an old house. But old houses groaned and flapped and creaked, they didn't make footsteps. Something rustled. Someone coughed.

I slipped out of bed, tiptoed to the door and peeked out into the dimness. Cigarette smoke hung in the hall, floating from the living room. I crept across the cool pine boards of the hallway and flattened myself beside the wall. I peered in.

Duke, hunched on the edge of the white sectional sofa with a cigarette between his fingers, stared out the big front window, where the first signs of dawn lightened the sky behind the pines. I stood and watched until he finished the smoke.

He jabbed his cigarette into the ashtray, got up, and limped through the other doorway. I crept back to my room and lay awake until the sun threw bars of light across my face, thinking of the way Duke's big hands had cupped his cigarette. Like he was protecting it.

From the wind. From the rain. From the enemy.

I didn't know then that the enemy was all around us.

Chapter Seventeen

Morning sun slanted in over the high bed, and the smells of bacon and coffee and biscuit wafted in from the kitchen. For a moment I stretched, my eyes closed, thinking I was seven years old, back home, breakfast waiting on the oilcloth-covered table. Chap would be hiding behind his newspaper, Ava would be heading off to school, and Momma would be stirring grits while the radio played and everyone pretended there would never be another war.

My eyes opened to the pale blue wainscoting around the room, the brownish stains on the ceiling. Momma was at the hospital and I was out at Sweetbay and Duke sat up at night and smoked, and my world was all whompy-jawed.

I pulled on jeans and a striped T-shirt, splashed water on my face, ran a comb through my hair, and slipped my feet into my old tennis shoes. In the kitchen, Ava was sitting in her place with both hands wrapped around her coffee cup, but Duke's plate was empty, streaked with strawberry jam.

Morning, I said.

Help yourself. Ava gestured vaguely toward the stove.

No eggs?

If you want to cook them.

I put Duke's plate in the sink, and then I took two biscuits from the pan and buttered them. The grits had gone cold, and I didn't feel like reheating them. I took the last strip of bacon, sat down, and roped syrup over the biscuits.

Ava, I began, something happened last night.

Oh? She raised an eyebrow and sipped coffee.

I thought I heard a scream.

Probably a screech owl, she said. She twisted a stray hair back into place and slowly got up from her chair. You're in the country now, kiddo.

It sounded like a person. And Duke was up smoking.

He gets up with the chickens, remember? That's farm life.

But—

At the door, she glanced back with the hint of a rueful smile. Do the dishes, okay? And don't forget the dogs. And then she walked out. I ate my biscuits. I dumped the leftover grits and biscuits and bacon grease into the big speckled pan they kept for old Mr. Dulany's hounds. Duke didn't hunt; he just let other people use them. From time to time he would sell one.

I stacked the breakfast dishes beside the sink and filled it with scalding hot suds, then washed the way Momma had taught me—glasses first, then plates, then silverware, then pots and pans. Outside the window over the sink, I saw Duke out at his truck. He waved when I went out with the dog scraps.

The hounds poked their noses through the wire fence of their kennel, tongues lolling, tails wagging. They were not pets, and I didn't stay long with them. It just didn't seem right.

That was no screech owl last night.

I walked over to Elzuma's bungalow and knocked. Maybe she'd tell me what was going on. Nobody came to the door. I peered in the window. She always kept the shades tightly drawn, but I could tell it was dark and empty.

Duke walked over. You looking for Elzuma, punkin?

Yeah, I said. I just wanted to ask her something.

Well, guess it'll have to wait. She took the bus yesterday afternoon to go see her daughter in Macon. There's a new grandbaby.

Oh. Where are you going?

Got to run into town for some feed. Want to go with me?

Sure, I said. I'll tell Ava.

I went running up to the house but Ava was waiting on the back porch and before I could get the words out of my mouth she said, I need you here today. I want you to help clean the pantry and some closets.

I ran back and told Duke what she'd said. He shrugged. Better do as she says, he said. Another day you can go with me. Let's keep the lady happy.

I'd hoped he'd stick up for me, but he didn't want to upset the apple cart. To me it was already upside down with apples rolling all over the place. Ava sent me into the room with the paint cans stacked in the corner.

Once we get those closets cleaned out, we can do the painting, she said. She gave me a broom, a rag, and a bucket, and I got to work.

Cleaning, Momma always said, is good for the soul. For me it was the opportunity to do some serious thinking while I sorted all the old stuff piled up over the years. I never understood why some people kept everything they ever had. Chap had told us if you had ever lived through the depression you would understand. Still, it was just old junk now. I unplugged the radio from the kitchen wall and took it into the spare room.

Duke wanted to be here, Ava didn't want to be here, and I just wanted to go home.

I grabbed a handful of wire hangers and poked them into a cardboard box. Lord, here were some of Duke's mother's old housecoats and a box full of empty jars and powder boxes. I pulled out a broken lamp. I found some old books and paged through them, losing myself in a story before I got back to work.

I was taking a box out to the back porch when I heard their raised voices. I hadn't heard him come back. Lord, how long had I been working? I stopped. Interrupt them or not? And then I heard my name.

Mae Lee can clean your office next, Ava said.

Nobody messes with my stuff, he said.

Why do you keep all that junk? That old army footlocker, for instance. It's just bad memories. That awful thing you have—

You have the rest of the house, he said.

That's what's wrong with you, Duke! You ought to trash it all. The pictures, the souvenirs. Then maybe you could forget.

Leave me alone, Ava. Just leave me alone.

You leave me alone too much, she said. You talk to Elzuma.

Don't start.

You like that old woman better than me.

Jesus. God. Please just shut up.

I hate it here! I wish I'd never married you! She burst into sobs and turned back toward the house, and I slipped back into my room just as she stormed through the door into the kitchen. Out my window, I watched Duke stride out into the yard and light a cigarette, taking deep drags, and it looked like his hands were shaking.

That afternoon, while he was out tending the cattle and Ava was out back hanging out clothes, I slipped into his office, curious about what awful thing he had, what they were fighting about.

I opened the closet door. The shelves were stuffed with boxes of papers, mainly, but on the floor was an olive-drab army footlocker. I tried the top, but it was locked. I heard Ava calling me and went back to the pantry, where I was supposed to be cleaning.

Momma didn't get out of the hospital that week. We went to see her every day, and she didn't look good. The exercises they were giving her were just tiring her out, and the medicines weren't helping much.

The nights were hot and I found it hard to fall asleep, even with a new fan. There were no more owls that I knew weren't owls, but I wanted Momma to hurry up and get well and let me out of this house of smoke and mirrors.

When the first day of school came, Momma was still there. Hurry up with those dishes, Ava said, checking her lipstick in the side of the toaster. What a pain, having to carry you to school.

A small price to pay for all this work I do around here, I said, hands deep in suds. I took a plate out and plunged it into the rinse water. Another month and I could get a driver's license, but please, dear God, let me be home by then.

Duke was still in the kitchen, jotting down supplies he needed to order. We need to take your momma's car to the shop to get it checked out, he said. Make sure the brakes are good before you get out there by yourself.

Chap used to fix it himself, I blurted.

We'll take it to the shop soon, Ava said. When Duke has time to help drive. But not today.

Sure, I said. A pang of grief for Chap, sharp as a knife, stuck in my gullet.

Be outside in fifteen minutes, Ava said, and walked out. Duke went out to the barn. I finished the dishes and took the pan of scraps out to the hounds. Francis, the mule, stood in the paddock flicking his ears, looking my way for a treat. Suddenly, he perked to attention.

Duke was coming around the barn on Nimrod, and I caught my breath. How splendid he looked, his black Western hat playing off the horse's black coat and white blaze, backlit against the morning sunlight. Duke on his horse was Duke before the war.

I stood there transfixed, watching him, and dimly heard the honking out front. At that moment Duke saw me and tipped his cowboy hat. Ecstatic, I dashed toward the house to get my books. That was a picture I wanted to hold in my mind.

During the five-mile drive, I expected Ava to light into me, but she was quiet, not even asking me if I'd hosed out the dog pan. Now that the closet's clean, are you going to finish the guest room, I asked, just to fill the empty space of her silence.

You planning on moving in? She stepped on the gas and the trees went whizzing by in a cool morning scent of pine.

Of course not. Nothing's going to happen to Momma.

We didn't make a lot of money this year, she said. God, I hate it out there. I didn't sign up for this.

You ought to be thankful, I said. Duke is a good man.

You can have him, she snapped.

My cheeks burned. Wash your mouth out with soap, I said.

You don't know the half of it, girl.

Half of what?

I lied. I have been lying to you all. It's hell living with him. He has nightmares from the war. Wakes up shaking, sometimes yelling, sweating. Then he gets up and smokes, stares out.

Not a screech owl, I said.

No.

Goes and talks to Elzuma, she said. Rides down to the swamp.

All those acres and nowhere to hide, I murmured.

Ava didn't hear me. What?

Nothing. I wish I was back home, I said.

Ava just looked at me. I could tell she was thinking she wished I was too, and wasn't going to give me the satisfaction of hearing her say it. She pulled up in front of the school. I'll pick you up this afternoon, she said. She looked around at the crowd of kids with interest. Which one is Glenn?

Shut up, I said, and hurried out of the car, slamming the door behind me. I had made the bad mistake of mentioning Glenn's name and she immediately figured out I had a bad crush.

I threaded my way through the throng into the hall. Velda Rafferty, who'd first told me about how it was between boys and girls, sashayed by in a tight pink sweater, though the weather would be too warm for sweaters by noon.

I felt something poking me in the back and I turned to see Starrett Conable with a pencil eraser in jabbing position. How's your momma? he said, sticking the pencil behind his ear.

I shrugged. About the same, I said, and kept walking. He walked on beside me.

I saw that good-looking sister of yours bring you, he said.

I hope you got a good look, I said.

She wear those rubies a lot?

Why not? Duke brought them back for her.

There's a story going around, he said. People said he killed somebody for those rubies.

I opened my mouth to say he would never do a thing like that, but then I thought about what Ava had just told me and the words died on my lips.

Here's my homeroom, I said.

Just then Glenn Dorris came up with Cathy Kelvey, the new girl at school—short and bouncy and giggly, with honey-blond hair. She's going to make a hell of a cheerleader, Starrett said with admiration.

Just what is it about cheerleaders? I said. I wouldn't be one if you paid me.

Starrett looked at me looking at Glenn and Cathy. So that's how it is, he said.

What do you mean? I said.

Hey, Glenn, come over here. Mae Lee wants to talk to you, he said.

Huh? Glenn said, looking blank.

I do not! I said, face flaming, and turned to go into the room. I'll get you, turd, I said under my breath.

The last thing I heard before the bell rang was Starrett Conable snickering.

When school was out, I sailed right on by Starrett, nose in the air, and hurried down the front steps expecting the white Caddy. What I saw instead was Duke's truck at the curb, Duke smoking, curls drifting out the window. I walked over and grabbed the hot door handle. Ava too lazy to come herself? I asked, clambering in, hitching myself onto the high seat. I whapped my books on the floor and sighed. I'm glad this day is over, I began, and then I saw his face.

Mae Lee, he said. He took my hand and patted it clumsily. Ava's at the hospital.

I looked at him and no words would come.

It's bad, he said. She had another stroke.

He turned the key in the ignition and started the truck. He drove the few blocks from the school to the hospital and pulled into the sandy lot behind it, under the pecan trees. The other cars there looked dusty and sad and tired, cars of people who lived on hog meat and hope.

He parked and stopped the engine. She's in a coma, he said. It's a matter of time.

He held out his arms to catch me as I collapsed into them. I never should have let her go out to hang that wash but she wanted to, I said.

It's not your fault he said. It's not. I shuddered and buried my face in his wooly jacket that smelled of mules and tobacco smoke. He stroked my back. Hush, now. Ava's feeling pretty bad. She wished she could have done more to help.

Sure, I said bitterly. Ava never did anything she didn't want to. And she had been there to tell her goodbye instead of me.

Duke released me and tipped my chin up. I know you're having a hard time, he said. You can still tell her goodbye. She'll know you're there. Be strong. He leaned over and kissed my cheek.

He got out of the truck, came around to my side, opened the door, and helped me out as if I might be made of spider webs and glass. He held my hand all the way into the hospital, and then the chlorine blood smell hit me again. We walked down the hall and I had this foolish hope that things would be as always, that when we pushed open the door she would light up, happy to see us.

But what happened was that Ava came up and gave me a hug. Why didn't you come get me sooner? I said.

There was no time, she said. She looked away.

I sat on the edge of the bed and held Momma's hand. Her eyes were closed and she breathed in and out, in and out. Momma, I said. Momma. Her eyelids flickered and her mouth moved, but no sound came out. Momma, it's Mae Lee. I'm here.

Look what your folks sent, I heard Ava saying to Duke, and I glanced at the vase of yellow roses.

The new Methodist minister at John Wesley stopped by and prayed with us, and I was glad he had come. After he left, Duke and Ava and I sat quietly while the dappled light danced through the venetian blinds as the tree limbs swayed, heavy with pecans. In a few months the pecans would lie on the ground, husks like black tulips against the sky, and I would be all alone.

Duke laid his hand on my shoulder and told us he'd leave Ava and me alone for a little while, and that he'd be back. The waiting stretched across the afternoon hours, lengthening like the green shadows on the wall, and by the time Duke returned, the sun was sinking behind the pecan trees in a blaze of fiery orange. Momma made a little choking sound, and I took her fingers. They gripped, then, harder. I looked up at Ava and she took Momma's other hand.

The pale eyes blinked open, and she looked from one of us to the other. Love each other, she whispered, and then looked up in the air. I'm ready, Jesus. She coughed and jerked, and a rattle sounded in her throat. Her hand grew limp and I clutched it harder, willing the life back into it, but it did not respond.

Then I felt a warm wind passing, and Ava was sobbing and pressing the bell and Duke ran into the hall shouting. I finally let go of her lifeless hand.

Chapter Eighteen

People deal with death in different ways, and now I understand what I didn't then, about Ava and Duke after the funeral.

I felt Momma's spirit all around us, when we were making plans, almost as if she was telling us what to do. I felt that she wanted Brother Ben Higgins who was here so many years ago to come from Augusta, where he was pastoring a big church, to speak over her. At the time I suspected Ava just wanted somebody important.

But when I saw Momma cold and dead in her casket, on that white satin, I felt that it could not be her, that it was not my momma in that casket. My momma would have no truck with being dead. She still had too much to do—to see me go to college, to see her first grandchild, to hug me goodnight before bed. How could she go off and leave us?

But she had, and the church was filled with people to tell her good-bye. All the students she had taught all those years were there, and my grandmother Mimi, willing herself to be strong. It is not a fitting thing, she said, for the child to go before the parent, as if admonishing God. Mr. Linley, my step-grandfather, did not come to the funeral, because he was already weak from the disease that would kill him before too much longer.

Ava set a black straw hat with a face veil on her hair, and I wore a black suit and little black crescent hat that Aunt Talley got me from somewhere. Ava arranged for a spray of white carnations, lilies, roses, and ferns for Momma's mahogany coffin that Duke's folks had paid for, as well as the rest of the funeral. At the cemetery, remembering what Momma had said about sweet shrub being not showy but mysteriously beautiful with its scent, my tears fell when I worked a couple of branches in when no one was looking.

Starrett Conable came over and took my damp hand. And I let him hold it, for just a little while, and he walked me back to the car. He gave me a hug before he opened the door for me to get in, and I gave him a sad little wave when we drove off.

After the funeral, I was back at the farmhouse to stay. I could not go to Mimi's house, not with Mr. Linley so unwell. I was confused and my tummy was tight. I didn't want to be there with Ava telling me what to do all the time, but I did want to be there with Duke and the horses to comfort me.

That night after we'd put Momma in the ground next to Chap, her name already carved on the double headstone, I lay awake in my bed until the moon rose high about the tops of the pines. Still numb with it all, I could not believe she was gone.

I wondered if Ava was awake and felt a strange yearning to talk with her, to be close like we had never been, so far apart in age. Maybe she'd be missing Momma too. I slid to the cool planks, wrapped my robe around me, and padded down to their closed door.

I raised my hand to knock and then heard a moan. I froze, and then heard the squealing of bedsprings. Oh God, baby. Harder, harder. That was Ava, then a keening, a wailing, a groan, and then a laughing hiccup.

Ava, Ava, Duke said. Oh, Ava.

My face hot as summer sand, I wanted to run away, wanted to cover my ears, but I didn't. I stayed until the sounds had died into a soft murmuring.

In the following months, after all the lights were off and the house was still and the moon made a shining crossbar on the ivory carpet of the living room, I would sometimes wander from my bedroom and lie on the sofa in the living room.

Sometimes I heard sounds coming from the bedroom at the end of the hall. Sometimes they were loud, and sometimes they were soft; sometimes there were moans and sometimes cries, and sometimes the sharp sounds of slapping, or growling, or panting, or soft wet sounds like the lapping of the lake on the shore, which made me feel like jellyfish were swimming inside my belly. I learned the music of the springs, their metallic swing beating out a rhythm of slow and staccato bursts that faded to a random sigh. I heard all these sounds and then softly stepped back to my bedroom to form pictures in my mind where it was me, and not Ava, floating in the lake of dreams.

And there were nights when he did not go to bed, but sat alone in his office and drank, and nights when he went to bed and there were no sounds at all. And those nights were coming one after another now, in an unbroken procession of silence.

On the farm, life went on, but with different patterns, as though a kaleidoscope had turned, the shiny colored glass rearranging in new and unfamiliar ways. Sometimes it seemed a deep river of cloudy water ran between me and the light. All I knew was to keep swimming.

With Momma gone, I had no grownup I could confide in. Ava, who had flitted through school like a dragonfly, breaking rule after rule and never getting caught, was not likely to understand. It seemed to me that Duke, with his long silences and his faraway looks, might be just as lonely as I was. I always hoped he and I might go out on the horses together, as we used to, but he was always working and I was always studying or doing chores. He belonged only in my dream world.

When Elzuma came back from Macon, we talked about Momma. Can she hear me? I asked. Does she know what I'm doing? Can she talk to Jesus? Is she with Chap?

Chile, she ain't settled into being dead yet. You got to give her time. Then maybe she gone listen to you. Elzuma ignored my other questions.

I felt her spirit go past me, I said.

Elzuma nodded. That do happen.

What can I do?

Jes' let yourself grieve, honey. Get all the sadness out, pour it all on the earth.

I started writing poems, that is, in between scrubbing the floor, feeding the chickens, and helping with the laundry. My English teacher saw some of them and told me I should send them out for publication. But my poems were about me, not about mythology or deep thoughts like Leda and the Swan or Ozymandias or The Rime of the Ancient Mariner. All I knew of poets were that they were usually dead before they became famous.

My teacher showed me what she called little magazines, full of poems and stories. She told me there were places that looked for young poets, and that I shouldn't be afraid to put my feelings on paper, or be afraid of writing bad poems. She said that sometimes we have to get the bad poems out before we can get to the good. She let me come by after school one day a week for extra help, when I could get a ride home with Lindy, and I began to feel my way toward the light.

Ava got it into her head that I was wasting my time with "that stupid poetry," and said there were chores for me at the farm. After all, she maintained, they were feeding me and paying my bills. Momma had left me her car and her meager savings and her wedding ring and her good necklace to help send me to college—she did leave Ava all the furniture in the little rented house—and Ava felt this was mighty unfair. Duke's family had paid for the funeral.

I still wrote poems whether Ava liked it or not. I wrote poems about the light on the broomsedge and the cows by the pond, their hooves scalloping the mud, and the horses—oh yes, the horses—and the glint of light behind Duke's hat (I didn't show that to anyone). I wrote about the frosty breath in winter and the yellow forsythias in the spring and the firethorn berries outside the house, of the late beautiful Hardy Pritchard, and I wrote about his hair and his dead feet, and the rosary and how I prayed, and I even wrote a poem for Ava.

I couldn't write poems about Momma. I wasn't ready yet.

I drove Momma's old car to school, and sometimes I would give Lindy Yarbrough a ride home, since she only lived a mile or so down the road. Since she'd gotten serious about riding, we didn't see each other as much, and she was always full of news about this show or that show or what ribbon she'd won.

When we crested the rise right before her place, I heard a terrific boom and saw a plume of smoke and my heart squeezed with fear. Good grief, Lindy, what's happening?

Oh, that's just the dynamite, Lindy said. She told me that her father was going to build her a ring so she could practice show jumping and not have to go out to Mr. Buckley's to use his.

Just the dynamite.

Daddy told me he would be blasting today, she said. A few stumps.

I hope Duke didn't hear that.

Why?

It reminds him of the war.

Oh. Does he have shell shock?

Is that what you call it?

It happened to my uncle, she said. He became an alcoholic and shot himself.

Thanks a bunch. Tell me about the horse show, I said.

That night, I stayed up reading, a circle of light on the page. When I found myself reading pages over and over I laid the book aside and closed my eyes. The book slipped to the floor sometime during the night with a thunk. Half-awake, I leaned over to turn off the lamp.

Through a drowsy curtain of sleep, I heard a rumble of thunder and then a moan. My belly chilled. Heavy footsteps shook the floorboards in the hall, followed by the clanking of bottles and glasses in the kitchen.

This must be a night for drinking. I cursed the thunder as my eyes adjusted to the darkness. I smelled tobacco smoke. I slipped out of bed, tugged on a robe, and found Duke hunched on the sofa holding a glass of whiskey, staring out the window at blackness, a cigarette trembling in his big hand.

I padded over and laid a hand on his shoulder. Can I help?

Nobody can help.

Maybe we have some grief together, I said, and felt how warm he was under my fingertips.

The rain's here, he said. And I heard it then, the first pattering drops, the rain smell, the sharp ozone of lightning. A steady drizzle began, electrical bursts flickering in the distance.

I sat down beside him. Tell me about it, the war.

Burma, he said. Nothing to tell a young girl about. The mud, the rain. Your boots mildewed overnight, you got dysentery, your damn insides spilled out on the ground. You can imagine the smell.

But your letters weren't bad.

He looked at me with a crooked smile. 'Course not. Not the kind of thing you talk about to your sweetie. It wasn't all bad. The natives were friendly, most of them. Great R & R in India, like a damned country club. Plenty of opium if you wanted it. Traders ready to cut deals on rubies.

I licked my lips and said, Starrett Conable told me there was a story going around you'd killed somebody over Ava's rubies.

He reached over and patted my hand. Sweet Mae Lee, you wouldn't believe the stories they tell on me. I never wanted to kill anybody. But they train you not to think of the enemy as human beings and you do your job. Even so, there was a time . . . He shook his head and lifted the whiskey glass from the floor. The rain pattered while he took a long drink. He finally said, you do what you have to do.

But did you?

Look, he said finally, and his voice was husky, some of that crap is true.

How charming. Ava's voice from the doorway felt like a slap. Don't you two look cozy.

We both turned to see her in the doorway, backlit by the light from the hall. Her yellow nylon nightgown fell in translucent folds around her breasts and ended just below the shadowy triangle at her thighs. She hadn't bothered to comb her sleep-tangled hair.

So what the hell's going on here?

Duke stubbed out his cigarette and looked at her, almost amused, almost tired. We're just talking, Ava. What's the matter? Jealous?

She crossed her arms and planted her feet like the Colossus of Rhodes in my history book. Of her? Hell, no. I just want you to come to bed.

Sixteen years of Ava's bullying had trained me, and I started to get up. He laid a hand on my arm. No, he said. He looked at Ava. I don't want her to go. We're talking.

The lightning crashed again, a blinding flash making our faces look like fright masks. His fingers on my arm trembled and then tightened. She walked slowly over to him, nightgown swaying, and reached out a hand. Come on, Duke, she cooed. Come back to bed.

Hell, he said. He straightened, ignoring her hand, and rose. I got to find me some peace, he said.

Ava's voice escalated to a shriek. You're going to that old woman, aren't you? Old women, little girls! Why, Duke, why?

He walked to the door and gazed back at Ava. His face looked long and weary. They listen, he said, and left the room. I heard the back door slam. He doesn't even have a coat, Ava said, and hurried after him. I followed her, but stopped at the back door and watched her run after him, catch him, pull at his clothes. He shook her off, yelled at her, and went on to the bungalow. Ava stood there out in the rain, watching Elzuma's door open, watching him disappear. Then she slowly walked back to the house.

She banged into the kitchen dripping wet, the gown plastered to her body, looking like one of those naked Greek statues. She pointed a finger at me. This is all your fault, she said.

How, Ava, tell me how this is my fault.

You little bitch. She turned on her heel, dripped down the hall to her room, and slammed the door. I got the mop and cleaned up the water, because I had just waxed that floor the day before.

I didn't sleep the rest of the night. I gazed out the window from time to time, where a beacon of light shone out from Elzuma's house. The light finally went out when the first rays of sun peeped over the fields.

Duke had already gone out to the fields by the time I'd dressed for school. When I came in the kitchen, Ava, in jeans, her back to me, was pouring herself a cup of coffee. Morning, I said, as if nothing had happened.

She wheeled around, her face ugly. You better stop talking to him.

Jeez, Ava, I live here. He's my brother-in law. I don't have a hell of a lot of family, you know.

She said nothing.

I spread my arms, tears rising in my throat. You are jealous of me? You look like a movie star and I'm just a skinny kid. Do you see any boys lined up for dates here? Huh? There was a huge lump in my throat but I wasn't going to cry. She wasn't going to see me cry. I grabbed my books, and dashed out the front door. I leaned on my car, the one thing I owned—not counting Momma's pearls and ring—and stared at my big feet.

She came to the door. You didn't get breakfast, she said.

I'll buy a doughnut at the little store across from school, I said.

I got in the car and turned the ignition key. Nothing happened. I tried again to make sure the damn car was really dead. It was too late to walk to the road and try to flag down the bus. I laid my head on the steering wheel and cried.

Ava drove me to school, deadly silent. When we pulled up at school, Starrett Conable was standing out front cool as you please, as if he'd been waiting for me. He saw us, brightened, and came over and opened my car door. He leaned in with that monkey grin.

Hello, Mis' Ava, he said.

Excuse me? I'm here too. My name is Mae Lee.

Ava leaned over me. Why hello, Starrett, she said. So nice to see you. Why don't you come out to see us sometime?

Well, now, I have been hoping you would ask.

Real soon, she said. I sure do miss seeing your momma and daddy. We'll all get together.

I've got to get to class, I said. You two can carry on Old Home Week without me.

See you, Mis' Ava. I'll walk with Mae Lee.

He walked me to class, then, without a word. When he left me at the door, I said, Thank you.

You're welcome, he said. You want to go to the drive-in Friday? The Streets of Laredo.

It would spoil our beautiful friendship, I said.

That night after dinner, when Ava passed around the pecan pie, she cut her eyes over at me and said to Duke, I think I might invite Mr. and Mrs. Conable and Starrett over Saturday night.

They were mighty nice to Momma all those years after Daddy died.

Please, no, Lord. I jabbed my fork into my piecrust, shattering it. I hoped we wouldn't get to reminiscing about Momma, for one thing. And I hated to be matched up with Starrett. I knew what she was thinking.

But Duke said, Not Saturday night.

Thank you, Jesus.

I scooped up a forkful of pie. Duke went on, I heard from my old army buddy Jack Austin today, the one who brought you that letter all those years ago.

I don't remember him, Ava said.

I do, I said.

Why are you blushing? Duke teased.

I'm not, I said, furious at myself, but I had been dazzled by that soldier with eyes as blue as the April sky after a rain.

Oh, really, to impress Mae Lee like that he must have really been something, Ava said, sipping her coffee, holding her mug with both hands the way she did.

Well, you're going to see him again, Duke said. He's coming to town for a few days.

Oh, no, Ava said, the guest room's not ready. It needs curtains and rug. Can we—

He won't stay here, Duke said. He'll find a boarding house. He's a crop duster, on his way to Florida, then South America.

A crop duster, Ava said. Ugh, what a job.

Duke grinned. It's a damn dangerous job, sweetheart, just right for him. That daredevil parachuted over the jungle when his plane went down, and it was lucky we found him before the Japs did. Since the war he's raced stock cars, barnstormed, flown anything with wings and some without.

Probably the dumb type, she said.

Duke looked at her as if he had a great big secret. Oh, you'll like him, he said. The ladies always did. He got up then and kissed Ava on the cheek. Got to see about some fences. Some of the cows got out yesterday, and it took Cyrus half the day to round them up.

He plunked his coffee mug down on the table and went whistling out the door. Ava told me to clear the table. I gathered up the plates without a word. Inside I was smiling.

Chapter Nineteen

S aturday morning, and this Jack Austin was coming. I wanted
to meet him, I wanted to see if he would remember that
child, I wanted to be that child who stood in awe, I wanted to
be a grown woman that he would notice. It was the first time
the clouds had lifted since Momma died. So many losses. Chap,
Momma, my home. I was ready for the world, or God, to give
me something back.

Why did I imagine love might come from this stranger?
Maybe because I wanted it to so badly. Little did I know.

I slid out of bed in the thin early sun and raised the window,
as if to let out all the ghosts of the past. The January thaw was
still with us, and the air was fresh and cool. Robins strutted
and pecked in the brown Bermuda grass, and daffodil shoots
were pushing through the pine straw flowerbeds by Elzuma's
bungalow. The day was going to be brilliant, and that was a sign
from the heavens.

I heard a whinny from the barn. Oh, that would be the very thing, to ride and ride till my cheeks were pink, to hold that warm sweaty brown neck, to feel my legs around that powerful body. I needed to get rid of the butterflies that were crowding my insides.

Morning sounds chorused around me as I pulled on my jeans and shirt: birds in the trees outside; Ava humming in the kitchen while the radio played; Duke scraping his chair back, then slamming the back door as he went out.

I didn't pick up on what was different until I got to the kitchen. The coffeepot was plugged in, but a lone box of cornflakes sat on the table and Ava was nowhere in sight. I shrugged, grabbed a bowl, and shook cereal into it. I'd almost finished when Ava, her arms full of sheets and towels, burst into the kitchen.

No eggs or biscuits? I joked. You p.g. or something?

She shot me a look of disgust. Look, Mae Lee. I've got a lot to do today. I'm going to Macon to buy liquor, I'm going to get my hair done, and I won't be back until late this afternoon. I'm depending on you to clean the kitchen, sweep the porch, and do the laundry.

But—

I've made it easy, she said. Just cornflakes.

It's a perfect day to ride, I said.

So work fast, sweetie pie. This is Duke's friend, and I want the house to look good.

I'm not your slave, I said.

She smiled sweetly. Yes, you are. Bless your little heart.

Then she turned and walked down the hall to dress.

I got up, put my bowl in the sink, and kicked the stove. I only succeeded in hurting my toe. I had to watch it. What would Jack Austin think if I came in all crippled up? I wasn't going to let Ava spoil my day. I stuck three carrots in my pocket, grabbed a bag of dog kibble off the back porch, and went out to the hounds, which were in a new pen away from the house.

Ava wanted the place pretty, and so Duke had built a new chicken house farther away and had torn down the old wagon shed. In the back yard, instead of plain dirt he'd installed Bermuda sod, a flowerbed, and a gliding swing. A fluffy hedge had been planted to hide the barnyard and dog pen.

I ducked past the hedge and fed the dogs. Elzuma's pet frizzledy chicken, Mooney, pecked around, getting all the stray bits. Mooney was called a frizzledy chicken because she had black and white feathers that were kind of curled on their ends. Some people claimed the feathers were in backwards, but that wasn't quite true. Some people thought frizzledy chickens had a special kind of magic, and I think that's why Elzuma had her.

The fine weather was making the horses frisky, and Dandy was tossing her head, sniffing the wind. I walked over to the paddock. Dandy trotted over and stuck her nose between the rails, daintily nipping a carrot from my outstretched hand. Francis, the mule, sidled over and took his carrot too. Only Nimrod stood aloof, remaining at the far end of the paddock. He swished his tail and rolled his eyes. I held out a carrot to him.

Come on, I said. Come on, Nimrod.

He let out a long snort and side-stepped.

Come on, boy. Don't you want this carrot?

Dandy stretched her head and tried to reach the carrot with her teeth, but I kept it from her, making my way down the fence toward the big horse. Come on, I whispered, holding it out. You know you want this carrot.

He shook his head and snorted. I didn't move a muscle. It was important to wait. Just when I'd about given up, he dipped his graceful neck and meandered over and took the carrot, as though he'd been meaning to all along.

I came in the back door of the house just as Ava was going out the front. I glanced through the living-room window. She swished around the car with a charged grace I hadn't seen lately, and she let the Caddy top down despite the morning's coolness. Then she draped a chiffon scarf over her dark curls.

I went back to the kitchen's laundry alcove and picked up a wicker basket. Balancing it on my head, I strolled back to her room. The bed was unmade, the velvet covers rumpled, and the hamper was overflowing. I separated shirts from jeans, Ava's lacy bras and panties from Duke's cotton T-shirts and shorts.

I separated out her hand laundry and put it back in the hamper. I made the bed quickly, smoothed the spread, then picked up the pile of shorts and T-shirts. I caught a scent, and then I lifted the clothes to my nose. The mustiness of unwashed clothes struck me first, but underneath it, Duke's smell, strong and animal-like, sent a feeling through me, a sharp-edged flutter in my belly like the feeling I got when I first saw the dark mystery of the river, the swamp, and the setting sun over the dark water. I dropped the pile of clothes in the basket as though they were on fire, then scooped up the jeans and shirts and dropped them on top of the whites. Red-faced, I took the basket down the hall and set it next to the unsuspecting washer.

Grabbing the broom from the closet, I attacked the front porch, sweeping with strong strokes, scattering leaves and dirt. When it was clean I stood on the steps, my forehead damp, feeling the sun warm on my face. I took in big sweet gulps of air, unquiet riding through me. I was still standing there when Lindy's new chestnut jumper, Belle, came trotting up our driveway.

She ambled over to the porch and I patted Belle's nose. Come on, Lindy said, let's go.

I can't, I said. I've got all these chores. I explained about Jack's coming and Ava's trip to Macon. Maybe I can go after lunch.

Come have lunch with me, she said, and do your chores afterward. I want you to come try out my new jumps.

I don't know how to jump, I said.

I'll teach you.

I had a thought of falling off and breaking my neck and spoiling the evening for everybody and never getting to meet Jack.

Another time, I said, and she got a disgusted expression.

What's the matter with you, Mae Lee? Where's your *spirit?*

Just then Duke's truck rumbled out from behind the house. He stopped when he got even with us, and I felt my cheeks flushing at the memory of the laundry. Hello, Lindy, he said.

Hello, Mr. Radford.

Mae Lee, I'm going into town to look at a new tractor. Are you planning to ride?

Well, I—

Dandy picked up a stone and her hoof is sore. You think you could handle Nimrod? He needs exercise.

I forgot all my hesitation, forgot all my chores. Oh Duke, could I?

Why not? You're a good rider. See you girls. He drove on off.

Lindy looked at me. Well! she said. That settles it.

My heart thumped wildly. Okay, I said.

When I cinched the girth on the well-worn stockman's saddle Duke always used, Nimrod caught my excitement, frisking and tossing his head. He'd skittered around while I saddled him, and Lindy helped me hold him. Could I really control the big horse? Duke had said I could do it, and I wasn't about to disappoint him.

I climbed on the block and hoisted myself onto Nimrod's back, but the stirrups were too long. I slid off and tried to adjust them, but the old leather was too stiff. I sighed and looked around for Cyrus, but he wasn't there.

Aren't there any more saddles? asked Lindy.

The one I use with Dandy, I said, the western saddle.

We went into the dusty tack room. I started to take the Western saddle from its peg, but Lindy spied another one. This one, she said. Put this English saddle on him, and then you can jump.

But—

She was already taking it down.

That's a pretty old saddle, I said, and grabbed a towel to wipe it off. I wonder whose it was. Maybe Aunt Talley's. Yeah, that's it.

When Nimrod was finally tacked out, I mounted the big horse and stood in the stirrups, testing them. They were perfect.

Cyrus came into the yard from Lord knew where and stood looking at me for a minute. You be careful, now, Missy.

I will, I promised. I'd be back right after lunch and get the rest of the chores done, then have time to fix myself up for the daredevil.

The big horse responded at once to my knees and we were off. Lindy and I cantered off through the pecan grove and turned down a dirt road that skirted her parents' farm, meandering a good five miles back into the country, the cool wind and warm sun bringing back the good feelings I'd had that morning.

Lindy looked at me. Race to the old oak tree?

Are you trying to kill me?

I just want to see what that big animal can do.

He can beat any horse around, but—

She didn't reply, but took off, the chestnut's flying hooves throwing up clods of dirt.

Nimrod strained at the bit, and, my heart in my throat, I let him have his head. His hoofs ate up the ground between Lindy and me, and I hung on for dear life, hunched like a jockey, my fingers clutching the base of his mane, the rest of it whipping my face. The huge, gnarled oak we used as our finish line was ahead, and I urged him on. He passed Belle, and we reached the tree two lengths ahead of her. I pulled him to a stop, my legs trembling.

Damn, Lindy said, laughing. At last you beat me.

You wanted to race, I said, giddy with relief.

Now we jump, she said.

I'll watch you, I said.

She cocked one eyebrow at me and we doubled back to her house, a low, rambling, wooden ranch-style with a red roof. Lindy's folks weren't real farmers. They'd moved to the country so they could have room for their horses. Lindy's father raised a few cattle, but buying and selling land was his real job.

The jumping course, built in the field to the left of her house, accommodated all heights and types of fences—split-rail and white board, adjustable, even a hedge with a ditch. I looked at it silently.

Lindy's mother came out, greeted us, and told us to be careful. Lindy set the rails low and put Belle through her paces. You can do it, she said.

It did look like fun. Of course you can, she said.

She explained exactly what to do. I circled Nimrod around the ring and galloped toward the first low jump, and when we got close I leaned forward, shifting my weight. Almost before I knew it, Nimrod was in the air.

When he landed, my rear end landed hard on the back of the saddle. I gritted my teeth at the stab of pain, gripped with my knees, and slid forward. I was going to be sore, but I hadn't fallen! I took him around again.

Now, let's raise the rails, she said. We took another round, and by this time I was flying high.

Lindy's mom came out and watched us for a time, and then she called us to lunch. She fed us sandwiches, chips, and iced tea. After we cleared the table, I saw Lindy's mom with a load of clothes on the way to the washer.

Oh my gosh, I said, I've got to get back and do that laundry or Ava will have my tail.

Mae Lee, said Lindy, as we mounted our horses, why do you let her tell you what to do all the time?

I haven't got a lot of choice, I said, looking up at the high thin wisps of clouds. A warmish wind ruffled the broomsedge in a field beyond. I'm kind of an orphan, you know. Where else could I go? An orphanage?

Quit being silly. You could stay with us.

They wouldn't let me.

So make some noise. If you let people walk all over you all you're going to get is footprints on your back.

I thought about that as we rode along. A mile along we ran into, of all people, Starrett Conable, on the old roan he kept at his grandpa's place, and he was impressed to see I was on Nimrod. He told us his grandpa had a litter of beagle puppies and would we like to see them. Of course, Lindy squealed and said yes, and for some reason I decided I just had to see those puppies.

We followed him back to his grandpa's place and played with the puppies, and his grandma made a big commotion over us and gave us some lemonade and fresh chocolate cake. Then wouldn't you know, Glenn Dorris came driving up and had some cake, too, and of course I couldn't leave then. We were all sitting out in the back yard having a good time when I finally noticed how low the sun had sunk.

What time is it? I asked.

Starrett yawned. Who cares?

See you guys later. I rushed over to where I'd tied Nimrod. I knew I shouldn't have been so jittery around him, but I couldn't help myself. Come on, Starrett, open the gate, I said.

What's the rush?

Just help, okay?

Anything for my proud beauty. Lord, I wish I had my wicked way with you.

Oh, shut up.

When he opened the gate, I gave Nimrod his head. His hoofs pounding the packed dirt roads, we flew past scraggly roadside weeds. Plum bushes whipped my legs and dust stung my eyes. Flecks of foam flew from Nimrod's mouth, and sweat lathered his flanks. We galloped through our gate full-tilt. I pulled back on the reins as we neared the barn, but Nimrod strained at the bit and kept going, heading toward the low hedge of the back yard. Barn cats leaped on fences in alarm, and the dogs in the pen began to bark.

Nimrod! Nimrod! The reins cut into my hands, I was pulling so hard. We were heading straight for the hedge. I spotted Duke standing on the back porch, watching in amazement, and I hunkered down, ready for the jump. Just then Elzuma's frizzledy chicken flew out of the hedge in a great flurry of wings and Nimrod skidded to a stock-still stop. I went flying out of the saddle, and my foot went through the bare stirrup. I hung suspended, upside down, pain shooting through my ankle. Nimrod, terrified, took off in the opposite direction.

My head bumped once on the ground, and then the worn leather stirrup-strap broke. I landed with a thud, on my back. Duke ran toward me. "Mae Lee! Mae Lee!" Dazed, I tried to sit up. "Lie down!" he ordered. "Don't move!"

I couldn't speak, for the breath had been knocked out of me.

He knelt and gathered me up and carried me toward the house. I stole a look at him through my half-closed eyes, and it frightened me to see that he looked scared too.

My breath came back. I think I'm all right, really.

You little idiot. When I think of what could have happened . . . damn. This is all my fault, for asking you to take him. Where does it hurt?

The right side of my head was tender, and my ankle was beginning to throb. He took me inside, sat me in a kitchen chair, and propped my ankle up, then tied some ice in a towel and made me hold it where it hurt. He filled an ice bag and put it on the sore spot.

Then I saw the basket of laundry by the washing machine.

Duke, I said in a small voice, I was supposed to do that laundry. Please don't tell Ava I went riding.

I'd better get you to a doctor, he said with a mixture of amusement and gruffness. To hell with the laundry.

But Ava will be back any minute, and your friend's coming. Really, I don't need a doctor.

I heard a noise on the back porch, and my heart flipped. Ava back already? But it was Elzuma. I seen that commotion, she said, opening the door. How is you, child? She came over and bent to see the swollen ankle. Mmm-mmm, she said, and shook her head.

What do you think, Elzuma? said Duke. She need a doctor?

Elzuma poked and prodded. She be all right, she finally said. You got some aspern?

Duke went to get the aspirin, and Elzuma eyed the laundry. She winked at me. Don't you worry none, she said. She shuffled her old frame over and started stuffing clothes into the machine.

Duke dosed me with aspirin and ordered me to my room with the ice pack. I'd better go round up my horse, he said. I lay back on the pillow, tears in my eyes. Some way to meet the famous Jack. If they would let me out of the room at all.

My ankle was wrapped with an Ace bandage and my head had quit hurting by the time Ava came home. I was in the kitchen, sitting in the chair with my ankle on the table, folding towels and dishcloths.

She bustled in and clanked down a brown paper sack on the counter, and fixed me with a stare. You should have had that finished a long time ago, she said.

Duke brought in two more sacks from the car. I had some outdoor chores for her to do, he said, without a glance at me. She fell in the barn, mucking out stalls.

Fine, slipped in shit, Ava said. I thought Cyrus was supposed to do that.

Hey, you got a haircut, I said.

Oh, she said, touching it. You like it?

It looks like Elizabeth Taylor's in that movie with Montgomery Clift where he pushes his wife in the lake.

That did not seem to bother her. I got up, put away the kitchen linens, and hobbled down the hall with the other clothes. Go lie down after you finish that, she said.

I'm all right, I said.

Then pitch in, she said.

I bathed as best as I was able and changed into a gray skirt and my best pink mohair sweater, the one that made my eyes look big. I couldn't get my shoes on so I put on my bedroom slippers over my bobby socks. I was in the kitchen clinking ice out of the ice trays into the wedding-present silver ice bucket when Duke came in, ready for the evening in tweed jacket and tie. Even dressed up, he never looked as though indoors suited him, but tonight he looked really good. He arranged the liquor bottles on a rolling side table he used as a bar when company came.

How are you feeling?

Better. I'd be dead if it weren't for you.

I had nothing to do with it. That damned old saddle saved you. I'm not going to even ask you why Nimrod thought he had to jump the hedge. I handed him the full ice bucket and got out the good glasses. Sit down, girl, he said.

All at once, the doorbell rang and Ava yelled at me from down the hall.

That'll be Austin. Duke headed for the door and I crab-legged to Ava's room to see what she wanted.

She waved a rumpled red silk blouse at me. Here, quick, iron this.

You have a closet full of clothes, Ava.

She cocked her head to one side. Somebody is not telling the truth about something, and I don't like it. Now play nice and iron this blouse, because we're taking him to the club tonight and this is perfect with my ruby earrings.

I listened to the voices in the hall. Not the time to pick a fight. I draped the red silk over my arm and turned back to the hallway. It would be so easy to scorch that silk. I eased toward the kitchen, but Duke heard my thumping shuffle. Mae Lee! Come and say hello.

I veered into the front hall, licking my lips from nervousness. And there Jack Austin was, in a black leather jacket, just as I had remembered him. His blond hair spilled over his tanned forehead, and his eyes were as blue as butterfly wings. When I'd been little, he'd seemed tall, but now I was as tall as he was, and he looked too young to have ever been in the war.

Here's Mae Lee, Ava's little sister, Duke said. He winked at me and turned to Jack. She's almost as much of a damned daredevil as you are.

I held out my hand, and Jack gripped it with both of his, grinning. Hiya, Mae Lee. Jack Austin. His eyes traveled down to my wrapped ankle, taking in my figure at the same time. So what you been doing, gal?

Duke drew me to him with a brotherly arm. Acting like you, trying to jump a horse over a hedge.

It was the horse's idea, I protested.

I stay away from horses, said Jack. Dangerous. Give me a parachute any day. I realized he was gazing at my sweater.

I've got to go, I said. Ava asked me to iron. I held up the red silk.

Ah, the famous Ava, Jack said. Can't wait to meet her.

Maybe we'll see her sometime this evening, Duke joked, punching Jack lightly on the shoulder. We might as well have a drink. We all trooped into the kitchen together.

They talked and laughed, opened bottles and poured Scotch, while I opened the ironing board and plugged in the iron. I finished the job as quickly as I could and hobbled down the hall to her room. My ankle was throbbing and pain shot though it with every step.

Ava, in skirt and lacy slip, was peering at her reflection in the dressing-table mirror, outlining her lips with a brush. She finished, pursed her lips, smiled, then with satisfaction, snapped the cap onto the brush. What the hell took you so long?

Silk's not easy to iron without scorching, I said, laying the blouse carefully on the bed.

Ava took a rat-tail comb and fluffed out her new hairdo. What did you think of Jack? Is he cute?

What do you care? I said sulkily. You're married.

She shot me a murderous glance. Hand me the rubies, would you? Second drawer of the chest.

Her elaborate Chinese jewelry chest of black lacquer and mother-of-pearl, painted with scenes of weeping willows and pagodas, sat on top of the dresser. I opened a tiny drawer and lifted the earrings from the golden silk lining. The ruby drops glowed like the heart of a pomegranate, like the last fire of sunset, like *bloude-red wine*. I remembered a line from a ballad from school, *The king sits in Dumferline town, drinking the bloude-red wine*. I gazed at the earrings, mesmerized.

Mae Lee, what the hell are you doing?

She snatched the earrings from my outstretched palm and poked the golden wires through the lobes of her ears. She smiled at her reflection, pleased at the effect of the rubies and the red silk blouse. She stood up, slipped into a black suit jacket, and walked out.

Her clothes littered the bedroom. Out of my habit of neatness, I picked up a rejected green dress and hung it in the closet, and winced as pain jolted my ankle. I sank to the dressing-table bench and picked up a jade necklace she'd carelessly left draped over her powder box. I stroked it. How cool and smooth it was, all polished swirling shades of green. I held it up to my throat.

We're going, Mae Lee, Duke yelled. I rose from the bench, slid the necklace back into the jewelry box, and closed the drawer. I shuffled out into the front hall, where Duke was helping Ava into her fur coat. Jack, lighting up a smoke, shook out the match and looked at me in that way he had, like he knew what the joke was and wasn't going to tell me. Mae Lee, he said. Wish you could go with us.

Oh, Jack, said Ava. Leave her alone.

He winked at me. I felt as hot and red as Ava's blouse. I slumped to hide my bosoms, and glanced over at Duke, but he was looking at his watch.

Wait, said Ava, rummaging through her bag. I need to get my lipstick. She clicked back to her room.

Jack edged so close to me I smelled Old Spice and leather jacket. He said, glancing back toward the hall, Let me tell you, Mae Lee, over there, half the guys—hell, all the guys—were in love with Ava. That picture of her –

Hey, Austin, she doesn't need to hear those old stories, Duke said.

Jack glanced over at Duke. One night somebody stole it. The picture, I mean. He didn't come back, I hear.

A load of crap, as usual, Duke said. That guy was on the squad that demolished a bridge.

Ava appeared, smiling sweetly, with a black chiffon scarf draped over her head. Come on, flyboy, she said to Jack, taking his arm. We'll show you a good time in the big city.

She took Duke's arm as well. Jack turned back and winked at me and then the door closed.

I felt like I was soaring over those jumps again.

I picked up three apples out of the fruit bowl, hobble-danced my way out to the barn, and gave them to Nimrod and Francis and Dandy, my breath coming in frosty puffs, as if to remind me it was winter after all. The stars cartwheeled above, and the moon was like a big slice of honeydew melon. Love and homesickness was the trouble with me, and I had no home, and love seemed as far away as the Big Dipper.

I called Lindy, hoping she'd come over, but she wasn't there. We didn't have a television set then. They still belonged to science fiction in our part of the country. I went through the pile of mail on the hall table again, in case I'd missed a letter from *Mademoiselle*, where I'd sent a couple of my poems.

Nothing was addressed to me. I took the rest of the mail, bills mostly, into Duke's office and plopped them onto the scarred old desk.

I'd never spent much time there, and now I looked around. On the wall hung his diploma from Georgia Tech, pictures of Ava in a bathing suit at the pool and in evening gown when she'd been Miss Sawyer High, photos of his momma and daddy and Talley and the Colonel and their kids, and the big stuffed marlin he'd landed in the Keys. The shelves held trophies for track and football.

And then there was the trunk, where something awful was buried.

Maybe I should have gone back to my room and played solitaire for the rest of the evening, or listened to the radio, or read *My Antonia* for English class. I didn't do any of those things. I looked in the top drawer of Duke's desk, where I knew he kept a set of odd keys. They were still there. I tried them, one by one, until I found the one that opened the footlocker in the closet where he kept the things from the war. I lifted the lid.

A handgun—drab, not chrome like the ones Jimmy Cagney used in the movies—lay on top. Was that the awful thing? I lifted it out, carefully placed it on the floor, then took out a Bible with stains that looked like blood. I laid it aside. I found two tattered paperback novels, a photo album, and a small leather-bound diary. I caught my breath, recognizing it as the book I'd seen in Elzuma's bungalow those years ago when Duke and Ava had been living there, the time when I'd been so sick and Chap had died. I hadn't understood it then. I wondered if I'd understand it now.

I put the photo album and diary to one side and laid the Bible back in the trunk beside a pile of letters, stacked and tied with string. Was the letter I sent him in that pile?

I lifted the stack of letters to see, and found myself looking at a bayonet. I picked it up and turned it over in my hands, and it chilled me to see the Japanese characters, picture-words, stamped into the dull metal. I wondered if Duke had killed the soldier who had owned it.

It had to be the awful thing. What did it feel like to stab someone, to push that blade into a living body? Suddenly I pushed myself to my feet and lunged forward with the bayonet like Errol Flynn in a pirate movie. I hobbled around, poked and parried, sliced the air. In my wild play I nicked Duke's chair by accident, splintering the wood. I gazed at the bright yellow gash and shuddered. I carefully laid the bayonet back in the trunk and settled down in the chair with the photo album and notebook.

I flipped the pages of the album. There was Jack Austin, standing with a couple of the natives. A scribbled note on the bottom read *Austin with Kachins*. He was clowning around even, mugging for the camera. I flipped the pages. Most of the pictures didn't mean anything to me—just soldiers and jungle, barracks, tents, soldiers. There was an airplane. Duke had written beneath it *Gypsy Moth*.

One picture stopped me. A Burmese or Chinese girl, about my age or younger, with bangs and lopsided pigtails, stood in front of a bamboo house with an old man, her grandfather maybe, squinting into the camera as though the sun were in her eyes or she was in pain--a smile or a grimace, I couldn't tell. *Li-Wei* was written underneath.

I closed the album, picked up the diary, and turned it over and over in my hands, not sure if I wanted to open it. Maybe it would give me a clue to Duke's nightmares. Maybe I didn't want to know what happened over there.

Chapter Twenty

The war, some people said, had been a great adventure. Oh sure, you worried about the boys out there fighting, but we were all pulling together, weren't we, on this great cause, and weren't we a blessed nation? The news came slowly and filtered and we were spared from the worst of it. That's why I had no idea what I was going to feel when I read the diary.

April 29. Washington. The men who are training us learned at a British camp in Canada. I'm learning to come to terms with everything I used to hate. Here honesty, decency, are words that are never used. Words used are tactics, outsmart, take out.

May 20. Joan gave me this book. She tells me writing breaks the tension. Well, I'm no Shakespeare but I'm going to write what happens. Joan speaks seven languages and they want her to go undercover in France. She's a smart, funny gal, a blond who knows it all and is not afraid to tell you.

June 1. We had a hell of a time getting passage to India. It was only when the colonel began making arrangements to charter a boat that somebody found room for us on a troop ship.

June 27. Soon we land at the Karachi and meet the colonel. I still don't know exactly where we're going. Maybe China. Hope Vinegar Joe has a plan.

July 4. Some celebration. We are cooling our heels as Stilwell is thinking about what to do with us. He doesn't want us in China.

September 13. We're off to Burma and see what chaos we can cause there.

October 5. The Brits have given us a tea plantation in Nazira, Assam, near the border. Behind us is jungle which will make good training fields for the recruits. Before us the valley rises into the slopes, and the tea plantings go on for miles, up the slopes.

I flipped through the pages, seeing names: Colonel Eifler. General Stilwell. Major Richmond.

November 20. We are near the Naga Hills where the Naga head-hunters live. We were in danger of being exposed by some Jap chutists and the Colonel sent the Nagas after them. They came back with a basket of six heads.

I swallowed hard and flipped a few more pages.

December [smudged] forward base will be established but I stay here. I have been given a Kachin trainee for an assistant. His name is Saw, but I generally call

him Mick, as in Mickey Finn. He's teaching me some
of the language, while I teach him the fundamentals
of espionage and sabotage, forgery and lock picking
and sentry killing. All this is right up his alley. He,
like most of his buddies, is short, rough, and tough,
a fierce fighting man, Mongolian looking, quick as a
frog's tongue. His teeth were black as the ace of spades
from chewing betel nut. The first thing he tells you is
that he hates both the British and the Japanese. The
word here is not to trust any native until you get to
know them well.

I kept reading, holding my breath, page after page of training,
of the heat and the long periods of boredom and the pure terror
of what they had to do. And little by little, I saw him becoming
blasé.

May 23. Monsoons started. We're in for months of
it, but we're not as bad off as the units down behind the
lines to the south. Sent a letter. Got a letter from Talley,
from Wilkes back in Washington. She's beginning to
regret he got me into this. I wrote her back I wasn't in
the mud, darlin'. Hell, I had to do something in this
war. That's what I told her.

June 17. It was a boring day. Rain sheeting down
outside, camp a mess of puddles. I was sitting here with
this book trying to think up something to write when
the colonel came in. His expertise with a pistol is a well
known story. He eyed the book pretty hard and asked
me how would I like for him to shoot it out of my hand.

I took the hint and got rid of it. I stuck it down in a corner of my kit, telling myself I'd throw it in the fire one day.

July 3. A Major Williams, a Brit who'd been in Algeria, came over with a communiqué from Dorman-Smith. We got into conversation and I realized he'd been in contact with Joan there. Now he was telling me she was dead, cover blown.

The next page was torn out, and the next few pages were blank. I started to lay the diary aside, but the blank pages were wrinkled, not smooth, and it seemed like there might be something further on. I kept flipping pages.

And then:

November 16. Writing this in hospital. I'm writing what put me here so I can forget about it.

Pat Robbins came in with us late, after we'd already been out for a year or so. A clean-cut farm boy from Kansas. He wasn't with the original group of boys trained in Washington. He was somebody the Colonel had met by chance in a Chittagong bar, decided he liked his style, and he'd gotten him transferred to our outfit.

Pat Robbins, once he got off the farm, developed a taste for the grape and grain, as well as adventure. And he had guts, and that's what the Colonel liked about him. What Pat didn't like was the jungle. He was from Kansas, you know, and from what he told me there was hardly a tree to be seen. Where he came from there was sun three hundred and sixty-four days a year.

Here, he was in the damned steam bath of the world. It was almost like those dog days of summer back home where a good rain hangs in and before you know it mold is growing out your wazoo.

But you have to hand it to him, he tried. I have never known a boy to try so hard. He had guts and when he was drinking got a little crazy, not being used to the stuff.

Said he was going in with his uncle in the auto supply business after he got back, said he had a pretty girl waiting for him. Well, I told him I had a set-up like that, and we came to be buddies. He had a picture of his girl. She wasn't a looker like Ava, but she had a nice and friendly face, and somehow I knew she'd make him a good solid wife, one who'd stick by him through thick and thin.

He had this idealistic streak in him, being a good old church going Kansan. He didn't know what to make of our Kachins. He couldn't believe they smoked opium all the time. Money, of course, didn't mean much in the jungle, and they'd get paid in opium. Pat thought this was un-American, but they didn't seem to get addicted to the stuff. Not so I could tell anyhow. Hell, it was true about Asians being hard to read.

By the time Robbins joined us he was behind the rest of us on his jungle training and he was always playing catch-up. He never quite got guerrilla fighting the way the Kachins did it. He knew that when you engaged the enemy, you fought. But from the Kachins we learned to attack quickly, do all the damage you can, then slowly melt away into the jungle.

Pat thought this was cowardly; thought you ought to stay and fight till the last man was down. This attitude was what got the Brits' ass whipped too many times before they caught on. Those Chindits of Wingate's put up a bloody good fight before they got driven back across the Irrawaddy.

Robbins was one of those gung-ho kids. We knew he would be a hell of a good agent if we could only get those ideas of honor and decency out of his head. We told him that the Japanese had a different kind of fighting code. You killed the enemy whenever you had a chance, by whatever means were at your disposal, and you tried to fake them, psych them. The little bastards would run at you screaming insults, like "Eleanor Roosevelt eats powdered eggs." We would scream, "Hirohito eats shit," before we blasted them.

Then the colonel got temporary duty to Washington. Col. Peers took over. He was a cool head, a military strategist. Robbins went to him and volunteered to lead a unit, wanted to get in on the action. Saw and I did not think he was ready, but there was no holding him back.

He was assigned to a unit to penetrate enemy lines and blow up a railroad bridge down near Myit.

Well, they had been out about three weeks and we lost radio contact with them. We couldn't get any information as to whether they had accomplished their mission or not. Then some word came back to us. The Kachins found it out through that damned jungle radar they have that our men had been captured by the Japanese.

The men at their outpost camp were stretched thin, so another detail was sent out to get them back and to blow up the bridge: myself and Saw Mick and two others.

We were careful. We were expecting ambush. We also had no way of knowing if the jungle information was true or false. You checked it out best you could and kept going.

The jungle is always full of sounds. You hear the cries of birds, the endless whine of mosquitoes, the crackle and buzz of other insects, the gurgle of water from a stream. What you don't want to hear is the crack of sticks as a tiger stalks you or the swish of a python in a tree.

You might see splintered bones on the path.

You might see the skeleton of a parachutist hanging from the trees.

You might see leeches every damn where on your body.

You will see buzzards for sure.

We parachuted in to where they had last reported and scouted the area until we found a village. Saw Mick questioned the people until we found out which way they had headed; we plunged through the jungle for pretty much a day and a night. On the second day we spotted signs of troops. A scrape on bark here, boot prints in the ground. We stopped to examine the treads. American boots can be told from Japanese by the tread—ours were a hell of a lot better and they would steal our boots given half a chance—and here, both treads were clear. At this part of the jungle the canopy was so thick there was little or no undergrowth and the prints stood out.

We followed the treads until we reached a wall of some razor-sharp grass. I felt we were nearing a river, and soon we came to a clearing.

The jungle was the unnatural heated quiet of midday, except for the far-off calling of a bird. I gave orders to my men to put rifles at the ready. We inched forward. I brushed aside a branch and stopped in my tracks at what I saw.

There in the clearing was Pat Robbins, tied to a tree. He was dead. Blood had crusted and dried on his uniform in a hundred places. He had been used for bayonet practice. The others were dead too, on the ground. As I stood looking at him I heard the cry of a jackal.

I stepped forward to cut the poor bastard down and then the crack of a rifle exploded from somewhere. We dove back into the jungle and waited.

And waited. The light was fading; through the trees we saw the sun blood-red through the thickets, setting across the grasslands of the river savannas beyond. The smell. We waited with the smell of blood and shit and rot in our noses and the screeches of birds and jackals in our ears.

Finally, when it was nearly dark, a patrol of Japs stalked out into the clearing, rifles at the ready, jabbering and talking. They went over to inspect the body. I waited long enough to figure they were alone.

We fired and got them all, all but one, who spun and fired in my direction. He hit me in the leg and then he took off running. Saw Mick chased my attacker and brought him down with a shot to the back.

He grabbed the rifle from the dead Jap and brought it back to me. We took the bayonet off the rifle and fixed it as a splint for my leg.

We buried the Lieutenant and the others in the jungle. My leg hurt like hell and we hadn't accomplished the mission. Saw Mick led us to a village where the natives hid me in a storeroom while the others blew the bridge.

By the time they got back infection had set in. It was painful to walk. We radioed to HQ and made it to the outpost camp where they treated it best they

could, despite Saw Mick's telling me the jungle cure was
to rub the ashes of a dead bat or something on it and
bury the rest.

The colonel's jerry-built Gypsy Moth managed to
meet us at the strip and we flew back to base. By the
time they got me to this hospital the infection was so
bad they had to work like hell to save my leg. And so
here I am lying up here not doing a damn bit of good
to anybody.

I dream of back home and my sweet Ava.

I couldn't bear to read any further. I felt sick to my stomach and went to get a drink of water. I looked at the clock. It was just about ten.

I didn't want to go to bed. I didn't want to take off my clothes.

I knew I should just put everything back in the book and close the lid on the trunk and never open it again.

But I went back to the chair and opened the book.

The next page was blank.

Maybe Duke had meant to fill it in later; maybe he hadn't. The page after that had one sentence:

I dream of old Sawyer and the folks, and wish I
had some of Elzuma's honest-to-goodness fried chicken.
I don't know if I ever want to see any more rice.

The next few pages were random thoughts about the war, and then it just fizzled out. There was an entry about the R & R place in India. And then there was nothing else to say. I held the book gingerly, as though it might suddenly burst into flame, slipped it back into the trunk under the other things, and laid the album and the bayonet on top. Then I closed the lid. I didn't lock it, but I returned the keys to the drawer.

I was curled up asleep on the living room sofa when the doorbell rang, making my heart thump and my dream of the jungle disappear with a pop, thank God, and then someone was pounding on the front door, big loud bangs. I nearly tripped over my feet as I jumped up, hurried to the door, and jerked it open.

Damn key won't fit, said Duke, looking up from his stooped position. Ava was leaning against Jack.

For a minute I didn't understand and then I did. Duke, you're really drunk, I said.

He just grinned. Not drunk enough, he said, and lurched in. He wove toward the kitchen through the living room, bouncing off Ava's white sectional sofa.

Ava patted Jack on the shoulder as if they were bosom buddies and had some secret between them. I'll be back in a minute, honey. I'm about to pop. After a minute the swishing sound came down the hall, like she hadn't closed the door to the bathroom.

Standing in the hallway with this man listening to my sister piss. He didn't seem to care. Little Mae Lee, he said. How old are you?

Sixteen, I said, and my heart started to thump.

I would've thought you were eighteen.

It's because I'm tall, I said. You look just like you did in the war.

Grin, snaky grin. So how do you know how I looked in the war?

Duke had a picture, I said, suddenly demure.

I'd like to see it, he said.

I swallowed. This way, I said.

He followed me into Duke's office. I opened the trunk, took out the album, and laid it open on the desk. Jack stood beside me and gently rested his hand on my hip as I turned the pages, and oh, God, I felt the heat radiating off his body. He pointed to the pictures.

The Colonel . . . the Gypsy Moth . . . Saw Mick and some of the Kachin rangers. He shook his head. Pat Robbins clowning around . . .

I turned my head away.

He took a sideways look at me. Duke tell you about that?

I shook my head. I read something he wrote.

He flipped the page, not looking at me. I'm surprised he showed it to you.

He didn't, I murmured.

Jack turned the pages, and I was conscious of his breath, my breath, his breath, my breath. He reached to the snapshot of the old Chinese man and the young teenage girl in pigtails, standing outside a village shop. I stopped his hand with my own. Who's that?

Gem trader, said Jack, with a funny look. Kid was his granddaughter. About your age.

What happened to her? I knew something did. I just knew.

Jack looked down and waited a long time before he answered. Japs took her, for the soldiers, he finally said. I guess you wouldn't know about that. They called them comfort girls. Mostly Korean, but they took some Burmese too. Some younger than that.

Oh God.

Duke tried to save her.

How?

Jack shook his head slowly. Don't know the whole story. He lowered his voice and leaned closer to me, and there was the scent of leather jacket and spice aftershave and the feel of his lips on my neck.

And then Ava was filling the doorway, flashing fire—all red silk and red lips and rubies.

What's going on here?

We both looked at her at once.

Her lip was curled. Duke's had it, Mister Jack. Help me get him to bed.

Jack winked at me. Don't go away.

I could hardly catch my breath, but I followed them out into the hall, where Duke had collapsed against the wall, legs barely holding him up, eyes seeing God knew what.

I looked away, tears springing to my eyes. Duke had been my hero, and he was still my hero, but oh God, what he had been through. My heart ached for him, and I wished there was some way I could help him.

Jack was helping him now, and he'd told me he'd be back. I felt as if I'd drunk a glass of that whiskey at the thought he liked me and I liked him. Was it wrong of me to be heartsick over Duke and excited about Jack at the same time?

It helped a lot that Jack had told me the story of the photographs.

I prayed for the souls of the dead that night. And whether she was dead or not, I prayed for the Chinese girl with the lopsided pigtails.

Chapter Twenty-One

The next morning, Sunday, when I got up everyone else was sleeping, and I knew they would sleep all morning. The weather had suddenly changed, with an icy, bitter wind whistling across the fields, slapping leaves across the windowpanes. I saw Cyrus, bundled up, going to the barn. I limped into Duke's office and replaced the picture book in the trunk.

Jack was out at the farm again Monday when I got home from school. It turned out that he was staying at Ida Duggan's rooming house, lining up jobs for the summer, working on his crop-dusting plane, and helping out around the farm. Duke had loaned him the old blue farm truck to get back and forth as part of the deal. No one mentioned the weekend. No one mentioned the war. Once in a while he would catch my eye, but that was all.

That week, he and Duke and Cyrus mended fences and hauled stumps, clearing land for more cotton. I mooned around, my ankle healing, writing his name over and over on my blue-lined notebook paper, and then I burned the paper in the backyard, afraid he would see it. Elzuma frowned at me and told me to quit lollygagging.

Ava and I were in the kitchen getting supper Wednesday when they came back late that afternoon, laughing and cutting up. They plopped into chairs and popped the top off bottles of beer, making me think of Chap. Ava watched the oven as though it might explode at any moment, and finally opened the door to peek.

What are we having? asked Duke. There weren't any pots on the stove.

Some of those new TV dinners, she said. I don't want them to burn. Don't you want to stay and eat with us, Jack?

No thanks, he said. I already put my name down at Mis' Ida's tonight, and she'd be pissed if I didn't show. Ava stiffened, because she didn't like profanity. Jack drained his beer bottle and set it on the table and gave her a puppy-dog look. Ava, darlin', wish you'd cook up some venison or quail. I'd be glad to shoot you some this weekend. How's the hunting here, old buddy?

Duke found something to look at out the window all of a sudden. Pretty good, but I don't hunt.

Jack was all grin and teeth, except his eyes weren't smiling. Not hunt? Come on. I thought everybody in this neck of the woods hunted.

I had enough of killing, Duke said.

Jack shook his head. You eat meat, don't you? That chicken in that TV dinner had its head chopped off.

I didn't do the chopping, Duke said. Somebody else can do the chopping.

Jack said nothing, and I saw a slow red flush creeping up Duke's neck. There were a lot of unsaid words there, charges of being unmanly, unsoldierly, as if he'd come by his war wound by accident. But Duke's jaw remained firm. You find somebody else to hunt with, Jack. I'll loan you my shotgun, if I can remember where it is.

I know where it is, I said.

You do, Missy, said Ava, and how is that?

It's in the tack room locked in a box, I said. I'll show Jack where it is, I said, since it seemed clear Duke didn't want to have anything to do with it.

Go ahead, said Duke, before Ava could tell me not to, because I was sure that was on her mind. He fished a key out of a dish on the counter and tossed it to me.

I walked out the back door with Jack and out to the barn. You got any idea what's going on with Duke? He said to me. I shook my head, keeping his secret.

When we got inside the tack room, we knelt down and unlocked the box. There were two shotguns there, and Jack took his time deciding before he chose one. When we stood up, we were close together and he looked at me in that lazy way he had and pulled me over to him and kissed me, long and slow. I had never been kissed before if you didn't count spin-the bottle at parties. This was a real kiss that I felt all the way down. And then he snatched himself back because Cyrus was coming into the barn. Cyrus gave us a glance and I told him Jack was borrowing the shotgun.

Just one, I reckon, Cyrus said. I needs the other for the varmints.

Sure, I said. I didn't know how he could shoot with only one arm but I guess he had it figured out.

Walk me to the truck, Jack said, and so I did. When we got to the truck he tipped my chin up like he was going to kiss me again and I pulled back. Everybody would say he was too old for me, and I suppose he was. He was twenty-eight, Duke had said. But he didn't look that old. He wasn't like these boys in school, wet behind the ears. Jack was a real man.

They might be watching, I said.

He glanced over to the house without moving. Finally he said, Sure, beautiful. See you later.

I hurried back to the house, feeling his eyes on my back. Laughter bubbled in my throat, feeling strangely like tears. He had called me beautiful.

Thursday afternoon Jack wasn't there when I got home. Duke and Ava rode over to look at a neighbor's prize bull, the one that had won a blue ribbon at the state fair. Duke was thinking of breeding some of his cows to it.

I was thinking about Jack so hard that when the phone rang, I grabbed it, hoping it was him, and it was, and my heart was in my throat.

Hey sweet thing, said Jack. Duke there? A deep, hollow pit formed in my stomach.

They've gone to look at a bull, I said. They ought to be back any time.

A bull, huh?

For breeding.

Is that a fact.

Did you go hunting today?

No, he said. Other stuff. Hey, Mae Lee, I been wanting to ask you, how would you like to go to the show tonight?

My stomach dropped to my feet. I can't. I have homework. Oh my God, my heart was racing like Nimrod on the dirt road.

Tomorrow night, then.

I don't know. I thought of the evil eye Ava had given me the night she'd seen us looking at the picture album together, and God only knew what Duke would think. The phone line crackled and I thanked Jesus and Southern Bell we didn't have a party line.

Don't you want to come, honey? That voice was making goo in my underpants.

I'd have to ask *them*, you know. No need to say who *them* were. I don't think they would let me.

Hey, you're a big girl, he said. Maybe they wouldn't have to know. They're going to some fancy party tomorrow night, right?

I knew this was true. There was a dinner party at Duke's parents' house. It was some kind of political thing and Ava was all excited.

We could be out and back before they got home, Jack was saying. Think about it and call me tomorrow at old lady Duggan's. Here's the number.

I grabbed a pencil and scribbled the number on the back of the phone book.

Ava and Duke came back from the bull viewing about seven. They'd stayed for supper talking breeding, and the neighbor had sent a plate of pork chops, vegetables, and lemon pie for me. Lindy called after supper, and I listened with half an ear to what she was telling me. Most of my mind was still on Jack's voice on the phone and the feel of his lips and the smell of him, and the damp in my pants.

Lindy was saying, aren't you listening, Mae Lee?

Oh sorry. What? . . . the weathered tan of Jack's skin and the muscles under his black jacket, his breath warm on my cheek.

You are coming to the game with me tomorrow night, aren't you? Some of us are getting together afterwards and I think Glenn's coming. You know he and what's-her-name have broken up.

I have to think about it, I said.

Jeez, Mae Lee, what are you talking about? All I've heard you talk about for the past year is Glenn. Now's your chance, girl. He's at loose ends.

I didn't want to tell her about Jack. I wanted to go with him, and I didn't. I wanted to sneak out and I didn't. But then again, sooner or later he would leave town and Glenn would still be here. Pick me up, I said.

Friday night Ava was dressed up fit to kill in a new green silk dress to match her eyes and a pearl-colored mink stole, off to cocktails and dinner. They said it was all right for me to go to the game with Lindy. I put on my gray wool skirt and my new red sweater and my bobby socks and saddle shoes and stared at myself in the mirror, trying to comb my hair this way and that. I pulled it back in a ponytail and then let it fall. I did not see any beautiful there. It was straight, the color of wheat, the color of Momma's hair.

Lindy was running late. I went to the phone and then I saw the phone book, the number I'd scrawled on the back, the boarding house number. I picked up the book, looked at it a long time, put it back down.

I gazed in the mirror by the door at my lips with their Tangee Natural orangish sheen. I wanted some red to match my sweater. Ava had plenty. Fire and Ice would appeal to Glenn. On her dressing table, the ruby earrings lay carelessly in a flowered dish. Tonight she'd worn the diamonds Duke had given her last Christmas. I went over and picked the rubies up.

Magic lay in my hands. I slowly raised the rubies to my ears. My gold studs came out, and the long gold Burmese wires were threaded into the holes pierced by Lourdes Sanchez's mother seven years before. In the mirror, the rubies' red fire blazed color into my paleness and lent my eyes their iridescence. Even my wheaty hair took on a sheen. I tossed my head as Ava might have, and smiled mysteriously. Right then the front doorbell rang—Lindy at last. Why didn't she just honk?

I hurried to the door, ready to dazzle her with the earrings. But when I flung it open, Jack was standing there. He gave a slow, lopsided grin when he saw me.

Mae Lee? Wow, you look great. He kept grinning, like a stupid idiot. Has Duke left? I just thought I'd bring this truck back and let him run me back by the boarding house on his way to his folks.

They've already left, I said. But you knew that, didn't you?

He spread his hands and grinned. Can't blame a guy for trying, he said, with mock-sad eyes. You never called me.

I've got other plans, I said, and looked beyond him to the road so he would get the hint. My friend is coming, I said. To pick me up.

He turned and looked. Nobody's there, and I was thinking we might never see each other again. I'm leaving tomorrow.

You're not coming back? I said.

Maybe I'd like to find a reason to come back, he said. I might even settle down here. Couldn't you just drive me back into town and meet your friend later?

It was the longest minute I ever spent.

She's late, I said. Let me call her.

That's my girl, he said.

I felt a fluttering in my belly as I picked up the phone.

Lindy's mother caught her going out the door, and she sounded breathless and impatient when she came on the line. Golly, Mae Lee, jeez, Louise, what is it? I know I'm late. Be right there. Couldn't help it. The damn horse stepped on my foot but nothing's broken.

It's okay, I'll meet you at the game, I said.

It's no trouble to come by. Really.

Nope, I gotta go, I said, and hung up. I would explain it all later.

My hand went to my ears. Ava'll kill me if she sees me wearing them, I said. I gotta take them off.

Honey, they make you look so sexy, Jack said. Leave them. You'll be back before she gets home.

I thought about all the kids at the game. I thought about impressing Glenn.

Sure.

He'd cleaned up the old truck, as though he was sure I'd come. He'd swept out all the dried clay and hay and draped blankets over the rumpsprung seats. He swung the door open for me with a flourish and bowed like a hotel doorman in the movies. I got in and smoothed the blanket. These aren't ours, I said.

Jack shrugged. Old lady Duggan likes me a little.

I'll bet she does.

He could charm the white socks off a horse, and by the time we reached town he'd talked me out of going to the game. We'll take in a movie, he said. We were hungry, so he took me to the drive-in barbecue place down by the river, and we sat in the glow of a blue neon sign, a tray clamped to our window, smell of barbecue and wood smoke all around. Frank Sinatra crooned on the radio, his tones floating in the marshy river breeze where the quarter moon was rising into the fading blue behind the mossy oaks.

The darkness surrounded us like a blanket, and with his arm around me I felt warm and safe, feelings I hadn't had since Momma died. I was almost sorry when he said it was time for the show.

But instead of turning west toward town and the theater, he headed east toward the drive-in movie. They were running *Tarzan and the Slave Girl* but I don't remember much about it. I remember the smell of the popcorn, the rows of cars with heads close together, the squawking speaker that never quite worked, the graininess of the moving shadows in front of us.

And Jack's hand around my shoulder, creeping over my red sweater. I slid that hand away every time someone walked by our car on the way to the bathroom or snack stand. The baby in the car in front of us began to scream, and the people in the car next to us got into a shouting match and started throwing popcorn. I looked at Jack. It was nice back at the river, I said.

He nodded. Sorry about this movie. Tell you what. How'd you like to see my plane?

Your plane.

I got a good little Piper. Yellow.

I stay away from airports, I said.

You scared of flying?

I've never been up.

Let me take you someday, he said. We'll fly high up in those clouds, and it'll be so clear, you can see all those farms and fields below us looking so pretty, and you'll feel like you never felt before, like you're part of the wind. Come on, let's just go sit in the plane. That's the first step.

I told him then about Chap, and the tears kept running down my face. He took out a handkerchief and wiped them away. Oh, God, honey. Don't you see you've got to go now? Just come sit in the plane. It will help you get over it. He leaned over and kissed me, that soft, soft kiss. I felt it, the goo.

The baby in the next car kept screaming.

We'd gone a few miles down the highway when Jack made a stop at a roadside market. You thirsty?

I nodded and he went in and came back with a paper bag. I looked in, expecting Cokes, but there were two tall cans of Pabst Blue Ribbon.

You do like beer, don't you?

Sure, I lied. I have it all the time.

We turned off on a county road before we got to the airport road, and then turned once again onto a sandy dirt road that threaded through tall pines. This is a shortcut to the airport, he said.

After we were deep in the middle of nowhere he pulled the truck to the side of the road, leaving barely enough room for another car to squeeze around us. I could just see the moon over the tops of the tall pines, but there in the trees' shadows, the road was black as the inside of a well.

He rummaged in the car pocket and brought out a church key. He ripped it into one of the cans, and beer foamed over the top, wetting his fingers. He licked them and handed the can to me.

I sipped the bitter foam. Yuk. How did anybody drink this stuff? I should have made him get me a Coke. Jack opened his own can, turned it up, and took a long drink. Cheers, he said, and clanked his can on mine. I took another sip, and it wasn't so bad. Under the foam it was kind of sweet.

It's nice and quiet out here, Jack said.

Spooky, I said, and shivered a little. It was so dark I could barely make out the outlines of the trees. I took another swallow. An owl hooted, and we sat there silently for a few minutes.

Mae Lee, Jack finally said, drawing my name out. Mae, that's a river in Burma. Where'd you get that name?

From great-grandmothers. I am really Mavis Leila.

Ouch. I like Mae Lee. Mae Lee, Mae Lee. He stroked my neck, giving me shivers and tingles, and kept going until he traced the outline of my ear, then played gently with the ruby earring there. He kissed my ear and then he took the whole earring in his mouth, tugging a little, and then he licked my ear and the sensation was strange, but the kind of strange you wanted more of, and then his lips left my ear and found my lips, and pressed so hard that I could scarcely breathe. After a few moments I felt dizzy, as if I was going to faint. I struggled for breath, and he drew back and traced the outline of my lips with his tongue. It felt dark and dangerous.

He kissed me again and again. My heart was pounding, the ruby earrings felt like fire, and down between my legs, I felt something needing to be filled, a pool of crocus blossoms, a yellow damp and sticky heat, and Jack's fingers were on my bare back, under my sweater, fiddling with the clasp of my bra and if I did not do something now I was going to be really sorry. And it was getting late and Ava and Duke would be home.

Jack. No.

Hush.

The clasps gave way and he lifted my sweater and there were my small bosoms not voluptuous like Ava's and I squeezed my eyes shut with embarrassment. Jack, I said.

Beautiful, he said.

We gotta see the plane. I gotta get back. But I sat there like a statue.

Plenty of time, you pretty thing. He leaned down and kissed the pale skin between my breasts. He kissed my closed eyes, my neck, my collarbone, and traveled downward. When his lips closed over my nipple I gasped, Lord, a flashing neon sign on a dark rainy street.

Feel good, baby? My mind was spinning, drowning in the electric goo, and he was over me, and zoop there was a zipper coming down. I took hold of his arm. He took my hand and put it on him, all hot and throbbing. Oh jeez. I pulled my hand back.

I can't, I said.

Don't you want to? he said.

I can't.

His hand had been sliding up my thigh but it stopped. Off the roof?

Duke, I said. Duke was all I could think about. What he would do if he knew. He might kill Jack. Shotgun or no shotgun.

Duke? Damn. He will never know unless you tell him.

He'll know, just like God.

The holiness of the body. The sounds from beneath the door. Ava in the yellow nightgown, beckoning, her tongue licking her lips. I could almost smell again the long curling smoke of the midnight hours. I don't know when I began to tremble. Please, I whispered. Please.

Jack pulled back and sat there for a few moments, and picked up his beer and took one last swallow. He picked up my can. It was nearly empty. You never did? With him, did you?

Good lord, no, I said miserably. He's like my brother.

But you want to.

No, no, no.

Zoop the zipper went up. We're going, said Jack, gimme that can. He drained mine and tossed the empties out the window.

The motor roared into life. The car spun through the sand, circling on the road.

I'm not going to see the plane, I crazily thought.

Jack was saying, you'll never get Duke. He's too good and noble. You know, there were some cute little Burmese gals in some of those villages, would give you anything you wanted. Thought it was an honor. Duke never took any. Had a gal waiting back home. Or two.

That's not what I want, I said.

We drove back the way we had come in a dull gray fog, in silence. I felt guilty, as if we had let the airplane down by not seeing it. When we turned into the farm, I said, Are you mad, Jack? Really mad?

No, baby, he said. One day I'll be back and you'll be ready. We rumbled on down past the fields to the house.

I didn't have time to think about it because there was the Caddy parked out front. Shit, they're home, I said.

Leave it to me, Jack said, and grabbed me and gave me a long, long kiss, one that stirred everything up again. I swallowed a lump in my throat and let him come around and open my door and help me out and walk me up the front steps, my legs unsteady.

Ava flung open the door before I could reach for my house key. Her hair was disheveled, but her makeup was on, and her red satin robe flopped at the wrap, showing plenty of cleavage. Her lips were curled up like a cat that has smelled another cat. God, Mae Lee, where have you been? I called over at Lindy's house and you weren't there. She said you never showed at the game.

Then she saw Jack standing behind me and folded her arms. What the hell, Jack?

Hi, sweet thing, he said, oozing charm. Sorry if we made you worry. Duke around?

She bit her lower lip. He's out. Hard work and bourbon will do that to you. Her voice became hard. Just what were you two doing?

He didn't miss a beat, didn't take his eyes off hers. Came out here to see Duke, forgot you two were going out. Thought I'd treat Mae Lee to a movie. All by herself on Saturday night. Didn't think you'd mind.

The two of them were talking about me as if I wasn't standing right there. I had a weird feeling something important had shifted.

You knew damn well I'd mind. She's just a kid. She turned to me finally, and whatever she was going to say died on her lips. Her eyes got big as cow pats. God, Mae Lee! My rubies! That does it. I have never.

Okay, okay, just shut up, Ava. I fumbled with the wires with shaking fingers. Tears streaked my cheeks and I swiped at them with my hand, getting the earrings wet and snivelly, then I threw them on the hall table. She snatched them up before they skidded and thrust them into her satin pocket. If you ever touch these again I will kill you.

She cocked her head at Jack. You'd better be glad Duke's asleep. I smell beer.

He jingled the change in his pocket. She didn't have any, he said.

The man could lie like a Persian rug, but right then I was grateful.

Go to your room, Ava said. I felt suddenly, violently, nauseated. I wheeled and ran to the bathroom off the back porch, where she wouldn't hear me, and gagged and choked and threw up and up and up, popcorn, barbecue, beer. My nose stung and I washed and washed.

When I felt better I walked into the kitchen for water and I heard her voice. Her soft voice. Her cooing, seductive voice. Why do you want to mess around with babies, big boy?

So Jack would take care of it, huh? I went back to the bathroom and was sick again.

In my room, I lay down on the chenille spread and closed my eyes, feeling as if I was being sucked into a whirlpool. Some time later I heard the old truck leave. I wondered if Ava was driving him back to town, but then I heard her footsteps in the hall, and then the angel of sleep spread great big floppy wings over me.

Or maybe it was the devil, I thought the next morning. My head ached and my stomach was still queasy. Nobody was up in the dark kitchen. I plugged in the coffee pot. Thank God for Cyrus, I thought, looking out into the dawn toward the barn where he was going in and out, seeing to the animals. I searched in the kitchen drawer and found one of Duke's BC powders. I left a note saying I was going out riding. Cyrus didn't say anything, he knew how things were when Mr. Duke was drinking, I guessed. I saddled Dandy and took her far, far out in the country. I avoided Lindy's place, going down roads I'd never traveled. I arrived back in mid-afternoon, my nose red and raw, feeling no better.

Duke's truck was gone from the yard. I draped the blanket over Dandy and walked her longer than I needed to. Still feeling awful, I walked into the kitchen.

The warmth of the house enveloped me like a blanket; I peeled off my jacket and hat and patted my chapped cheeks. Ava was wielding a spatula, buttering a rectangle of dough. The smell of cinnamon was in the air.

This was so unlike her I felt as if I'd landed on Mars.

What are you doing?

She laid the spatula down and picked up a shaker of cinnamon sugar. Making cinnamon rolls. You smell of horse, she said.

So kind of you to notice, I said. Where's Duke?

Not gone to beat up Jack, she said. I told him you and Jack had gone to the show and had a flat tire on the way home. She shook sugar all over the rectangle of dough.

Did he believe you?

Why not? She said. All Jack has to do is stick a hole in the tire, have it patched, and Duke will even pay him back. A small price, don't you think?

You're really sneaky, you know, Ava, I said.

I call it smart, doll baby.

So what's with all this cooking? I said.

Hunt breakfast, she said.

Hunt what?

Duke suddenly decided they're going deer hunting before Jack leaves.

He's really leaving?

That's what he said.

They're going deer hunting?

You sound like a parrot, Mae Lee.

But Duke doesn't hunt, I said.

I guess he changed his mind. I guess he wants to be gung-ho, she said. I guess he wants to do something for his friend. He's that kind of guy.

He's not a killer, I said slowly.

Mae Lee, he's not going to shoot anything. He's just going along.

But the noise, Ava.

Oh, he's over that, she said.

Was she lying, or was she fooling herself?

Chapter Twenty-Two

The party gathered the next morning in the kitchen, and Ava had fixed eggs and sausages and the sweet rolls, biscuits and peach preserves and bacon and a huge pot of coffee, and made me mix up a pitcher of orange juice from the freezer. It was ungodly early, the dawn just peeping over the fields when the blue truck rolled into the yard. I held my breath when Jack got out, dressed in camouflage. Then another truck rolled in behind him and it was Mr. Elmo Conable and Starrett and then a station wagon pulled up and it was Lindy's dad.

The men stood out in the yard for a while talking with Duke and then they all trooped in. The dawn was taking a long time coming up; the air was full of dew and heavy with clouds.

We had set the table and now the men tucked into the breakfast. Jack didn't glance my way, avoiding me, I was sure. They talked about the things men talk about when they are going out to kill things.

Duke didn't join in, making sure that everybody was fed plenty. The talk turned to the weather, whether it would rain. Some thought it was likely, some thought it would hold off till late. Rain and thunder were as bad for Duke as gunshots to my way of thinking, but I held my tongue. What else could I do?

They headed out in good spirits. There was an old deer stand back in the woods that had been there since before the war and I thought that's where they might be going. I prayed to God that the deer would all go into hiding.

Sure enough, it started raining hard around lunchtime and then sleet began to come down about an hour later. They straggled back from the fields, cold and hungry and wet and complaining. Duke changed clothes and the others let us take their camo shirts and stick them in Ava's new electric clothes dryer.

Not one deer did they see. Not even a whiff of one. Ava had counted on them staying out all day and eating the sandwiches they packed, so she didn't have any lunch ready. We broke out jars of Elzuma's home-canned vegetable soup to go with the sandwiches and we still had the rest of a pecan pie, so they ate pretty well.

Starrett Conable got up from the table and came into the kitchen where I was eating pie and looking at a Sunday paper. He was in a T-shirt and camo pants and I suddenly realized he had muscles I had never noticed before. It made me disoriented, like the stubble on his face. Your childhood buddy, the pebble in your shoe, should not suddenly sprout a set of muscles and whiskers.

We should have gone to my granddad's place, he said. Plenty of deer over there.

I just shrugged.

So where were you Friday night?

I had other plans, I said. I put down my fork and inspected my nails.

Have anything to do with that guy in there?

I couldn't play dumb and ask what guy, because Jack was the only one who wasn't a parental figure.

Why do you ask? I said coolly.

Because you keep looking at him.

I do not.

I saw you, Mae Lee.

You lie.

Have it your way, he said.

Do you want some more pie? I said. I found myself looking into his eyes, which were as hard as I have ever seen them.

You don't know what I want?

Be nice, Starrett. I took a last bite of pie and licked my fork.

Goddamn it, Mae Lee. He grabbed my wrist, but just then Ava came into the kitchen to get pie for somebody and he let my wrist go.

You kids behave, said Ava.

I'll check and see if the shirts are dry, I said. The sleet was still coming down outside. It was like the whole sky had opened up. I jumped up and went over to the dryer, opened it and felt the shirts. Almost, I said, and Starrett had followed me.

Ava had gone back in with the pie, and he slid up close behind me and touched my shoulder. What is it with you, anyhow, Mae Lee?

I wheeled to face him. What makes you think there's anything? Just leave me alone, Starrett Conable. But his face was inches from me and I was afraid he would grab me right here in my own house and kiss me like he owned me. I stifled a sob, because he could be so great a friend sometimes and now he acted like this. I ducked out and burst into the dining room. I'm sure I must have looked stupid.

Does anybody need anything? I gulped.

Jack looked over at me.

I've got things taken care of, Mae Lee, Ava said.

The phone rang and I went to answer it. It was Aunt Talley, for Duke. The fourth baby had come, and they were going to name him Robert Dulany Davies.

The weather didn't improve. Monday morning when I got up for school I looked out on rain sheeting down in slivers, puddling in the brown grass, riddling the barnyard with channels of mud.

The hallway was dark, except for a light from the kitchen. The rising damp had settled into everything. Even the white kitchen curtains drooped like a miserable old lady. Duke was out checking the livestock. Ava stood at the stove wrapped in a robe, stirring a pot of grits.

Good morning, Mae Lee, she said. Butter wouldn't melt in her mouth.

What's good about it? I poured myself a cup of coffee, hoping it would be strong. She ignored me, humming, and spooned up grits and eggs into a plate and handed it to me. Biscuits aren't done. Got up a little late.

I'm still not caught up on my sleep, I said. I hope I don't sleep through class.

And I have to go to Macon today, Mae Lee. Can you get supper?

Macon? Why? When will you be back?

Doctor, she said. Thought I'd do a little shopping while I was there. I don't want to rush.

You don't look sick, I said. I sat down at the table and broke the yolk on my egg, stirred it into the grits.

I'm not sick, but I don't have a baby.

Holy moley, I didn't know you had any motherly instincts.

She gave me a murderous look and slid the biscuit pan out of the oven.

Is it 'cause Aunt Talley had number four and named him after Duke?

Duke's sister has nothing to do with it. I *want* a baby. She jabbed the spatula at the biscuits just as Duke opened the back door. A biscuit flew off the pan and landed at his feet. He picked it up, dusted it off, and set it on his plate. He scooted back a chair and sat down. Ava went behind him and kneaded his shoulders. Today I'm going to see that doctor in Macon. Mae Lee's going to make supper if I'm late.

He patted her hand and his smile was like a lightbulb had been switched on behind his eyes. We'll do whatever he says. Get the best doctors.

He had never talked about kids before, so I didn't know how he felt on the subject. But now he was saying, Pick up a little something to send to Talley and my li'l namesake.

Okay, she said. Silver maybe.

I finished up my plate, gathered up the dirty dishes, and ran a sink of soapy water. I wondered what would happen if one day I told her I wasn't going to wash the dishes. What kind of hell would break loose? What if I sailed them around the room and let them crash into the wall? I hated those tacky swan dishes, anyhow. What had happened to Momma's dishes, the blue willow? I plunged one of the swans into the suds, drowning it. When I finished them, I left them on the counter for her to put away. If I didn't hurry I'd be late for school.

I grabbed my jacket and books and dodged through the steady rain to Momma's old Ford. I turned the key. The machine that Chap had always kept in perfect running order coughed and sputtered, but it started. I breathed a sigh of relief when I hit the highway. I was glad to be putting road between me and Ava that morning.

I knew it was Talley's baby. Ava was jealous of the attention Duke was giving her. I thought about the way Ava had been flirting with Jack, the way she'd spoken to him. Was she trying to make Duke jealous? There was some kind of restlessness in her, the restlessness I'd seen when Duke had been overseas. Oh, hell. Maybe a baby would calm her down.

I was sitting in the Cremee-Freez with the kids after school, but I just couldn't join in the giggles about Glenn Dorris. They said he was out parking with somebody and got his car stuck in a ditch and missed curfew and his parents grounded him and the coach was fit to be tied because they wouldn't let him go to practice. I should have been interested but I wasn't. I slid out of my booth. I've got to go home and start dinner, I said.

Cinderella goes back to the hearth, Lindy said.

And there's no handsome prince, I said.

Starrett Conable gave me a lopsided, knowing smile as I rose. Doesn't matter, he said. Your big feet would break the glass slipper.

I hate you, I said.

He laughed. I just love you when you're mad. And then he winked at me. Oooh!

Ava wasn't home when I got there, which was good considering my mood. It was too soon to start supper. I changed into jeans and a warm sweater and riding boots. A few minutes later I was in the tack room looking over the torn saddle. Since my tumble, the saddle had just lain in the corner gathering dust. I lifted it and picked at its brittle leather straps and dropped it. Just then Duke came into the barn. Thought I saw you home, he said.

I want to jump, I said. Can we fix this?

I'd have to find somebody. Saddlemaker.

Oh, damn, oh, shit, I cried, and turned to the wall.

Hey, punkin, strong language for a pretty girl. I turned back and he looked at me wryly. What's wrong?

I want to jump. I want to do something dangerous. Maybe I can climb up on the barn, huh? I clenched my fists and looked for something to beat on, but I saw only Duke's chest and I couldn't beat on that.

What's eating you? There's something between you and Ava. What?

Nothing. Then as he waited, I'm sick of her bossing me, I said.

So stand up to her.

You don't, I said, and a curtain drew behind his eyes.

That's different, was all he said. He stepped out of the tackroom and looked up, hand to his forehead for shade.

I stepped out, too, and looked up at the late afternoon sky, at slanting rays drawing long shadows from the fence posts, at clouds reflected in puddles left from the rain. The horses came out into the paddock and stuck their noses over the side, looking for a treat. I rubbed the mule's nose. I'm supposed to be doing something about supper.

I'll have the saddle fixed. He turned to me. Put on the Western saddle, he said. Let's go for a ride, you and me. I want to talk to you anyhow.

What about? I said, my voice getting thick. Ava will be mad if I don't have supper ready.

Soup and cornbread's fine, he said. We've got plenty of bread from last night. Heat it up with a little butter.

Hokay, chief, I said, and went for my saddle.

We took the horses down the road that led through the cornfields, the road that led to the far fields, the fallow fields, on the very edges of Duke's land. We passed the artesian pond, the sky throwing long streaks of gold across the falling indigo, reflected in the dark, wind-rippled water.

We crossed the cow pasture where the land rose to a small hillock, sloping to fields and woods beyond. I loved the quiet of dusk, and here there was a fragrant evening smell, and owls tu-whooing in the distance.

Duke pulled Nimrod to a halt under a spreading pin oak. I stopped beside him and waited. I could hear myself breathing. The horses snuffled and blew.

You've been in my footlocker, he finally said.

Oh, Lord, oh, Lord. I'm sorry, I said. I was bored. I was curious. He looked out at the setting sun. It was private, Mae Lee.

I'm so embarrassed, I said. I heard Ava say there was something awful in there. I did put it all back.

You left the photo album and bayonet out.

I won't do it again, I promised. My ears were burning and my heart was thumping and it was like a great big watermelon was lodged in my throat. But there was one thing I wanted to find out, one thing I wanted to know, and now that I was caught, I could ask.

I read your diary, Duke, I said. And there is no excuse for that, I know. But I just have to know. What happened to the girl? Did you ever save her? Jack was going to tell me, but—

Duke eyes bored into mine. Jack don't know squat, he said. I never told him the story. He would have fed you some bullshit to impress you. Nobody knows the whole thing. Except Elzuma.

Is that why you go to see her?

One of the reasons.

He wheeled his horse around. Come on, I'll tell you on the way back. Stay close, now, 'cause I'm not going to repeat myself.

I did as he asked.

The old man. The gem trader. I first met old Mr. Shen from the village near our post when I was thinking of bringing something back for Ava. He dealt in raw stones, bought them from rogue miners down Mogok way. I had never seen such stones, even raw—that rich red, pigeon's blood, they call it. Told me where I could get them cut and set in Calcutta.

Wanted a king's ransom, of course. The Japs had shut the mining down. I kept coming back and making offers. Shrewd and stubborn, that old fellow. He had a second sense how much I wanted them and wouldn't come down. Kept telling me that some Brit was going to come for them any day now. High brass.

A bunch of bull, of course. He kept holding out. I took a liking to the old fox and we became friends.

I would stop by there from time to time to have a cup of tea with him and talk. I would tell him about America. He thought maybe his granddaughter would go to America someday, after he was dead, of course. Her role was to look after him and help him in business. She was fifteen, and her name was Li-wei. She was an obedient granddaughter.

What happened to her parents? I wanted to know.

His only son had been killed by the enemy. His daughter-in-law was kidnapped. I don't like to think of what might have happened to her.

An orphan like me, I murmured.

Yep, Duke said. The old man's wife had died and his grand-daughter was all he had. He took out a cigarette, and lit it with his Zippo, and we continued on. The sky was darkening, and soon we would have just the moon to guide us.

Little Li-wei reminded me of you, in a way, Mae Lee. She was smart and hardworking. I was fond of her. He let out a little hollow laugh. She was merry, full of fun, made the most of every minute. With all that had happened to her, losing her parents, the war, she could have been sad, but she wasn't. She had quite a crush on me, would just light up when I appeared. She would have done anything I asked her.

He looked at me then, and I was glad he didn't see my cheeks turning like the sunset as I recalled what Jack had told me. I had too much respect for her and her grandfather to take advantage, Duke said. He wanted her to make a good marriage.

He let the moment hang, still in the hush of the rolling fields, while I could find no words to say. He continued, I think the old man knew the score. He asked me to find some way to get her out of Burma until we had beaten the Japs. Safe territory somewhere. Had a cousin or something in India.

We made a sort of deal. He finally came down on the rubies and I was going to try to find a way to get the girl safely out to India.

I asked a special friend of mine, a woman correspondent, if she could help. We had a thought of dressing Li-wei up like a nurse, where we were going with that I wasn't sure. We'd have to get her some false papers. It would be difficult.

I remembered Joan, the woman from the diary. Had they been lovers? It didn't matter, did it? She was dead. Still Duke went on and I dreaded what he had to tell.

It proved to be more complicated than I thought. Before we got very far on the Li-wei project I got sent on that damned mission and got injured. It was months before I got back to the village.

When I got there, the village was deserted. The people, who had fled to the hills, filtered back slowly. It seems the village had been raided and the girl had been kidnapped by the Japs. The old man was dead.

I was furious. I had never been so angry. Up until then I had just been doing my job of soldiering. Nothing personal. It was my job. Not even what I'd been through got to me like that.

After that I started to enjoy booby-trapping and killing. One day I was out scouting, my buddy and I were spread out, and I came on a hut in the jungle. I went inside and there lying on the floor was a wounded Jap. Starving, skinny, looking at me with the last remains of hope. I didn't want him to look at me, didn't want to see any humanity at all. I leveled my gun and shot. Mae Lee, I blew his brains out, all over the place. And I left the body and walked away.

There was a long, long silence.

Duke, I said, choking up, God will forgive you. It was war.

I never liked killing, he said. Until they took Li-wei. That got to me. It was like my nerves had been scraped raw. After that, I hated.

Hated, Mae Lee.

The sun was giving a last splash in the west, a fiery rim on the edge of the land, pink shading up to a purple sky.

He spoke on, quietly. Forgot everything Mr. Shen ever taught me. It was like my soul had been ripped out, that part of myself that cared about people, leaving a big bloody hole. Nothing was left in that hole, not even Ava. Not myself. I didn't care of I lived or died. I just lived to kill the enemy. They were all Japs, you see, just evil to be smashed. God knows, they had no hearts, no dreams, nobody to miss them as far as I was concerned.

But, Duke, I said, you're not like that now.

He finished his smoke and dropped the butt into the dirt. How can you be so sure?'

But I know you, I said, realizing with a chill that I really didn't.

Tell you something, kid, he said. Every day I live with the terror I've lost all my humanity, all my decency.

No, you haven't, I cried. Look how you hired Cyrus. You care for this farm, for your animals, for . . . I spread my hands helplessly. You're a hero for that.

He smiled then, a smile ripe with gratitude, I think. When I came here, it helped me remember what Mr. Shen taught me, he said. Nature was the Way. To follow nature. He told me there was gentleness in the male nature, and toughness in the female. Yang and yin.

So the farm, I said, is a way back? Warm tears tracked across my wind-cooled cheeks, and I swiped my face on my sleeve. I wanted my illusions.

Gentleness is more victorious in battle than force and holds its ground. For do not the softest things in the world overcome the hardest? That was what he said, Duke told me. He gave Nimrod a nudge and galloped ahead of me. I let him go.

He had given me a lot to think about. I could see what he meant about himself. He was trying to forgive himself for doing something he felt was wrong. It sounded right. It sounded good. But how did that apply to me? Did that mean I shouldn't fight Ava so hard, be gentle toward her? Why should I? She wasn't gentle toward me. Duke had gone out there and fought. Chap had gone out there and fought. Chap had fought all his life. And oh, how I missed him. He'd probably think what Duke said was foolishness. But would he have been happier if he had learned to take things easy? Would he still be alive if he hadn't been so impatient to get that plane in the air?

Soon I could see the welcoming lights of home, Ava back in the kitchen, maybe with news about having a baby. Would it make any difference between them? Could he tell her what he had told me?

She wasn't soft. She wouldn't understand. She'd laugh at him.

Duke was washing up at the sink when I walked in. I held my breath when I looked at Ava.

You cool her? He was talking about my horse.

I did.

The soup was in the pot, bubbling away and the cornbread was heating in the oven. Ava was in a good mood.

Good news? I asked.

Maybe, she said. We have to wait for the tests to come back. We know *this* guy is okay. She patted Duke's shoulder.

How do you know? I asked.

He got tested last year, Miss Nosey, Ava said. Lots of wiggly little buggers there.

Well, excuse me, I said, turning red as the soup beneath my spoon.

How was the big city? Duke asked Ava, to change the subject. I think he was a little embarrassed too.

Oh, fine. Busy, she said. I bought the baby present. She buttered a corn stick. Yum, she said.

Eating for two already, I said.

She pointed her corn stick at me like a gun. Pow, Mae Lee.

Cut it out, girls, Duke said.

I think I'll make an apple pie tomorrow, Ava said. Look here, there's some of your momma's chocolate cake left for dessert.

Turn on the radio, Duke said.

She scraped back her chair. I'm bushed, she said. I'm going to lie down. She switched on the radio before she walked out.

I cut Duke a slice of the chocolate cake his mother had brought over Saturday, and I cut a slice for myself. We listened to the news for a while and when they started talking about Korea he put his cake dish on the drain board and wandered out. I got up to switch the station to music.

I cleared the table and ran some hot water and put in soap. *The Third Man Theme* came on, and I thought about Harry Lime running though the sewers. The last zither notes had barely faded away before the announcer broke in. *This just in. Sheriff Dolphus Gray reported that the two escaped convicts are back in custody after a massive manhunt. A roadblock on the Macon Road, which tied up traffic for hours, managed to trap the stolen car. . . .*

Funny Ava hadn't mentioned it. The dishes didn't take long. I left them to drain and dried my hands. There was a paper bag on the counter, and I opened it to find a white jewelry-store gift box. Inside, nestled in tissue paper, lay a silver baby rattle. I closed the box and put it back in the bag. The ticket was marked ten dollars. The ticket was from a store right here in town.

Lying beside the bag was an appointment card from the doctor. She had another appointment in a week, at 11:00. The doctor was in Macon.

So she might have come back early, before the roadblock was set up. Where had she been?

The next morning the sun broke through, just a little ray of light splitting the heavens, and it cheered me up. But on the way to school, I thought about Ava's day away from the farm, trying to add up all the bits, and they didn't seem to work: the doctor, the roadblock, the shopping. Usually when she went shopping it was Katie bar the door, with Duke hollering about the money and Ava hiding shoes and pocketbooks under the bed.

Standing in the cafeteria lunch line, I got to wondering if maybe she didn't have some dress boxes stashed in the car to bring in when Duke went out to the fields. Lindy was a few kids ahead of me and I hollered at her to save me a place. Lord, it was hard for her to hear me over the din in the big brick room. The other kids jostled and shoved; I pushed my tray down the line, while the lunch ladies spooned up roast beef, gravy, mashed potatoes, field peas, and banana pudding onto my divided plate.

Lindy waved to me from a table on the far side and I headed over with my tray. I had to pass by the table where the basketball players ate, and Starrett Conable was leaning against it, holding a bottle of milk. He stepped out and blocked my way.

Hey, Starrett, I said. Move over.

Hey, Cinderella, I got some news about the prince.

What are you talking about?

Starrett carefully peeled the aluminum foil cap off the top of his milk bottle. That pilot guy was on the airport road yesterday.

Well, no hock, Sherlock, where else would a pilot be?

Oh, I forgot to tell you. On the back road.

There went my stomach. So what were you doing there?

Skipping school. I like to go out there and hang around.

Okay, now you've shown your tail. Let me by.

Not so fast. I haven't gotten to the good part yet.

The good part?

Your sister was with him. He made a ball of the aluminum foil and flipped it at me. How about them apples?

He took a long swallow of milk, turned around, and walked away.

What happened after that I don't remember. Mr. Johnson, the principal, told Duke that Starrett had gotten two tables away when I grabbed my dish of banana pudding and threw it at him. It hit him square in the back of the head.

He yelled, wheeled around, and threw his milk bottle in the direction the dish had come from.

It whizzed by my nose and smashed into the brick wall behind me. I heard the crash and then I felt a sharp icy pain across my face, and I put my hand up, and when I brought it down it was covered with blood and I heard screaming screaming screaming.

I remember the emergency room as a big blur and confusion. They told me later that when they called the house, Duke had been out in the fields. Ava had come to the hospital wearing a white angora sweater and black slacks under her trench coat, and when she saw me she gave me a little cry and went to hug me and the nurse said be careful and she got blood on her sweater, and in my mind I can still see that blood on the sweater and her mouth all round like a Revlon ad for Fire and Ice.

When we got back to the house, Duke was standing out front waiting for us. Ava stopped the Caddy and he opened the door on my side. Let me see, he said.

I put my hand to the bandage over the ugly black threads that held my cheek together. It still felt numb from the anesthetic, though not as numb as my heart. Ava's betrayal made me feel humiliated, but Jack's betrayal had hit me like a stomach punch. The two punches collapsed me like a deflated balloon, hollow and hopeless.

Duke looked at me with a different kind of pain. Tell me, he said. Tell me what really happened.

I looked away. I don't remember, I said.

Ava put her hands on her hips. I can't get anything out of her. The other kids seemed to think she threw some food at Starrett and he threw a milk bottle. It hit the wall and a piece of glass ricocheted and got her cheek.

Shrapnel wound, Duke said. What got into you, punkin?

My lip began to tremble. Starrett made me mad. I guess I went a little crazy.

What did he say?

I stood there and looked down. I had never lied to Dulany Radford in my life.

Starrett's been suspended, Ava broke in. He's not talking either. Come on, honey.

I shook my head. He was teasing me. Being mean. Telling lies about something he saw. Out by the airport.

My heart was filling my throat, and Ava was looking at me in a strange manner. Okay, she said in a little strangled voice. Okay. Maybe you ought to lie down. She needs to rest, Duke.

He put his arm around Ava's shoulder. The airport, he said.

I burst into tears, and they flooded down, soaking my bandage. Duke turned away and kicked a rock, hard. It scudded across the dry grass of the front yard and bounced off the wheel of Ava's Cadillac.

My knees felt like jelly. I tried to take a step forward and sank to the ground. Through a gray fog I heard Ava and Duke quarreling as he carried me into the house.

Chapter Twenty-Three

For days after the accident, I lay in the high old bed under a pile of quilts, my ruined face to the wall. I did not come out except for necessary functions, and I think that time was the most alone I have ever felt in my life.

I didn't feel alone after Chap died, because I had Momma and Ava and Mimi. And after Momma died, I had Ava and Duke and Mimi. And now all I had was Duke and Mimi. Duke went places I couldn't reach, and Mimi was looking after her beloved Mr. Linley, who was going to leave us too. And Starrett? He wasn't my friend any more.

Ava brought me breakfast on a tray that first day as though she was a zookeeper and I was some kind of tiger or crocodile. She edged through the door with a kind of fake concern, ooh, honey, does it hurt bad and all that, now don't you worry, blah, blah. Made me want to puke and I didn't eat a thing. She finally got the idea of sending Elzuma, who fluffed my pillows and sat in the rocker and told me I had to eat because it was worrying

Mr. Duke plumb out of his mind and she had made me a boiled custard special. So I ate it while she rocked with that dip of snuff in her cheek and told me the Lord was carrying me with his wings, and I told her he might as well carry me on up to Heaven. She said it was not my time and I should rise and take up my bed and walk, if Jesus could do that for a dead man he could do it for me.

Where was Jesus when the milk bottle went flying? I wanted to ask her, but I knew she would just shake her head and tell me not to talk like a heathen. And why did Starrett do it? If he liked me as much as he pretended, then why did he try to hurt me? Or was it an accident, like he said? Maybe he didn't mean for it to hit the wall, but me. Just as bad.

I wanted to scream, but I didn't.

Duke poked his head in the door every now and then, but didn't know what to say to me. Nobody said anything about Jack. And then came the morning the doctor visited, one of those days where the sun glinted off my mirror bright and hard as steel.

Ava slipped in the door after he left. Get up, she said. The doctor says you're fine.

I'm not getting up. I'm not going back.

What do you mean?

I'm not going back to school. Never never never.

Well, just what do you intend to do?

I can work on the farm. Slop the pigs.

We don't have any pigs.

We can get some.

She snorted in disgust. What would Momma say about you, Mae Lee?

Momma is dead and buried.

Ava pulled out a cigarette. She's looking down on us. Wash out your mouth with soap.

I started working the fresh adhesive tape loose, and before she could stop me, I had the gauze pads off. I slid out of bed and looked in the mirror at the ugly track that just missed my eye and curved across my cheek. She stopped with the lighter halfway to the cig and I swear she blanched. I was glad. All for you, Ava, I said.

What the hell is that supposed to mean? She lit the cigarette but her hand was unsteady. She took a deep drag and blew out the smoke. I didn't get to savor the moment because Duke appeared in the doorway. He laid his hand on Ava's shoulder and she grabbed it like she was going down for the third time.

What's all the shoutin' about? he wanted to know.

She says she's not going back to school, Ava said.

Let her be, Ava, said Duke, eyeing my scar. Give her more time. We can work something out. I knew why he didn't try to talk to me, talk me out of my swamp. It was too close to the bone.

Duke called the school and made arrangements for me to study at home with the Visiting Teacher for another week or two. Hank, Lindy, and Starrett Conable came to see me, but I turned Starrett away. He left a bouquet of flowers and I threw them in the trash and Ava took them out and set them on the dining room table. Or so I heard from Elzuma. I told her she could have them. My English teacher brought me a book of poems by Dorothy Parker thinking they would cheer me up. *Might as well live.* I knew her secret message was in case I was suicidal. Even as I thanked her, I knew my poem-writing days were over forever.

What had my teacher told me? *A poem is a vicarious sense impression.* Right now my only sense impression was a dark foggy blob shot with pain, and I couldn't see it getting better. Writing poems had been fun, they had been a way to make sense out of my world. Now nothing made any sense. I was going to be scarred for the rest of my life. I might as well *not* live.

In my spare time I played solitaire with Elzuma's cards out of the chifforobe. When she came to visit with me, rocking with snuff in her cheek, I asked her to teach me to tell fortunes, but she claimed she didn't remember how. She told me tales of the farm when Duke was a boy, when he would come out and go fishing with his granddad and about the time he almost lost his finger to a snapping turtle but it healed up and worked just fine now.

The week stretched into the next, and slowly the fog lifted, like layers drifting away, so I could see a vase of flowers and two presents on top of the chifforobe, which I finally opened, and found a bottle of Evening in Paris perfume from Starrett and a flowered neck scarf from Lindy. I was glad of the scarf and wrote Lindy a note.

One morning when I woke up early, the pink sunrise creeping over the treetops looked so joyful and hopeful that I couldn't help but smile—for just a minute, because it hurt—and I thought maybe I wanted to be here for more sunrises. It was that very same day that a new face appeared at my door with my lunch tray, a girl who looked not much older than me, pretty, with short nappy hair. You gone get up today, ain't you?

Who are you?

Iris, she said. Elzuma is my granny.

Why aren't you in school?

They need me at home, she said.

Where's Ava?

She gone to town, Iris said. Now you eat up, I got to get back to my wash. And sure enough, I heard the washing machine running in the kitchen. During the day, I heard her as she washed and ironed and cleaned, humming all the while. I wondered what she had to be so happy about. Can't go to school and work in Ava's house. I wanted to get up and talk to her, but I stayed put. Elzuma liked to sing gospel songs, but Iris kept the radio turned to rhythm and blues from a Macon station.

Ava came in finally. I bought you a new school dress, she said.

It stayed in its bag until Iris came in the next day and hung it up. You better try this on, she said. You lucky to have it. She looked down at the black dress Ava had bought for a work uniform.

That made me feel bad but I still did not move.

Iris talked to me about all her sisters and brothers, and the one named Otis that needed help, and she was working to help with his doctor bills, and that's why she didn't have any decent clothes. I told her she could have the school dress, and she said oh no, Mis' Ava would get mad at her.

Duke came in and told me he had gotten the saddle fixed. I thought of riding across the fields with Duke, and how I wanted to do that again, but still I did not move.

And then, nearly three weeks after my accident, I lay awake, listening to the waver of a screech owl down in the marsh. Thunder rumbled a long way off, and then the furnace roared and groaned, drowning the night sounds. I slid out of my bed and tiptoed into the empty living room, dragging the old quilt from the foot of my bed. I sank down on the white sofa, drew the quilt across my legs, and looked out at the clouds floating across the moon.

The furnace clicked off, and the room began to get chilly. I heard the screech owl again then, and it was so still that I heard the faint chuffing of the 1:15 train, and then its mournful moan swelling and receding. The moon flooded the room with light, and all around me it was light and shadow, light and shadow.

The floorboards creaked. I looked up. Duke was standing in the doorway.

I put my hand to my long red scar. Duke flipped his lighter. The flare cast devil's mask shadows into his eyes and deep hollow cheeks. He lit his cigarette and drew on it deeply, then let out a thin stream of smoke.

It looks like you and I both have bad dreams, kid. He did not mention that I had finally risen from my bed. He sat down beside me so quietly he hardly disturbed the stillness. Smoke from the cigarette he held between two fingers rose in a steady stream, and then shivered into fog, floating out toward the moonlight.

Tears choked me, then, and finally spilled over, and I blotted them with the hem of my nightgown, and I laid my head on his chest, and the tears soaked his T-shirt, and we sat like this for a long while, looking out at the pines.

Why can't you move on? he said. You have to move on.

It's Ava, I said.

What about Ava? His voice became guarded and I could feel his muscles tense.

I don't trust her, I said, and neither should you.

I have to trust her, he said. I owe her a lot.

What?

I would have died without her, there in Burma, he said. The thought of her was what kept me going. Some of the guys got those Dear Johns; they were the ones that messed up their missions and didn't make it. It saps your will to survive. The heat, the mess, the goddam boredom sometimes . . . sitting in the jungle, waiting, waiting, for a supply drop, for the sound of a twig to break, for the rain to stop. You think about all kinds of things, you think about your girl . . . oh yeah, you think about food, and bed, and dry clothes . . . other times the enemy is a few yards away . . . quiet as a snake on a limb, it's kill or be killed, you think, I can't let the men down, I can't let my girl down. And you, too, punkin, you're like my baby sister. Like the little Chinese girl I told you about.

He touched my nose, stroked my hair. I settled back against him. He felt warm and safe and solid. He needed his dream.

Dreams are the only things that keep most of us alive, aren't they? Dreaming one day we'll be happy, one day our prince will come, one day we'll wake up and be beautiful. If we dream it hard enough, maybe it'll come true. He'd dreamed of home, of Ava. He made it out of the jungle. Now he needed to keep that dream alive so he could stay out of the swamp. The thunder rumbled again, but more faintly.

I pressed my lips together, because they were starting to tremble. Tears ran down my face again, scalding hot. I took a deep breath. What happened to Jack? I asked.

Duke turned away and looked out at the full moon now sinking behind the pines at the edge of the yard.

Said he was clearing out. Said he was going to South America, work the crops there.

Ava was so mad at me that night. For wearing her rubies. I didn't mean any harm.

Of course not, sweetheart.

I held him tightly then, buried in his warm rough scent, and something came over me, something dark and sweet. I brushed the palm of my hand over his bristly haircut, and then ran my fingers down his face and then I put his hand on my scar.

No one's ever going to love me, I whispered.

He turned away, and then I pulled away the quilt that was covering me. All that was between us was the thin cotton of my nightgown. The sharp male smell of him was like the striking of a match.

He held my face with his hand and leaned toward me; our lips came closer and closer. They touched, and I felt myself trembling.

Jesus God, what am I doing? He pulled back; his hand left my face and covered his face. His breath was coming heavy.

Things got very quiet then with the breathing and the stillness, not even the owl hooted in the soft dark night, and the hand came away from his eyes, and he turned and looked at me with those golden eyes, with all the sadness he had carried through all the years of the war.

I heard the noise of the springs from the back room, squeak squeak squeak. Ava was rolling over in bed. I caught my breath.

Duke reached for the quilt on the floor and pulled it over me. You are too beautiful, he said.

He told me to go to sleep, and went into the kitchen and got a drink of whiskey and went out onto the back porch, and soon it was all quiet once again. And I cried, and whether the tears were of joy or of sorrow I did not know.

Was I sad that he hadn't taken what I wanted to give him, that he'd stayed the Duke I knew and loved, my big brother who wanted to do the right thing? Was I happy that he had almost kissed me? What had I really wanted last night? Had I wanted to take him away from Ava, claim him for my own? And what would have been the consequences?

One thing I knew. He had called me beautiful.

Chapter Twenty-Four

You are too beautiful.

Early morning, me before the mirror before dawn. There was the scar, puckering at the edges, angry pink like bad lipstick. Sloe-eyes, mouth too wide, too tall, taking after Momma's side of the family, not skinny any more but willowy, I guess you could say. Hair long, silky, never could do a thing with it except maybe comb it over that scar like Lauren Bacall.

It took ruining my face to appreciate what I'd been given. All my life I'd felt ugly, comparing myself with Ava, who had Chap's wild, dark looks. She was still beautiful, but spitefulness had spoiled her mouth, and indulgence was nudging her curves outward. She was starting to wear too much make-up. She was starting to see me as a threat.

And I was. Hadn't I always wanted him?

But he loved her, in spite of all. There was nothing else to do but leave. Now.

I didn't know where I was going or what I would do. There was the little bit of money left from Chap's life insurance. I could go somewhere nobody knew me and get a job. Maybe in a drugstore, like Ava.

I pulled on a pair of jeans and a shirt and walked through the light and shadow of the hall to the kitchen, where the red lamp of the percolator glowed in the blackness. I poured a cup of black coffee and drank a good slug of it. Duke was getting dressed, I reckoned. I slipped back to my room and heard his footsteps in the hall as I packed my small suitcase. A few minutes later I heard him go out and slam the back door.

I lugged the suitcase out to Momma's old car, along with all the books I could carry. When I got to the kitchen, Ava was up, mixing biscuits in her robe. You're out of bed, she said. At this hour.

I'm going to school.

So you saw the light, she said with a tight smile.

You might say that.

After the biscuits were done she called Duke to come in for breakfast. I poured everyone a mug of coffee while Ava set out plates of grits and biscuits and scrambled eggs and sausages. I sat down at the table, and I knew something had changed. Something in the air. Something between Duke and me, something that if started would be as hard to stop as a runaway train. Something in the way he shifted, turned toward me slightly, beyond brotherly love.

I'm glad to see you've decided to go back to school, Mae Lee, he said and reached for the butter. I studied his hand. There was a scar where the snapping turtle had bitten it.

It was time, I said. There is a time for every purpose under heaven.

Maybe I can let Iris go, said Ava.

She needs the job, I said.

Duke looked from Ava to me, not wanting to get into it. Knives and forks clinked. Cows mooed in the distance. I kept my head down.

He cleared his throat. Dandy's been missing you. How about riding her today?

Dandy's not my horse. Not really, I said, and Duke sat back in his chair and I could see things playing out behind his eyes.

We'll get you a horse, he finally said.

Oh? said Ava. Iris, and now a horse?

Now, Ava, said Duke.

There is a time to keep silence, and a time to speak, I said.

Will you just shut up? said Ava. She took another biscuit and slathered it with peach jam, then licked her fingers with a wet tongue.

I've got to go, I said. There is a time for school.

It's still early. You do those dishes, now you're up.

Not this morning, Ava. I held my hands tightly together to keep them from trembling.

Leave her alone, honey, said Duke.

Why are you taking up for her? Her eyes narrowed and she looked from him to me. But he slapped on a mask of indifference and got up from the table. I've got business in town today, he said. I'm going to see about selling a few of these acres.

Sell them all, she said. Let's get out of this place.

Well now, he said. I'm going to see Momma and Daddy and eat dinner with them. Maybe go out to the plant. Don't expect me back until late.

All right, she said. Cyrus appeared at the back door, wanting to talk to Duke, and he went outside and I saw them walking toward the barn.

Was he serious about selling this place? If he didn't have the farm, he might as well be dead. Those night dreams might take over. And what would become of Cyrus and Elzuma?

This is all for you, I said to Ava. How could you do that to him?

Do what? she said.

I know about you and Jack Austin, I said.

You don't know anything, Mae Lee. She laid the remains of her biscuit on her plate almost daintily, wiping her fingers on her napkin, Miss Priss to the core.

I've seen you flirt with him. I've seen you going out when Duke was busy, not to the Piggly Wiggly in that white spangledy western jacket. You were going to meet him, weren't you? I'll bet he's never left town.

Her lip curled in a sneer. What right have you to talk to me like that?

I jerked the hair back from my face. Every right, I said. Take a good look, Ava. Starrett Conable said he saw you and Jack on the back airport road. You came back from Macon early. Don't bother to lie, I know about the roadblock. Starrett was telling me this right there in the lunchroom. That's why I threw the dish at him, I said. Jack Austin took me to the airport road, I said, and let it hang there in the air.

She wiped a smear of jam from the corner of her mouth and her eyes were sharp as steel blades. Did he screw you? Was it good? What would Duke say about that?

My stomach dropped to my feet but I stood my ground. Nothing happened, I said. I was too scared. And so he went to you. Old war buddy Austin, it would break Duke's heart if he knew, so I didn't tell him. I held my fingers an eensy bit apart. Ava, I breathed, you are that close to losing him.

She leaped up and gave me a stinging slap across the face, close enough to my scar that jagged warps of pain shot through my head. Not to you, you little bitch.

It hurt, it hurt, and I sank sobbing to the floor.

She stood there mute for a minute.

You have everything and I have nothing, I said. But you know what? There's biscuit on your face. I hope Duke comes in right now.

She swiped the crumbs off with the back of her hand. She looked shocked all of a sudden, like she did think how it would look if he came in, and she came over to me then, knelt down, and put her arms around me. Oh, honey, I'm sorry, I was a little crazy.

I would not be sorry to leave. She brisked around the kitchen, finding a cloth and wetting it, coming at me with it. I don't need it, I said, but I took it and put it to my cheek to appease her.

She sat down and lit a cigarette then, tossing the match in the pie plate, and her face softened. The dimples appeared, the ugliness became pretty again. Crocodile pretty. She said softly, Mind your own business, Mae Lee, and we can get along. Now get along to school. You have just enough time to make it.

Outside, Duke was getting into the truck. Ava walked back to the bathroom at the end of the hall and started running a bath.

I slipped into Duke's office and got the keys out of the desk, unlocked the trunk, and took out the scrapbook. I wanted to look at all the pictures one last time. I might never see them again. I flipped the pages to Jack's picture, the blond hair blowing in the breeze, the toothy grin, the squint against the sun's glare. I wanted to hate him, like I wanted to hate Ava, but there was just a long, melting, cockeyed, crazy sadness. That moment passed, and anger surged up in me.

I put it back and then I saw the glint of the brutal bayonet, the souvenir Duke had taken the night they found the lieutenant.

I pulled it out looked at it with new interest. Its edges were beginning to be pocked with rust, but its tip was still sharp. I hefted it again, feeling its weight. I thrust it ahead of me. My cheek still stung where Ava had slapped me, and I tightened my grip. She would be naked, helpless, in the bath—

I stared at the cold object in my hand.

I shuddered and dropped the bayonet into the open trunk. I closed the trunk, tossed the keys on the desk, and hurried out. It didn't matter anymore. Let him think what he wanted. I got my jacket out of the hall closet and walked out to the car.

I drove to town, not sure where I was going. I circled the school, hoping to find Lindy and tell her I was leaving. The bell hadn't rung yet, and kids were milling around outside, the younger ones eating sticky candy and Kool-Aid powder they'd bought at the store across the street.

I parked in the lot across from school, got out of the car, and stood on my tiptoes looking. Suddenly a hand gripped my shoulder, and I spun around. Oh, jeez. Starrett Conable, I said, get out of my life. Haven't you done enough damage?

The smile faded. I said I was sorry. I sent flowers. I tried to see you.

I don't forgive you, I said.

He dropped to his knees. Please?

I flushed. Get up before somebody sees you, stupid.

He didn't get up.

Okay, okay, I said, but crossed my fingers. You are forgiven.

He got to his feet and dusted off his jeans. Walk you to class.

I've got to talk to Lindy.

Well, I'll be damned. You don't know?

Know what?

She broke her collarbone falling off that fool horse. She's home today.

She didn't call me?

It just happened yesterday afternoon. I only know because her momma called mine.

Thanks, Starrett, I said, and turned to head back to my car.

Where are you going? Aren't you coming to school?

I've got to talk to her.

Wait, wait, he called, but I was already in my car and peeling out of the parking lot.

I called Lindy from a pay phone next to the Shell station downtown. I wanted to say good-bye, I said. I explained what had happened. She said she was okay but the doctor thought she ought to rest for a couple of days, not carry any books.

She was always the voice of reason for me. You just can't go off like that, she said. You need a definite plan, or they'll catch you for sure. Maybe even send you to reform school.

I snorted. They can't do that.

You want to bet? she said. Juvenile delinquent, they'll call you. Runaway. Did you take any money? They'll get you for stealing.

I've got my own money, I said. In the bank. I'm going to draw it out.

Be sure to act cool.

I bit my lip. Would they call Duke?

Not if you act like you're supposed to be there. Come out here, said Lindy. Momma's got a dentist appointment in town about eleven. I'll help you. I've got maps and everything.

I don't know, I said. They might see me on the road.

You can't just take off without a plan, she said. You need money, gas, extra food, a first aid kit, and a map.

Okay, I said. I can do that.

I went to the bank and cleaned out my savings account, and nobody batted an eye. I went to the service station and got the car filled up and they gave me a free map. Then I walked over to Dr. Weir's drugstore to buy a Coke and some cheese crackers and peanuts and a first aid kit. The old pharmacist was still in back, with even less hair. I sat on a stool and asked for a Coke in a bottle to go. The freckled blond woman didn't know me.

What are you doing out of school? she said.

Dentist appointment, I said. I'm early.

He'll tell you to lay off the Cokes, she laughed, pushing the drink toward me. I was just preparing to pay her when a black truck pulled up outside.

Duke. There was no way out. Had Lindy called and told him?

He got out of the truck, closed the door, and walked up to the drugstore.

Wait, I want a magazine, I told the girl and walked over to the magazine section where I hid.

He opened the glass door and came in. I watched him walk to the back of the store. Mornin', Doc, he said, and handed over a prescription. I thought I could sneak out without him seeing me. But damn. I had to pay. I went up to the register, dollars in hand, paid quickly, said keep the change, and was pushing the front door when I heard him behind me.

Let me get that for you, Mae Lee, he said calmly, and pushed it all the way open. Our eyes locked, and my heart sank way past my knees.

Come on, he said, indicating the truck. I saw your car.

Trembling and with a huge lump in my throat, I climbed into the passenger seat. He didn't say anything, but drove down to the empty lot of the drive-in by the river where Jack Austin and I had eaten barbecue and listened to Frank Sinatra. He looked into my eyes, daring me to lie to him. What's this all about? You change your mind about school?

I shook my head.

I'm sorry about last night, Mae Lee. It'll never happen again.

Then the tears came. Between sobs, I said, I'm leaving, Duke. I can't stay in the same house with Ava. And with you, I silently said.

You have nowhere to go. I'll look after you.

I don't want your pity, I said. And it's the dream. You can't sell the farm. That was part of your dream.

Sometimes you wake up, punkin.

I think I'm just now beginning to dream, I said. I'm not going back, even if I have to jump out of this truck.

He shook his head slowly. Then I'll just have to stop the truck and scrape you up off the pavement.

Let me go to Lindy's for just a little while. A day or two. Maybe I can go stay with Mimi. Please?

He considered this for a few minutes. Let me see a couple of folks first, he said. And I'm going to drive you to Lindy's, if that's where you want to go. You're not having that car until we work this out. Hand over the keys.

I pulled them out of my pocket.

I'll arrange to get the car to the farm, he said. Then he drove to his father's office at the plant. I waited with the secretary, reading magazines, while he talked to his father behind closed doors. He told me I could use the secretary's phone to call Lindy, and so I did. When he came out he gave me a wink and a nod, and I followed him out.

We started back home, though it had never really been home to me. He looked straight ahead and I gazed out the window, feeling like a prisoner on the way to jail, although Lindy's house was nice and her mom brought orange juice to her in bed every morning.

The miles melted away, and we were driving by the familiar fields of Sweetbay. Cows huddled at one end of a pasture near a bubbling artesian well under a stand of pin oaks. Gazing at the cows, I was stopped short by a flash of yellow against the green, half-hidden beyond the stand of trees. It looked very much like the tail of an airplane. I gasped.

What?

Over there, I said.

Duke slowed and looked and then he drove on down about a hundred yards, turned into a dirt road, unlatched a gate, and we bounced over the ruts until we reached the cows. We got out and before we'd walked very far we saw the plane in all its yellow glory.

Austin's plane, he said. He walked over to it and all around and then he looked into the distance and saw Sweetbay house on the rise. Then it was just as if wheels were clicking into place on a slot machine. He raced back to the truck and I hurried after him, stumbling through the uneven grass. He gunned the engine, and the truck jostled and rumbled back to the paved road. Duke didn't stop to latch the gate. The cows! I shouted.

Damn the cows! We were speeding down the tree-lined road that led to Sweetbay.

I turned cold all over. He swung into the circle and screeched to a stop. Stay here, he commanded. He ran in.

I was trembling. Shivering. I waited. And then I heard a scream, long and piercing.

I leaped out of the truck, chest hurting with the effort to breathe. I ran inside to a chaos of shouts and screams. When I reached the bedroom Duke held the bayonet, and Jack, wearing only a pair of jeans, gashed arm pouring blood, was trying to wrestle it from him.

I froze, horrified. What could I do? I looked from one to the other and screamed, Duke! Stop!

Ava, naked, was scrambling madly for her clothes, whimpering. She scooped up a pair of lace panties and tugged them on, never taking her wide eyes off Duke. Now he bent Jack's arm back, forcing the bayonet toward Jack's neck. Suddenly Ava leapt from the bed onto Duke's back, clawing and scratching. He let Jack go and whirled toward Ava with the jungle in his golden eyes.

I ran up and grabbed Jack's arm. Do something! I screamed at him. He's going to kill her!

Jack shook me off like a mosquito. Then he grabbed his shoes and ran out the door.

I wanted to follow him, tell him he had to help, but he was going pell-mell. How could he just run off like that! How dumb I had been, how childish to fall for him! He was gone and it was up to me now. No more death. No more. I was shaking and there was a huge lump in my throat. I had to save them. They were my family.

Duke and Ava struggled. The bayonet, sharp and bloody, danced in my sight. My scar throbbed. I took a deep breath and knew what I had to do. His mind had turned Ava into the enemy he had to kill, and I had to make him see where he really was. I made my voice soft and advanced toward them in a dreamlike state. It wasn't me doing this.

Duke, Duke, put it down, I said.

He looked then, from Ava to me, eyes blank, not really seeing me.

It's me, Mae Lee, I said. He looked confused, glanced at his weapon, then back to me, trying to make out where he was, who I was. Get out, Ava, I said under my breath, without taking my gaze from his. Get out quick.

Li-wei? said Duke. His tongue was thick, a drunkard's tongue.

Yes, I said softly. I'm Li-wei, Captain. Come and talk to my grandfather. He will tell you not to kill. Still Ava did not move, her hands frozen on his, the bayonet inches from her pale throat. Twist around! I shouted to her. Duck and run! I picked up the shirt off the floor and flung it at her. Duke, surprised, relaxed his grip.

Cover up and go, dammit! I screamed. She scrambled for the shirt and made for the door.

He lunged after her, then, lunged with the bayonet, and I saw a thin stripe of blood where the point raked her perfect pale back.

She screamed again, then, and raced outside, right through the front door that Jack had left hanging open. Duke was hard on her heels. She grabbed for the car door, but he stayed her hand. She broke loose and raced around the car, then when she saw she couldn't get in, she ran across the driveway to a hogwire fence and scrambled over. She raced across the hard-packed field of waving weeds toward the plane, its propellers already turning, its motor sputtering.

Duke shook his head then, and his mind must have cleared somewhat. Ava! yelled Duke, staring pitifully after her. Ava!

Captain! Captain Radford! I yelled, and then, when he didn't move, I walked up to him, my hand outstretched.

Cyrus must have heard the commotion, for he came running up. Cap'n! he called out. Cap'n! Duke turned back toward us, gave a long, anguished yell, dropped the bayonet, and sank to the ground. The bayonet lay at my feet, and there were drops of blood in the dust.

Almost like a ghost, Elzuma appeared behind me. Using a rag from her pocket, she picked up the bayonet and gave it to me. Wash this, honey, and put it away. She led Duke inside and, speaking very softly, made him change his clothes, as though he were still a small boy. Her steadiness calmed me and I was able to help her clean up the spots of Ava's and Jack's blood, change the sheets, and tidy the room.

I washed the bayonet. I remembered how I had sliced the air, thinking of Ava. I laid the bayonet back in the trunk and this time, locked the lid.

Now you call Mr. D.B. Radford, Elzuma said to me.

Clutching the red and crystal rosary for dear life, I did.

Duke's father arrived in twenty minutes and took charge of the situation, even getting a doctor out there right away. The doctor said Duke's battle fatigue had been triggered by the shock of Ava's desertion.

Duke was sent to a private mental hospital—the same one where Celia Pritchard had been sent so many years before.

I went to live with my grandmother Mimi and Mr. Linley in South Georgia, at the peanut farm where she was looking after him.

It was hot and dry there, and the dusty air smelled of feed and hay, fertilizer and bug spray. One movie theater and one soda shop entertained the kids in the sleepy town nearby where I finished high school, but there was also a junior college, and the train to Florida hooted its way through every night at 11:00. It reminded me that I would someday leave.

Mimi kept me busy with chores, and I was glad. Carrying chicken feed and gathering eggs, watching the barn cats, folding the laundry, and going to town on errands kept my mind from dwelling on everything I'd lost.

At school, the other students were curious about "the new girl" but didn't go out of their way to include me in their cliques, and that was fine with me. I didn't want them asking too many questions about why I was there. If anyone did ask, I just said that my parents had died; I said nothing about having a treacherous sister who had flown away with her lover boy and left her poor war hero husband who went out of his mind and tried to kill her. No, I would not tell that story to anyone.

And then there was my scar. I wore my long hair down around my face, but if people saw the scar and asked what had happened, I told them a horse had thrown me into a barbed wire fence. That usually shut them up.

Back in my room, on the yellow desk that matched the yellow bedroom furniture with blue painted flowers, I lined up pictures of Chap and Momma and Duke, Duke from the wedding picture they'd given me. I'd cut Ava out of it. Gazing at Duke in his "monkey suit," I wondered if I would ever see him again. Mimi said that people sometimes recover from madness, but not always. I hated to think of him being in that hospital for the rest of his life. I wrote him a long, friendly letter, not knowing if he would be able to answer.

Duke wrote me two letters. I have them still, tattered and torn from so many readings. In the first letter he said how he missed Ava and he missed me too and he'd soon be coming home to us, as soon as the g.d. war was over. That one broke my heart.

In the second letter he sounded as though he was getting better. He said he missed me and the farm and Ava. He wrote that his daddy had kept on Cyrus and Elzuma and some of their kinfolks to keep the place running until he could get back to it. He said that he wrote Ava every week but she never answered. That second letter broke my heart again.

I could see in my mind the letters piling up on the hall table, letters from the mental hospital. One after another. I was afraid that if she never answered, he wouldn't get better, just like him giving up when he was in the Army.

I wrote Duke and told him that she wanted to answer but that she thought he wouldn't forgive her.

And that is when the deception began.

PART IV

Chapter Twenty-Five

It all began with a call from old Elzuma.

She ain't showed up to your place, is she? Elzuma said.

Ava's not ever coming back, I said bitterly. She's probably in Timbuktu.

No'm. But it's these letters.

Letters? I asked. Was she writing Elzuma?

They keep comin' in the mailbox from Mr. Duke, and Mis' Norma, she say just toss 'em out. I hate not to mind his momma, but I don't have the heart. What if Mis' Ava show up at the door one day, and say, where my letters? And him up there in that hospital missing her something powerful? He ain't going to get well that way, with no word from her.

Let me call Mis' Norma, I said. I had always gotten along fine with Duke's mother, unlike Ava, who felt they wished Duke had married somebody else and so was prickly and defensive around her.

What do the doctors tell him? I asked Norma Radford. Do they tell him Ava is gone?

They do not, she said, on the chance she may come back. They said they can deal with that part when they have to. They think it's good for him to write to her. Mae Lee, he may be there for a long, long time. I want him to have peace of mind. When I go to see him, he is so—she paused, looking for the word—*earnest* in his belief that she will wait for him. I can't shatter that. But then she never writes back. He'll have to face that eventually.

That's just it, I said. Would you mind if I wrote him back, pretending to be her?

Well, why—I never thought of that. Oh, dear.

Mis' Norma, Duke needs the will to get well, just as he needed the will to live out there in the jungle.

Let me think about it. I'll ask the doctor.

In the end, they agreed, with reservations. They'd see how it went.

I sent Elzuma a packet of brown envelopes addressed to me. Once a week she would mail me the letters that had come for Ava, and I would send her the letters I had written in Ava's hand, for her to put in the mailbox for the postman. I knew how Ava wrote, knew all her expressions, and it was not hard to sound like her. I filled the letters, written on creamy paper printed with roses, with tenderness and hearts and Xs and Os, written with her favorite purple ink.

The hard part was reading all the sweet stuff he wrote to her and knowing it was not for me.

The pecans cropped out and spring came and tassels formed and made a new crop by fall, and I filled baskets and shelled them and looked after my grandmother and helped around the house and studied and finished high school. I wrote to Lindy and found she had dreams of going to the Olympics as an equestrienne. I entered the junior college there in town and studied history and religion. I was interested in Asia.

And I wrote letters to Duke. When I sat down at the desk and took up that pen with the purple ink, it was almost as if she was inhabiting my body. I wondered if she was dead and had come back to haunt me.

We'd left all the rest of her things at the farmhouse, in case she came back. Mis' Norma said we shouldn't dispose of them until we knew for sure. The thing was—nobody much wanted her back, except Duke. Myself, I wasn't sure. She had done all of us dirt, but she was my sister, and after Mimi was gone she would be my last link to my old life. That's how I thought of it, the old life, when times were good even when they were hard.

I clung to the night long ago when we sat around the oilcloth-covered table eating chops and cornbread while Chap bragged about the airplane he was building, and Ava talked of letters from her soldier, and Mama's cheeks flushed with love and pride over one of the poems I had written. I missed writing poems, but they wouldn't come now that I was inhabiting Ava's skin.

I was becoming more like Ava with each letter I wrote. Without knowing why, I found myself at ease with the boys in my classes. My wardrobe became brighter and tighter. My grandmother gave me a pair of red spike heels that hurt her feet.

They fit me fine, and I wore them. I was gaining some of Ava's strength, some of her determination, which I was going to need, as it turned out.

Mr. Linley died after a long period of not knowing where he was. Mimi went into black and vowed she would wear it forever.

My scar faded to a thin pale line. I told people I met that I'd suffered it learning to fence. There were those who thought I'd run *into* a fence, but I let it pass.

I got a letter from Starrett Conable, at Georgia Tech studying aeronautical engineering. He told me once again he was sorry for what he did, that he had been a real jerk to tell me about what had happened with Ava and Jack. At first, I touched my cheek and crumpled the letter up. And then I got to thinking—it would have come out sometime. And the same thing might have happened. We were all scarred, every one of us.

I saved the letter. And then one morning I decided to really forgive him. One morning, when I'd seen the sun rising over the fields and birds taking flight, I thought of what Duke had told me from Mr. Shen, the Chinese grandfather, about living in peace. I let my anger go, let it rise and fly away like the wheeling swallows, and I felt the lightness of the pale blue sky.

I wrote Starrett and told him that I forgave him everything.

He wrote me back and told me how much it meant to him. He told me about his engineering studies and asked me what I was going to do when I graduated. I told him I was going to be a teacher, like Momma had been, and maybe share my love of poetry with high school students. And we kept writing each other. I hadn't expected that he, of all people, would be my link to my childhood, when we were all together, Momma and Chap and his folks, with the card games in the lamplight.

I was expecting a letter from him that November day three years after Ava had left. I walked to the mailbox, swishing my shoes through drifts of pecan leaves, nuts crunching underfoot.

The envelope from Elzuma was there. I took a handful of mail to Mimi, where she was paying bills and filling out government forms for the farm. That kind of work was becoming hard for her, but she wouldn't hear of my doing it. I carried the brown envelope to the yellow-painted desk in my room, stenciled with blue flowers like the bed, chest, and nightstands.

White dotted-Swiss curtains hung at the window; a stairstep calico quilt covered the bed. The flower pictures on the walls had been torn from Christmas seed store calendars and framed. A picture of me on the front porch at Sweetbay, framed by its live oaks and moss, was taped to my mirror, and I had arranged pictures of Momma and Daddy, Ava and Duke, on my mantel.

I sat at my desk and looked out on the fields behind the farmhouse. The sun was streaming in. How many letters would I have this week? I carefully opened the packet and shook it.

Only one letter tumbled out. Only one?

I tore it open so fast I ripped the envelope, and winced as though it had been my own skin. I unfolded the standard lined tablet paper.

My Ava,

Looks like your old soldier is coming home pretty soon. Pop got up here and talked to the docs and they said I could go back to the farm. I sure am looking forward to being back there with my girls. How is Mae Lee? You never talk about her, looks like she'd be missing the horses. Thanks for the news about Dandy's colt. He might be a fine horse for the girl when he gets bigger. I guess she has gone off to college by now. Time sure flies when you're having fun. Gosh, I'm so happy. Maybe next month they said.

God how I want to hold you.
Your loving husband,
Dulany Radford

Why hadn't the Radfords called me and told me? Just possibly they had forgotten all about me, about the letters, and that Ava would not be there when he got home. Numbness filled me. What had I been thinking? That he would stay in the mental hospital forever? He'd be coming home and somebody would have a hell of a lot of explaining to do. My letters had done their job too well. He'd recovered faster than anyone predicted.

Just then, the phone rang, and it was Norma Radford. She apologized, saying the release had caught her by surprise too. Can we have Ava meet with a sudden accident? She wanted to know. No, I pleaded. What if she turns up? Can we hire a detective?

Can I hire one, you mean. She laughed. I think it would be better if we just faced the fact she's gone. Let her be dead. That's what I'm going to tell Duke. A car accident. He can take it now. She won't come back.

It might cause a relapse, I said. Let me try to find her.

You? A girl of nineteen?

A woman of nineteen, I said. I've been through a lot. She ought to be there to welcome Duke when he comes home.

I want him to have peace, she said.

He'll have no peace without Ava.

I could hear a long, long sigh. All right. I'll permit you to go ahead. But think of this, Mae Lee. What if she's dead? Or what if she refuses to come back?

Then we can go with the car accident. But I have to know, Mis' Norma. Maybe for myself.

All right. Good luck.

I'd need it. I couldn't go to the sheriff again and have them start asking questions I didn't want to answer. All I knew was that she had flown off with Jack, and no telling where he was by now. South America, he'd told me once. You have to move around and find crops to dust.

On the third day after I'd received the letter from Duke, I sat down and took up the purple-inked pen and wrote back with the misspellings she always used.

I'm just wild that your coming back, I have missed you every nite and every day that you have been gone, my arms ache for you, I long for your kiss. When you come back, we'll go dancing the way we used to do, long before you ever went away.

Hurry, hurry

Out of ink. I dipped my pen and filled it. This was going to be a hard letter.

I called information in Atlanta, Savannah, Birmingham, Mobile, New Orleans, Miami, all the cities I'd ever heard her mention, all the cities where she might have gone, and asked for a listing under Ava Radford. There wasn't one, nor was there an Ava Willis, nor A.W. Radford, no A. Radford, nor A. Willis. Jack or John Austin? A few of those. I called all around the state.

I was scattering buckshot. Through Lindy's father, I got a list of farmers who might have employed Jack for crop dusting and called them all. None had seen him since the time he'd been in Sawyer staying with us. One hearty lady laughed and said, I 'spect you aren't the first girl who's been calling here looking for Mister Austin. She gave me an address and a phone number he'd given her once.

The person at the number had never heard of him. I wrote to the address in Memphis, Tennessee, and the letter came back *Addressee Unknown—Return to Sender* with a huge purple finger pointing back at me.

I called the old lady, by this time almost deaf, who ran the boarding house. JACK AUSTIN, I hollered into the phone. THREE YEARS AGO. A CROP DUSTER PILOT. She said she would look. Maybe she had kept those past guest books, maybe not. I called three more farmers on the list and got nowhere.

At one farm that Lindy's father told me to try, I never could get an answer. I drove out to the place. The farmer was outside, repairing a tractor. Wife died a couple of years back, kids all gone, who's gonna take over the farm? he asked me rhetorically. He leaned against his tractor, spat a wad of tobacco juice, and said to me, I remember that feller. Yellow plane. Cocky sort of guy. In the army, weren't he? If I was you I'd try the army. They keep records.

I tried. You have to be kin.

The time had come to pay a visit to Sweetbay and see if I could turn up any clues there.

The branches of the live oaks still swept the ground, trailing moss; a carpet of crackly brown leaves shone underneath. The drive was well-swept and the yard was mowed; the porch and front columns shone with fresh paint.

My heart seemed to fill my chest, and I swallowed, thinking of that day I left the house for good three years ago, crunching across the oak leaves, leaving behind those columns and the pines that had towered under the moon.

I walked slowly to the front door, looking around for ghosts, but there was only the swaying moss.

Iris, Elzuma's granddaughter, opened the door. She looked up at me shyly. Cyrus and I got married, she told me. It's good to see you, Mis' Mae Lee.

Just call me Mae Lee, I said. I need to go in Mr. Duke's office. I'm looking for something important.

Mis' Norma say it's okay?

She did, I said.

Come in, then, Iris said. We're keeping it for him so it'll be just like when he left.

The office was cleaner than it had ever been when I lived there. I slid open the drawer, drew out the key chain, and unlocked the rusty lock of the footlocker in the closet. Iris left me and went back to her chores.

I didn't see the bayonet at first. Someone—Elzuma, probably—had buried it beneath the papers, photos, old magazines, books, and uniforms. The diary was still there. He'd never burned it. I leafed through it, and then laid it carefully back in the trunk and examined the letters. None from Jack. They had apparently never written each other.

I shrugged and looked through the photo albums. Nothing there. I winced as I saw once again the old man, Mr. Shen, and the girl Li-wei.

I searched the desk, the yellowing papers in the old farm files. Nothing.

I called for Iris and found her on the back porch, sweeping it clear of leaves. Three bushels of pecans waited to be shelled and picked. Is this all? I asked. Have you seen any more papers anywhere else? In the bedroom?

No, ma'am, she said, and I winced at the *ma'am*, but I knew she would not call me Mae Lee, not as long as she worked here.

I glanced out at the paddock, at the horses grazing, at the old blue truck. Funny it was still around. I thought of the night Jack and I had listened to Frank Sinatra, down by the river in the soft blue night.

Has anyone cleaned out that blue truck?

She shrugged. I don't reckon, she said. No need.

I remembered that Jack had cleaned it. For me.

Is it unlocked?

She grinned. Yes, Lordy. Nobody'd want to steal that thing.

I walked outside, went over to the truck, and climbed in. The rubbery, musty smell made me shiver. I opened the glove compartment: Jack had not bothered to clean that out. There were gasoline receipts in Duke's name, a screwdriver, some dried-up cheese crackers, half a ball of twine, a church key, greasy machine parts, and scraps of paper. I searched through them all, and found a matchbook folded inside a cash receipt. Written on the matchbook was a number and the name of a girl, or somebody. Viv.

Cyrus said the matchbook sho' wa'nt his. I had never heard Duke mention a Viv, or a Vivian. And there wasn't an area code. The number was not from our town.

I pocketed the matchbook. It wasn't much. It could have been Duke's from long before. But it could have equally been Jack's. The cash receipt was dated from the time that he'd visited us.

I thought I'd come to a dead end. All I had was that matchbook. I pondered the problem all the way back to Mimi's and didn't come up with a solution. That number might give me a clue to Jack, but it could be anywhere in the United States.

Driving home, I remembered something Starrett Conable had written me. They were going to get a big computer installed at Tech, one that could be used to solve the most complex problems. What I had was a complex problem. When I got back to Mimi's, I called Starrett.

He was happy to hear from me until I told him I was trying to find Ava, and why. When I mentioned Jack, he became quiet. I told him about the matchbook and Viv. I was afraid he'd tell me to hell with it. I held my breath.

I'll ask around, he told me.

He called me back a day later. There are only X number of telephone exchanges per area, he said. He'd come up with three cities where that number might be likely. One was Miami, one was San Francisco, and one was a small town in Iowa. I could breathe again.

I called the Miami number first. No answer. The Iowa number said they'd never heard of a Viv or Vivian. The San Francisco number had been disconnected.

In the meantime I got a call back from the old lady in the boarding house. She'd remembered that boy Jack. He had registered in her book from an address in Memphis, Tennessee.

Oh. I already knew that one was no good, but I thanked her for taking the trouble. I was about to tell her goodbye when she said I remember him now, a good-looking young man, flirtatious-like. That boy could charm the spots off a snake. I knew it was all a lot of hogwash, you know, but he got to me anyhow. Once he brought me oranges. He loved oranges. Said he had worked the groves.

A Miami number. It made sense.

I called the number again. Still no answer.

It was a long shot, I knew, but I felt if I could just get to Miami, I could find this Viv, and she would know what had happened to Jack, and hence to Ava.

Like any student, my bank account was miserably low. I went to Mimi and asked to borrow money for a bus ticket and motel room. Mr. Linley had left her fairly well off, even though after she died the farm would go to his two sons from his former marriage. She was renting out her acres now.

Mae Lee, she said, it's out of the question. Going to Miami alone? I won't hear of it. You're only nineteen. The town is full of gambling, prostitutes, drugs. Just like Havana. Crime, she said.

I won't get mixed up with any criminals, I told her. I'm just going to look for Ava. A lot of perfectly nice tourists go to Miami and come back alive. It can't be all bad.

You don't even know she's there, said Mimi.

I know. And I want to go anyhow. Mimi, I've never been out of the state of Georgia. It's about time I had that kind of education. I don't want to live on a farm all my life.

It was good enough for me, she said. She grumbled for half a day before she got on the phone to some of the friends she'd known when she lived in Florida with my grandpa. She found a reasonable mom-and-pop place in Miami she trusted, waited while I made a reservation, and the next day, took me to the bus station.

When I arrived in downtown Miami and disembarked, I walked out of the reek of diesel fumes right into a fragrant balmy breeze. I could see why Ava might like it. During the taxi ride to my motel, we passed pretty pastel buildings and palm trees, everything new and strange, and somehow I knew it was the kind of place my sister would find agreeable.

The motel was a small motor court in Coconut Grove, and the man and woman who ran it were salt-of-the earth retired

Yankees, friends of friends of my grandmother. The room was small and mint green with white curtains and pictures of parrots and macaws on the wall. The bedspreads were the corded kind you find in college dorms, tropical blue.

I sat on the bed and dialed Viv's number. No answer. Outside, the sun was going down, splashing the sky with neon orange and pink behind the weedy, sandy vacant lot across the street. I cranked open my jalousie window to take in the balmy, salt-and coco-scented air, with hints of plaster and grass and heat and asphalt. Just for a moment I felt like a tiny rowboat in a big ocean, and then I remembered that I had to put my hand to the oar.

My motel was too small to have a restaurant or a cocktail lounge, but it did offer a rack of brochures and maps. I took a handful of them and wandered down the street until I found a fish shack and bought a grouper sandwich, slaw, and fries. I washed it down with a big glass of sweet tea and read the brochures. One offered a bus tour of the city.

When I got back, I called Viv again. Still no answer. I kept trying. Right around ten, a woman answered. Viv? I asked. Vivian?

Who wants to know?

You don't know me, I began, and she hung up and let it ring when I tried to call back.

The next morning, with nothing else to do, I signed up for the bus tour. We went out to Miami Beach and the grand old pastel-colored hotels and toured the streets where the mansions rose, the older ones neglected and crumbling, the newer ones swank and grand.

That was the kind of life Ava had wanted: the life behind those gates and bougainvillea. Not likely to find it with Jack, I thought, unless he had turned to some sort of crime.

We passed the public library, and something clicked. I asked to get off.

You sure? asked the tour bus conductor. I nodded. It's real important, I said.

He stopped the bus half a block beyond.

I asked the librarian for a city directory. She fetched it for me: a big book, with names and addresses of all the people in the city and their occupations. But there was something else, I knew. In the back, in green pages, were lists of telephone numbers and the names of people who owned them.

Cross-referencing, I found that the number belonged to a Vivian Fox. *Vivian Fox!*

I looked her up. Profession: entertainer. All right. I copied her address down, ending with Number 115. Apartment house?

I looked up the street on the big city map in the library. The librarian, seeing me puzzling over the streets, asked if she could help. I told her where I wanted to go. You sure? she asked. I'm sure, I said. It's very important. I'm looking for my sister.

She had tanned skin and black cat-eye glasses and black hair in a bun. Be careful, honey, she said. You don't want to go to that neighborhood after dark. It's dangerous.

I won't, I said. Just tell me how to get there. I'll go tomorrow.

She found a bus schedule and copied the information down, and I took a bus back to the motel, watching the flamboyant sunset splash across the sky.

The motel owners were called the Pacellis, and they invited me to eat spaghetti with them that night, but I told them I had already eaten. The truth was that I didn't want them asking too many questions. I ate peanuts and a Coke that night, and the next day ate a big breakfast at a cafe down the street, waiting until late morning. I had a hunch Viv slept late. With the bus information in hand, I traveled to the street where Viv lived.

In late-morning haze the bus dropped me across from a brooding, mauve, five-story building called The Alhambra. I gazed up at the flaking plaster and rusty wrought-iron balconies. Men loitered on the sidewalk, cigarettes between their lips; women in full skirts walked with bags of groceries from corner stores. A few children, faces thin, chased each other.

Uneasy, I jaywalked. A warm, fetid wind skittered trash around my heels. Passersby glanced at me, the stranger. I walked up to the entrance past a bedraggled palm tree covered with dust.

I pushed through the revolving door into the building and found myself standing on cracked tiles in a lobby with faded velvet rumpsprung chairs, upon which two elderly men sat, reading newspapers and smoking cigars behind plants that looked like they had died years ago. The men looked up and then went back to their papers.

The elevator, with a tarnished brass door, stood at the far left of the lobby. On the door was a hand-lettered sign, OUT OF ORDER. From the curled and dirty look of the paper, the elevator had been out of order a long time. To its right a bank of numbered mailboxes stood. To its left, a door labeled *Office* was tightly shut, frosted-glass pane dark.

Broad steps covered with threadbare carpet ascended to my left, and I hoped these led to the first floor. At the top of the steps, a hallway covered with carpet that might have once been green stretched left and right. Four doors down, again on the left, I found number 115. The wall beside the door was dark with smudges, as though many hands had leaned there. I pushed the bell.

You're early, a voice yelled from inside.

Early for what? I looked behind me, to see if anyone was coming. But the hall was empty. Of course—I was early.

She opened the door five minutes later, a poofy blonde with sleepy eyes whose dye job was way overdue. She was wrapped in a silk kimono, red with embroidered dragons, that did not quite cover up her black lace bra. Wobbling a little on her red satin mules, she grabbed at the gaping kimono and scowled.

Who are you? Where's Marvin?

I don't know any Marvin, I said.

What the hell are you doing here, kid?

Are you Viv?

She peered at me. Your boyfriend ain't here, and neither is your daddy.

I must have turned forty shades of red. I'm looking for a Jack Austin, I said. I held out the matchbook.

She took it and looked it over, then handed it back to me with a tiny flicker of a smile. Honey, there are a lot of Jacks in my line of work.

A pilot, I said. But she was looking over my shoulder. I turned to see a bald man with jug ears, who reminded me of the man in the game I'd once had—the magnetic man you fitted with hair, mustache, and beard by pushing around iron filings with a magnet. Marvin, she said, and then to me, Sorry, I gotta go. Nothing personal, just business.

She grabbed Marvin by the arm and pulled him inside and shut the door, saying there oughta be a law against these magazine people.

By now sweat was running down my forehead and my sides and the building's funk of grease and moldy carpet and decay was filling up my nose. Maybe I should just give up. But I couldn't—I'd come all this way, and she knew Jack. Maybe I'd try again after Marvin left. I had a feeling it wouldn't be long.

I walked back to the lobby and sat on one of the ratty up-holstered benches. If Jack wasn't here, then what had become of him? Had he gone on to South America? I had a feeling he'd never come back anywhere near our town again. I didn't want to see him anyhow. I just wanted to find Ava.

Cigar smoke drifted my way, along with pairs of curious eyes. The ancient men were still there. One of them got up and came toward me, and I decided to wait outside. At the revolving door I stopped to let in a woman wobbling on impossibly high heels, clutching a bottle in a brown paper bag. Her hair, wild and dark and dull, looked as though it hadn't been combed for days. Retired hoods, prostitutes, winos—

The woman tripped, on a loose tile I guess, and dropped the bottle, and it cracked in two like a gunshot. She gazed down at the spreading dark puddle and shrieked, convulsing with wild, wailing sobs.

A numb feeling spread over me. I knew those sobs. I walked over, and she looked at me with a scowl which melted like an ice cube on the sidewalk back home and said, My God. Mae Lee.

Chapter Twenty-Six

Ava put her hands to her face. I grabbed her shoulder and shook her. Ava, come on, get up. Is there anybody who can get this cleaned up? Does the building have a janitor?

She just stared at me dumbly. One of the old geezers ambled over, chewing on his cigar, and looked more kind than menacing. I'll get McGillicuddy, he said.

A woman in housecoat and curlers emerged from somewhere as I was trying to persuade Ava off the floor. I'm the resident manager, she said and looked at Ava. You again.

She tripped, I said.

Can't stand up, said the woman. I'm sick of it. She toed at the puddle. Fred will take care of it. Not that she will be grateful, she said to me.

She's my sister, I said.

I pay my rent, Ava said.

You've been warned, said the manager. We don't want trouble here. This is a quiet place.

I've come to see about her, I said. My eyes met the woman's, asking for a little compassion. The lines in her face unfolded a little. Relieved, I suppose, that someone had come to take charge.

I'll go get Fred, she said, and left.

Come on, I said to Ava, taking her arm. The old guys were standing there watching as I hauled her up the stairs trailing an odor of staleness and sweat, of rancid hair. I found the stairwell and walked her up to the third floor, and she let herself into apartment 302, fumbling with her key.

Good Lord.

In the dingily-lit studio we stepped onto a rich-looking Oriental carpet. Make yourself at home, Ava said, dropping her handbag—which looked like alligator—on one maroon velvet chair. I laid my own bag on the chair's twin and stroked the soft velvet. Silk, I'd bet. The covers were still rumpled on the round bed which stood against the far wall, but the covers were gold satin and the sheets were shiny and black. French bistro posters hung on the wall. A wilting red rose drooped in a glass vase on a black lacquered table.

Lie down, I said. I'll get you something to drink. She followed me into a tiny alcove to the right. Under fluorescent light her skin looked yellow, almost jaundiced.

I opened the refrigerator to more mildew than food—a bottle of milk, a jar of pickles, and a half brick of cheddar cheese with dried edges. I sniffed the milk and poured it down the sink. A small glass jar with a gold label, way to the back, caught my eye.

I pulled it out—quarter full of cherries in brandy. No meat, no milk, no vegetables? I said to Ava.

I eat out a lot, she murmured. Gimme. She grabbed the cherries, opened the jar, and fished them out with her fingers. I'd forgotten they were there, she said. How could I have forgotten those? Albert gave me those. She turned up the jar and drank the brandy. Aah, she said. God. There were dribbles on her chin.

I need a real drink, she said. She swiped the dribbles off with trembling hands and opened a drawer and pulled out a pack of cigarettes. She shook one out and lit it with a kitchen match.

No, you don't, I said. I pulled open the freezer compartment, frosted over and empty except for two aluminum trays filled with ice. I took one out, yanked the lever, poured the ice into a bowl, refilled the tray, and put it back. You're going to tell me everything that's been happening to you.

Ava was talking all right, wailing again. My wine, my wine, disappeared into the cracks of the goddamned Alhambra. Fred probably lapped it up. That was my last five bucks.

Is that all you think about? I said.

She picked up the empty cherry bottle and gazed at it. I didn't ask you to come.

Tell you what, I said, looking in the rusting metal cabinet for a glass. You take a bath and change into some clean clothes. Wash your hair. Then I'm going to go out and get us something to eat. And if you eat what I bring, I'll buy you some wine. And then we're going to talk. I found a glass that looked like some kind of wedding crystal and filled it with ice.

She stuck out her lip at me, and I saw the girl who had stuck out her lip at Momma over being made to go to church. I filled the glass from the tap with water smelling of sulfur and handed it to her. Drink this, I said.

She took a few sips, made an ugly face, then walked over to the bed. She set the glass on the bedside table and flopped face down on the rumpled covers. I walked into the bathroom and looked at the tub. I chased the spiders out, found a plug, and screeched open the faucet. Water gushed out brown and muddy before it ran clear.

I looked for shampoo; an empty bottle lay behind the toilet. A cake of soap had curled up and died in the recessed soap dish, but it would have to do. When the tub was full, I walked out and shook her shoulder. Get in, I said.

Why are you doing this? she said.

Just do it.

When Ava was clean and wrapped in a parrot green nylon peignoir, torn at the hem, I left her sitting in the velvet chair and went out. Following the directions she gave me, I found a deli on the corner and bought Cuban sandwiches and two quart bottles of Pabst Blue Ribbon beer. No one asked for I.D.

Beer, she sniffed, when I set it on the table.

That's right, I said.

She drew herself up, and for a moment became the old haughty, glamorous Ava. And then the illusion dissolved, and her eyes looked frightened, and across the kitchen table from me sat a pathetic woman.

Eat, I said. I bit into my sandwich.

She looked at the sandwich suspiciously, picked it up, and nibbled on the corner, and then disregarding me, dug in. I figured she hadn't eaten for a while. In spite of the bath, she hadn't managed to clean her fingernails, flecked red from a long-ago manicure, and grime remained under them.

We ate in silence, wary of each other, like two strange cats.

Her sandwich was half gone, along with most of the beer in her quart, when she pointed her sandwich at me, curled her lip, and said, I suppose you and Duke are shacking up.

The bedraggled kitten, dried and fed, had become a saber-toothed tiger. I forced myself to take a deliberate swallow of beer before I answered. You don't have any damn idea what you did, did you?

She tossed her hair and smoothed a forefinger across her lip to wipe away the beer foam. I don't know what you're talking about.

I don't suppose you would, I said. Duke has been in a mental hospital for the last three years. He's getting out soon. He's coming home. And he expects to see you. He thinks you've been waiting for him. Like you waited for him while he was in Burma.

A mental institution? Her face changed, and I couldn't read it.

I leaned forward and my eyes bored right into hers. That night made him go over the edge. He was awfully close to it for a lot of years. You knew that.

Her eyes slid away, she opened her mouth, and then . . . she dropped her head into her hands. God, Mae Lee. If you only knew. Living with him was hell.

Did you ever try to understand? I asked softly.

So? *You* were going to understand? She pressed her lips together.

I shook my head. So where is Jack? And where did all this stuff come from? Did he buy it for you?

She sighed and drained her glass and wiped foam again. Jack and me, we didn't last long. We had a lot of laughs while the money held out, and one night he balled me three times and the next day he flew off and never came back. I couldn't go back home, could I? Face Norma Radford and her clan? Have Duke slam the door in my face? I sold my wedding set, bought some clothes, and got a job as a restaurant hostess.

I shook my head slowly. He would've had you back in a heartbeat.

She got up, found her bag, and pulled out a cigarette. She lit it and tossed the matchbook on the table. Her little gold lighter, I guessed, was long gone. I picked it up and noticed it was from the same bar as Jack's matchbook, the one that had Viv's name and number.

The smoke curled out of her mouth and shimmered to the ceiling. What did you ever know about me and Duke?

Oh, more than you can imagine, Ava, I wanted to say, but didn't. She took a deep drag, sucking like a baby. The smoke flowed out her nose. I told you I was a hostess. Vito came into the restaurant a lot, and we started going out. He liked to spend money on me. Then I met Bernard, Vito's boss. She paused, waited to hear whether I was going to make any comment.

Okay, I said. Go on.

Bernard was older. Married, she said. I looked good then. He set me up in an apartment, bought me anything I wanted. I had the life, I did. Go look in my closet.

I just looked at her. Go on, she said, *look*. Then I'll tell you the rest.

In the bedroom, I opened the tiny, grim closet. It was crammed with clothes: fancy gowns from Saks and Bloomingdale's, snug-fitting linen suits, hats in boxes, spike-heeled shoes. All limp and smelly, because dry cleaning was a waste of good liquor money.

I had a fur but it's gone now, Ava called.

A fur?

He took me to New York sometimes, she said.

I walked back into the kitchen. Ava was pouring beer from my bottle into her glass. So what happened with Bernard? I asked.

She shrugged. One day somebody shot him, she said, flipping ashes off her cigarette onto the sandwich wrapper. Outside, it was now dark and through the filmy curtains I could see a big, round Miami moon.

Did you care? I asked.

What do you think? she said. I had to get out of my apartment. It was his, after all. His wife was very ugly about it. I was lucky to be able to keep all my stuff.

How did you wind up here?

She blew out smoke. Jack and I stayed here for a couple of months when we first came to Miami. It was cheap.

You're lucky you didn't wind up dead, too. I said.

I was talented, she said.

You need to get out of here, I said. For your sake as well as Duke's. My voice went up a few notches. I'm just glad Momma and Chap aren't here to see this.

You came down here to get me to come back? Well, I won't go, she said, and you can't make me. She drank the last of my beer. The bottles were empty and the sandwiches were gone, and the chips. Her head fell forward and she passed out on the table.

Somehow I got her into the bed and pulled the sheet over her. That round bed was one she had made, and maybe she ought to lie in it. Maybe I ought to go back home and forget about the whole thing. I sat there at that table with the two empty beer bottles and the ashtray full of cigarette butts and the remains of the sandwiches and I balled the paper up and threw them all in the trash. I found a tattered phone book and copied down the number of a taxi company. I could go back tomorrow and say I hadn't found her.

I looked out at the moon and thought about the moon above the pines and the night Duke and I had looked into one another's eyes, and he had pulled away. How I had wanted him not to pull away. What if I let him think she was dead? What would happen then?

And what would happen to Ava when she had sold all her clothes, when she had sold the chair and the rug and the bed?

What would happen to her tonight, when she woke up from her drunk and I was gone? She would dress in one of those silk dresses that smelled of cheap perfume and the sweat of men and she would go out, that much I knew.

I still don't know how I did it. I went into her closet. I dressed in one of her outfits. It didn't fit me too well, but so what. Tight in some places, loose in others, way too short, but it was black and red. I fluffed my hair over my face and put on some of her red lipstick. And then I went out to the liquor store. Guys called to me from the cars but I didn't turn my head. I hustled there and hustled back, clip clopping in her heels that pinched my big feet with a bottle of gin in her big swinging pocketbook. No one asked for an ID in the liquor store and I didn't figure they would.

She woke up an hour later raging for a drink, and then I proceeded to get her drunk, hoping that if she got drunk enough she would come with me. I would keep her drunk until we got to the bus station. That was my plan, anyhow.

It didn't quite work out like that.

She decided I was boring her and she wanted me to go away but leave the gin. She wanted to go out, she knew a guy. She lurched into her closet and pulled out a teal dress which looked awful against her sallow skin. They wear that color here, she said. Bernie loved that color. What the hell are you doing in my clothes.

I stripped them off and got back into my things and took the dead soap and scrubbed every speck of makeup off my face. I can't wait to get out of here, I said. Why did I ever try with you?

A sob escaped my throat, and tears started leaking down my cheeks. I had failed. I had found her; I had gone on a bus and stayed at a motel and made phone calls asking questions like some private eye, all to try to find her and bring her back to Duke. And she didn't want to go. So she liked living here in the smelly tatters of her life? In this squalor? Selling herself for a bottle of booze? I was heartsick and disgusted. I took a Kleenex from my pocket, blew my nose, and dried my eyes. I swallowed hard. Let her rot, then.

I called the taxi.

Ten minutes, the guy said. I grabbed my pocketbook; I'd wait in the lobby. I thought about leaving her a twenty while I waited. No. I would not.

Just as I got out the door I heard her retching.

Talking on the big white telephone, they call it now. Hand and knees on the cold white tiles, except here in the Alhambra they were sandy beige and teal. She could drown in that commode for all I cared. Mae Lee, she croaked. Mae Lee, help me.

I'm through with you, Ava.

Mae Lee, I'm bad sick.

Sure, Ava. sure.

Mae Lee. I love you. My baby sister.

You lie, I thought, but it was like a stake in the heart.

Mae Lee. I'm scared.

That did it. I grabbed a wet towel and hoped the taxi would wait.

You're coming home with me, I said. I grabbed a suitcase out of the closet and started filling it with whatever I could lay a hand to.

If I can have a drink, she said.

We both rode the bus back to Mimi's. It had taken me more than a week to find her, and it was less than three weeks until Duke was coming home. Jesus was right about that damn prodigal son. You should have seen Mimi. I'm glad she didn't have any cows because one would have been slaughtered for sure to provide Ava with some veal cutlets. As it was, Mimi let her stay in the best room while Mimi moved over to the one that had been Mr. Linley's.

Still, Mimi was Mimi and didn't let her off the hook.

Look at you, she told her. You look like a tramp. She was referring to shiny black satin toreador pants and a low-cut lace blouse.

Nobody in Miami was complaining, Ava said.

You're in the country now, Mimi said. She bustled around with her walking stick, poking at the clothes in the suitcase. She made me take them to be cleaned. She made an appointment for Ava with her hairdresser. And then she let herself be kind. You're going to the doctor, she said. You're going to be the same Ava that he left behind. And no booze.

I can't do this, Ava said.

Be there for Duke when he comes home. That's all I ask, I said.

Why are you doing this? she asked again.

I confessed to her then how I'd been writing to him all this time, pretending I'd been her. I didn't explain how the writing had changed me, giving me some of her strength, some of her determination. I was going to give some of her own back, if I could.

My God, said Ava, as I handed her the packets of letters now, all tied up with ribbons, three years' worth of letters, twice a week, letters, one hundred and four letters per year, three hundred letters for Ava to read.

She sat there and untied one of the ribbons. I could swear she took out the first one with a shaky hand, from emotion or lack of booze I wasn't sure. She read it all the way through. Then she put it back and took out another. She read that one all the way through, then put it back. She carefully re-tied the little bundle with ribbon. She leaned back in her chair and lit a cigarette. She was thinking.

No doctor, she finally said.

I had a pan of butterbeans in my lap. Mimi had her priorities. You know you're sick, I said, and ran my thumbnail along the edge of a bean.

Mimi's already gone to a lot of expense for me. I just need rest and I'll be fine.

The doctor will tell you to stop drinking, is that it?

She cut her eyes at me. Maybe I don't want to.

You'll die, I said.

Maybe I want to die, she said.

Wash your mouth out with soap, Ava.

I don't think I can face my loving husband without some fortification. I looked over at her, and sure enough, there was the ghost of a smile.

Are you kidding or not kidding?

That's for me to know and you to find out. She rose and strode back into the house on those long legs, leaving the basket of letters, and then she came back and got them. I never saw them again.

Chapter Twenty-Seven

We never did get her to go to the doctor, but we got her looking good.

The day before Duke was to arrive home, we took Ava and her things out to the farm. She had insisted on keeping the Miami dresses, but Mimi had bought her a couple of pairs of jeans and some striped shirts. You'll need these, she said.

Ava greeted Iris as if she'd been away only a week. She walked around the house, looking in all the rooms, and checked out back to see if her Caddy was there, and was pleased to see it alongside one of the trucks in the shed Cyrus had built.

I can unpack, if you like, Mis' Ava, Iris told her.

All right, she said, but I'm not staying here alone tonight.

You won't be alone, Iris told her. Me and Cyrus stay to the bungalow.

Mimi and I would stay too. The guest rooms had been finished.

There are ghosts here, said Ava. She had been three weeks without a drink and her nerves were on edge, so I didn't blame her. She hugged herself. I might go back to Miami, she said. My rent is paid till the end of the month.

You will do no such thing, Mimi said. I will arrange to have your things there sold.

Not yet, Ava said. Not yet.

The next day we were all ready an hour before Duke was to arrive. Ava wore black slacks, spike heels, and a low-cut red rayon blouse. She took a deep breath and went to her room and walked over to her dressing table, now empty of all her jars and bottles. She fingered the empty porcelain dish on her dressing table.

My rubies, she said. Where are my rubies? She walked over to the Chinese jewelry box and opened each silk-lined drawer. She turned to me, a flash of anger in her eyes. All my jewelry is gone, she said. Did you—

Your jewelry's in the safe deposit box in town, I said. Mis' Norma thought it ought to stay there until you settle in. But I kept the rubies. If you never came back. I reached into my pocket and pulled out a silk pouch. I handed it to her.

She gave me a long, hard look. Then she shook them out and wordlessly fixed them to her ears. She threw the rhinestones she'd been wearing into the trash.

Mimi and I waited in the living room for Duke's arrival, reminding me of the time we had all waited for Duke to come home from the war. I tried to keep still and not let Mimi see now nervous I was to see him. Would he be like the old Duke, or would we be meeting a stranger? Had the doctors managed to take his nightmares away? And would he remember what had happened that horrible night?

Back then, I had been holding my joy to welcome him home, sitting on the front steps with the waving daffodils. Now, I was holding my breath. Different songs were playing on the radio, and this time there were no daffodils, but waving broomsedge. It was Indian summer: a warm spell in October, the late crops in, and a light fragrant breeze wafting sweetness our way. Outside, the horses frisked in their paddock, and the new colt, a bay, had grown up to be a beauty called Ranger. Cyrus had trained him well.

Ava prowled the house, unable to sit still, looking into cupboards and closets. Iris, flouring chicken for frying, had cooked all day the day before, butterbeans and corn and slaw. I helped her make a lemon cheese cake, stirring the mouth-watering lemon filling on the stove until it got just right, creamy and translucent. Cyrus was out back with the horses, and Elzuma, wad of snuff under her lip, sat in the kitchen stripping turnip greens for supper.

The breeze outside died down, and it felt like the world was holding its breath. I glanced out the front window where I had spent so many nights looking out at the pines. The trees were taller now, the lower limbs higher from the ground, so you could see more of the road. And now a car was coming up the drive.

When it pulled into the circle and stopped, my heart jumped and I looked over at Mimi.

Ava slipped into the room from wherever she had been.

The door finally opened and Duke stepped out from the passenger side. His father emerged from the driver's side, and Duke, leaning on his cane, opened the back door for his mother.

He then turned, straightened, and looked toward the house. His face had become more lined and his eyes more deep and thoughtful. I crossed my hands over my heart and pressed, as if that could force it to slow down.

Ava stood stock-still at the window, watching Duke heft his bag and walk up the steps. This time, she didn't run out to greet him, didn't throw herself into his arms. She seemed unable to move, one manicured hand resting on the back of the white sofa she'd chosen a lifetime ago.

How can you be so calm? I asked her. He was so thin. His hair had turned entirely gray. A lump rose in my throat.

I'm not calm, she said. I'm numb.

Numb?

You did this for me, she whispered. I still don't know why.

Since she couldn't move, I went to the door and threw it open, standing back, so he would see her first. The look on his face when he saw her was like the sky lighting up, the brilliant gold of the early dawn.

She ran to him, then, they wrapped their arms around each other, and then he held her back, looking at her for a long time, the way he had done after the war.

Welcome home, soldier, Ava finally said.

Duke brightened when he finally saw me, and hugged me next, and I swear he looked at me as though we shared a secret.

Mr. D.B. Radford and Mis' Norma came in and stayed about an hour. Mis' Norma sat and watched the two of them as if calculating how things were going to be. We served coffee and tea and sweet rolls and talked about how the town was changing and about the farm and what Duke was going to plant next spring. And then the Radfords said they couldn't stay for lunch, they had to go.

I walked outside with them. Norma Radford looked at me. I still don't know if this was the right thing to do, Mae Lee, she said.

It was right, I said. Did you see his face?

I would never tell her of the condition I'd found Ava in, or the apartment in Miami she could still escape to, or the life she had lived, or not lived, there.

Mis' Norma looked back at the house. They'll need a lot of support, she said. They are both damaged.

Yes, ma'am, I said, wondering how much she really knew.

Ava and Duke stepped out to the porch then to wave them off.

Mimi and I stayed for lunch because they insisted, and Iris had planned on it, and afterwards Mimi and I decided we had to let them be alone at last, and the last thing I remember of that day was the both of them as Mimi and I were driving away, their arms around each other's' waists, waving good-bye as the sunlight glinted off the rubies.

Ava stayed with Duke, her restlessness gone. She looked after Duke pretty well, given her tiredness, which we all put down to her years of heavy drinking. She didn't mind when he went off riding on Nimrod. Both of them were growing older, and she had regained her love of life and fun, as much as she was able. She made the sun shine for him, and for all of us.

She avoided doctors for three years, until one day in 1957, not long after my twenty-second birthday, she felt too sick to get out of bed. The flu, she thought. Iris could bring her soup and she'd be better in no time. Duke wasn't having it. He told her if she didn't go this time, he'd drive her there in the truck and carry her in himself.

The flu turned out to be cancer.

She went into the brand-new hospital in town—the small hospital where Momma had died had been torn down to make room for an office complex—and there in the room with its pale pink walls Ava lay hooked up to tubes and monitors while the doctors did what they could.

She hated it and begged to go home.

Duke sat by her bed and held her hand, talking about old times, their happy times. I hoped that sometime, in Miami, so far from all her dreams, with men she had latched onto out of desperation and spite, she had cried and repented of what she had done, and she wanted to come back to be with Duke, who really loved her, and maybe she had drawn deep from that love, that love that never had left him, love enough for two. And maybe she drew from the love our momma and daddy had given us, deep down, before the devil got into her, filling her with so much wanting, with so much anger that it drowned out the real beauty in her, the beauty inside.

But all Duke's prayers, all his caring, couldn't save her. She died after a month in the hospital, protected by morphine oblivion. As much as I'd hated her earlier, I missed her now. It was like a radiant star had disappeared from our skies. I regretted I hadn't spent more time getting to know her in these last years. Now I had only Mimi and Duke in my family, and I was worried about how Duke would take her death.

I did have my friend, Starrett Conable. He came to Ava's funeral and hugged me, and we stood together by the mossy gravesite where she would be buried in the Radfords' plot. He held my hand.

Afterwards, we lagged behind the others walking back to the car. 'There's something I want to ask you,' he said.

I stopped and looked up at him, so tall and lanky, with the same freckles and light brown sun-bleached hair. He brushed back my hair and touched my scar. 'You've really forgiven me? It's hard for me to forgive myself,' he said. I only opened my trap because I couldn't stand thinking of you and that guy. Hell, Mae Lee. You know how I've always felt about you. Do you think . . . maybe . . .'

I felt my face becoming warm and tingly. Hush, Starrett. Not now.

We walked on and were passing behind the mausoleum, out of sight of the others. He leaned down and kissed me.

And I threw my arms around him and kissed him back.

Duke had a relapse after she died. Or so I heard from Elzuma, because a few months after the funeral I was finishing up my

schooling and looking after Mimi, who had fallen and broken her hip. I knew she would never be the same again, for her mind was going too. I had to stay with her and look after her, after all she had done for me. I was doing my practice teaching at the same time and writing to Starrett. He had just graduated from Tech and had found a job.

I couldn't let Mimi down, after all she'd done for me when I had had no place else to go. And Starrett did come from Adanta to spend time with me.

It was Starrett who told me to go see Duke, and I was glad I did, because he only lived a year longer after Ava died. Some said it was a heart attack, but I knew it was a broken heart. When I went one Indian summer day to see him at Sweetbay, I had written Duke that I was coming, but he'd never answered. Lindy had gone over and told Elzuma of our plans to visit, so I went to Lindy's house first.

She saddled two horses for us and we took the back roads, past abandoned cemeteries and rolling fields and plum bushes. She told me he didn't see many people. She'd heard that he thought Ava still lived there and talked to her out loud. We rode for a long time, with me wondering if I really wanted to go.

We finally turned our horses toward Sweetbay when the sun was going down, the October moon was rising, and the air was getting chill. Smoke drifted over from somewhere. And there we saw him, Duke, rocking on the front porch and smoking. Cyrus was sitting on the steps, and Iris was sitting beside him wearing a flowered skirt.

Two brown children were running and chasing under the pines, lobbing magnolia pods at each other. Elzuma sat, elbows on a table, and smoked an Indian pipe. I looked again to see what she was doing.

One by one, she laid out cards.

As we watched, another horse ambled up behind us. I turned, and there he was, Starrett Conable, meeting us like he'd said he would. Have you told Lindy our news? he called.

I shook my head.

What news? she wanted to know.

Just wait, I said. I was saving this for everybody.

We rode our horses up into the yard and tied them to the hitching post that still stood there. There were happy hugs all the way around, and then the three of us stood in front of Duke.

How are you? I asked.

Fine, punkin. His golden eyes searched my face. It's good to see you looking so pretty. By now the scar had faded to a thin line, and I never thought about it anymore. Why don't you go in and see Mis' Ava?

My mouth opened. I looked over at Starrett, at Lindy, my heart in my throat. I glanced over at Elzuma and she shook her head ever so slightly. Later, Duke, I said. I've got something to tell you. Starrett and I are getting married. We're going to move to Atlanta where he works at Lockheed and there's a nursing home for Mimi.

Well, I'll be damned, he said. That'll make Mis' Ava mighty happy. I've got something to give you, punkin. It'll make a fine wedding present.

He went inside, motioning for us to stay on the porch. He came out a few minutes later. Hold out your hands and close your eyes, he said, just the way he'd said it the day he put the bunny rabbit into my hands.

When I opened my hands, I looked at him, unable to speak. Mis' Ava wants you to have them, he said.

I stared at the red fire in my hand. I didn't want them. Not now. Duke stood there, waiting for my happiness, my joy. I smiled at him through tears, kissed his cheek, and thanked him. I slipped them into my pocket.

You children are going to stay for supper, said Elzuma, looking intently at us. Cyrus cooked some of his barbecue, and we got plenty.

Yes, do stay, said Iris. I made a pound cake.

Suits me, said Starrett, grinning broadly.

Me, too, said Lindy.

The wheel of fortune turns continuously, Duke told me. The first shall be last and the last shall be first. We like to talk about love being forever, and maybe on some level, love is. But the form of love changes as the wheel goes on.

The sun went down that October evening in a blaze, splashing blues and oranges through the Spanish moss of Sweetbay, while we sat on the front porch with Duke, plates on our laps, talking of times past, the way everybody talks of times past, as a time when the world was fine and beautiful and a great mystery to be lived.